Arthur A. Macdonell

Camping Voyages on German Rivers

Arthur A. Macdonell

Camping Voyages on German Rivers

ISBN/EAN: 9783337237899

Printed in Europe, USA, Canada, Australia, Japan

Cover: Foto ©Andreas Hilbeck / pixelio.de

More available books at **www.hansebooks.com**

THE WERRA AT MEININGEN.

CAMPING VOYAGES

ON

GERMAN RIVERS

BY

ARTHUR A. MACDONELL, M.A.

CORPUS CHRISTI COLLEGE, OXFORD

Olli remigio noctemque diemque fatigant
Et longos superant flexus variisque teguntur
Arboribus, viridesque secant placido aequore silvas.

VERGIL.

WITH FRONTISPIECE AND TWENTY MAPS

LONDON: EDWARD STANFORD

26 & 27 COCKSPUR STREET, CHARING CROSS, S.W.

1890

DEDICATED

‘

TO THE

five friends

OWING TO WHOSE COMPANIONSHIP

THESE VOYAGES ARE AMONG

THE PLEASANTEST MEMORIES OF MY LIFE.

PREFACE

THE subject of German rivers from the point of view of boating expeditions has never before been treated as a whole. The author having navigated a distance of nearly 2000 miles in Germany has at least the qualification of a more extensive knowledge of that subject than is possessed, he believes, by any one else. Brief accounts of the whole or part of some of the streams described in the following pages have been written by others. The Weser is treated of in a small work entitled *Camp Life on the Weser* (pp. 53 ; London, 1879). The experiences of a voyage on a part of the Rhine and on the Main from Würzburg in flood-time are narrated in the *Log of the Waterlily* (pp. 59 ; London, 1852). *The Waterlily on the Danube* (pp. 216 ; London, 1853), and a chapter of *A Thousand Miles in the Rob Roy Canoe* (pp. 318 ;

London, 1866), by my countryman, Mr. John Mac-
Gregor, contain accounts of excursions on different
parts of the Danube.

The present work, on the other hand, may claim
a certain completeness as describing, with one exception, all the German rivers which it would be
worth the while of Englishmen to attempt to navigate. The Oder, as well as the lower courses of the
Elbe and Rhine, traverses regions so extremely flat
and uninteresting that no one would think of going
down it except for the purpose of rowing or sailing only. But the streams treated of in the following
pages flow through all the finest river scenery in
Germany, constituting in fact a large proportion of
the natural beauties of that country in general.

The one exception above referred to is the Lahn.
The course of that tributary passes through a very
picturesque region. It is navigable from Wetzlar, a
distance of from seventy to eighty miles. The locks on
it between that town and its confluence with the Rhine
are, however, said to be rather old and neglected. It
would doubtless be possible to come down this stream
from Marburg, a town about 100 miles from its mouth,
in a canoe if not in a rowing-boat.

The writer hopes that the perusal of his book may suggest some charming haunts to many of those who prefer to recruit their strength far from the madding crowd. A boating excursion is, however, certainly the most delightful way of spending a holiday in the regions he describes. It combines the most healthy form of physical exercise with absolute freedom from the dust, the stifling heat, and the worry of railway travelling in summer. The voyager, while passing through some of the finest scenery in the country, is always at liberty to refresh himself with a bathe or rest in the shade on the banks whenever and wherever he pleases. He also enjoys many opportunities of visiting interesting places, often not easily accessible in any other way, as well as of becoming acquainted with the natives in a manner which would otherwise not be possible.

If the expedition is a camping voyage, it is at the same time the cheapest form of travelling on the Continent. The expense of a month's holiday thus spent need not amount to more than £20 at the outside for each member of the party. This sum would include railway fares, freight of boat and luggage, cost of boat, tent, and the remaining requisites for camping. It is in the long-run decidedly cheaper to buy one's equipment. For it could be sold on one's return at a loss amounting to less than the sum paid for hire ; while if it be retained till used again, the expense of each subsequent voyage would be reduced to half that of the first. The cost of living when camping is extremely small. The writer, for instance, remembers once spending during the voyage on the Neckar no more than five shillings on a twenty-four hours' supply of provisions, including beer, for five men.

The author trusts that the reader may also derive some amusement from the experiences recorded in the following pages, as well as a certain amount of instruction from the information which, scattered throughout the book, and in many cases not otherwise accessible, bears on the characteristics, the scenery, the inhabitants, and the historical associations of the river valleys described. He only regrets that owing to the press of work entailed by professional duties, no less than by various necessary avocations, he has been enabled to devote but a very small amount of leisure to writing this book, much less to rendering its style as attractive as he might have hoped to make it under more favourable conditions.

The work is based on notes taken down each day during the course of the voyages which it records. The maps of the Werra and the Neckar, as well as of the upper courses of the Main and the Danube, which it contains, may be regarded as thoroughly trustworthy, being reproduced from the maps of the German Ordnance Survey. The additional details as to obstructions, such as weirs and mills, given in them, being supplied from the personal observation of the writer, are not obtainable elsewhere, and should therefore prove of value to those who may use them for practical purposes.

The large general map, besides affording a comprehensive view of the river system of Germany, furnishes, along with the letterpress, as much information as the navigator wants with regard to the railways and towns on the banks of the larger rivers.

An Appendix, giving tables of distances and lists of obstructions, besides other practical details, has been added.

The book concludes with an Index, which will

PREFACE

probably enhance both its practical value and its general interest.

In conclusion, the author ventures to express a hope that such of his readers as may navigate the streams he describes, or other German waters, will, through his publisher, bring to his knowledge any inaccuracies they may discover, or new information they may acquire. He would gladly incorporate their notes in a second edition, should this work ever attain to that distinction.

LONDON, 28*th June*, 1890.

CONTENTS

CHAPTER IV

THE NECKAR

CHAPTER V

THE RHINE

CHAPTER VI

THE MOSELLE

CHAPTER VII

THE MAIN

CHAPTER VIII

THE MOLDAU AND THE ELBE

CHAPTER IX

THE DANUBE

CHAPTER I

" Come, my friends,
'Tis not too late to seek a newer world.
Push off, and sitting well in order smite
The sounding furrows."—TENNYSON.

Early voyages—India—Germany—English rivers—Preparations
for a continental voyage.

THE writer of the following pages was born in Behar,
the Palestine of Buddhism, near the banks of the
Gandak, a stream whose shores were hallowed by the
last wanderings of the great reformer in the fifth
century B.C. His first voyage was made on those
waters in early infancy, when on the outbreak of the
Indian Mutiny he escaped with his parents in a
native boat to the shelter of a neighbouring fort.
He still has vivid recollections of accompanying his
father and mother on a trip down the Ganges to
attend the races at Sonepore. Well can he remember that mighty river's high sandy banks, from which

B

now and again fragments would break off and fall
into the tawny waves below; he can still recall the
small cabin of the house-boat and its unwieldy rudder,
and the native servants preparing the evening meal
on the low sandbanks, to which the vessel was moored
at night. To this voyage may perhaps be traced the
fascination which travelling by water has always had
for him. From his later boyhood, which was spent
chiefly in Germany, he has pleasant reminiscences of
numerous adventures shared with two enterprising
German schoolfellows on the Leine, near the University town of Göttingen, and on the winding and
beautiful stream of the Werra, between the castle
of Hanstein and the village of Witzenhausen. The
charm of these trips was in no degree diminished
by the fact that they were always undertaken in
boats of almost prehistoric uncouthness of build, and
with oars which would have appeared primitive to
Noah himself. An Undergraduate's life at Oxford,
that city of many streams, yielded almost unequalled
opportunities of indulging a passion for boating;
and while still *in statu pupillari* the navigator of
the German rivers hereafter described was already
familiar with the course of the Thames from Lechlade
to Richmond, and had acquired a love of camp life
on its peaceful and verdant banks. A continued
residence at Oxford led in 1881 to an acquaintance
with the beautiful shores of the Wye, and a camping
expedition in a pair-oar on the Severn from Welsh-

pool to Tewkesbury and up the lonely and charming Avon from the latter city as far as Warwick.

Recollections of his boyish experiences on the Werra soon afterwards suggested the idea that a camping voyage on this little-known river, many parts of the valley of which are noted in Germany for their beauty, would combine all the attractions of exploration and adventure with a holiday in fine scenery safe from the invasion of the tourist. The plan gradually matured, but detailed information was hard to obtain. However, as the German encyclopædias of Brockhaus and Meyer both stated that the Werra was navigable for rafts from Themar, a small place not far distant from its source, Meiningen, as being the only town of any size some way lower down, was finally fixed upon as probably the most suitable starting-point.

A letter addressed to the proprietor of the principal hotel there soon produced an answer to the effect that there was plenty of water at Meiningen to float a boat of the draught of an oak-built pair-oar such as had been described. This was satisfactory so far; but as seemed probable at the time, and as later experience invariably showed, information of this kind throws hardly any light on the lower course of a river. The ignorance possessed by riparians, not only of distances, but of artificial obstructions, such as weirs and mills, situated within a few miles of their native place, is positively amazing.

They never seem to have walked more than three
miles from the house where they were born, or to
have heard even faint rumours of anything beyond
that charmed radius.

Two enterprising college contemporaries, who had
been companions in previous camping expeditions,
expressed their eagerness to bring up the crew to
the full complement of three; and it was finally
arranged to leave England for Meiningen on 30th
June 1883. A strong oak skiff, with all fittings—
one pair of oars, two pairs of sculls, a boat-hook,
towing-rope, mast, and sail—was purchased second-
hand from Mr. John Salter, the well-known Oxford
boatbuilder, for the sum of £15. A gipsy tent
(9 feet by 7) was hired from Messrs. Piggott of
Bishopsgate Street, and the necessary camping utensils, such as tin plates and cups, knives and forks,
lamps, filters, and last, but not least, a small portable cooking-stove, containing a number of pots
and pans, which fitted into one another like Chinese
boxes, were bought at the Stella lamp shop in
Oxford Street, of Mr. Potter, who for many years
equipped Mr. John Macgregor for his famous canoeing expeditions in the *Rob Roy*. A table with
movable legs, three camp-stools, a waterproof ground-
sheet, some blankets, and a yachting bag each, to
contain their personal effects, completed their out-
fit. A pound or two of good tea, some tinned
soups and meats, besides a few pots of jam, were

added in the way of provisions not obtainable in Germany. For a full month before starting the writer used to practise the elements of cookery every morning on his own breakfast, working through in rotation a programme consisting chiefly of chops, steaks, cutlets, buttered eggs, and eggs and bacon.

Good charts of the river were an essential part of the equipment for the proposed expedition. These the writer prepared, not only for the first trip, but also for the subsequent voyages, by mounting tracings from German ordnance maps on canvas, and cutting them into squares of a uniform size. The squares were folded double and fitted into a case, from which each could be withdrawn separately. The maps illustrating the present work are, including the large one, derived from the same source.

The day of departure having been fixed, the boat was despatched through the medium of an agent three weeks before, to await the arrival of the travellers at Frankfort-on-the-Main. In passing, it may be mentioned, for the benefit of any reader of these pages who may wish to send a boat to Germany, that in order to ensure its arrival in good time not less than twenty-one days should be allowed for transmission. Disagreeable delays at the other end of the journey may result from neglecting to take this precaution, as will appear in the chapter on the Danube.

The party started on the evening of the appointed

day with light hearts, but comparatively heavy purses.
No incident worth mentioning occurred on the way
viâ Flushing to Cologne, except at the German
frontier. Here the custom-house officials spent so
much time in scrutinising and weighing the various
appliances of the three friends, that all the remaining
passengers had long re-entered the train. A pompous
Prussian guard of more than ordinary corpulence,
who was fretting and fuming up and down the platform, kept repeatedly shouting *einsteigen!* (take your
seats), but without producing any effect. At length
the trio issued from the custom-house, and he whom
we will henceforth call the Professor, sauntering
leisurely up to the irate official, inquired with great
calmness and an air of childlike simplicity: *Wie
lange Aufenthalt* (how long does the train stop)?
The great man turned a deeper purple, but having
his breath completely taken away, remained tongue-
tied, while the insolent foreigners entered their compartment amid the laughter of their fellow-passengers.

On arriving at Frankfort the party at once proceeded to the office of Herr Joseph Wirth, a well-
known boatbuilder, to whom the skiff had been
consigned. She had, it appeared, arrived safely some
days previously, and was now immediately despatched
to Meiningen. As two days would be occupied in
transit, the friends resolved to utilise the interval
by visiting Heidelberg. When about an hour's distance from their destination a genial old gentleman

got into their compartment after gallantly taking leave of some young ladies who had accompanied him to the station. He soon fell into conversation with the party, in whom he began to take a keen interest, after hearing about their projected voyage. He told them he was a retired judge (*Oberamtsrichter*), eighty years of age, and lived at Heidelberg. He was certainly wonderfully well preserved, not looking more than sixty. "Though I have passed the usual limit of old age by many years," he continued, "my spirit is still young; and," turning to the Interpreter (as he will now be called), "if you should see Max Müller when you are back in England, you must tell him you met in Germany an old man, from whose heart, though he is eighty years of age, the *deutsche Liebe* (German love) has not yet quite faded away."

On taking leave he promised to call for his new acquaintances next morning. And, sure enough, punctually at ten o'clock the old gentleman appeared in a carriage and insisted on driving them up to view the castle. That he had not exaggerated his youthfulness became pretty evident in the course of the day. After showing the friends over the ruin, and discoursing on the merits of the monster barrel preserved there, he conducted them to the restaurant to refresh themselves with a glass or two of beer. But finding it poor stuff, he constrained them to accompany him down to Bremeneck, a well-known students' beer-garden at Heidelberg. Here he quaffed two or

three additional glasses by way of a morning freshener
(*Frühschoppen*, in students' parlance), gaily chaffing
the waitresses the while. It being now one o'clock,
the three friends asked the festive old gentleman to
do them the honour of dining with them at their
hotel. He gladly accepted the invitation. He was
a connoisseur in wines, as in all else that pertains to
the life of a German student. For had he not belonged
to a distinguished *Corps* in his early days, and taken
part in many a *Commers* (drinking-bout) at his old
University in later years? And so, with much
appreciation, he disposed of a bottle and a half of
a brand he had specially recommended. After dinner
his friends regaled him with coffee, liqueurs, and
cigars in the garden. Unable to prevail on them
to stay another night, he was fain to accompany
them to their train. The farewell scene he concluded
by saluting the Professor, to whom he had taken a
particular fancy, with a sounding kiss on both cheeks.
What country but Germany can produce old boys
like this, who enter into the feelings and enjoy the
society of young men of twenty-five? The friends
had grave misgivings that that day's festivity might
have injured the constitution of one so aged; they
had probably little ground for fear. At all events,
the old gentleman was, a year later, as they were
glad to hear, flourishing exceedingly.

After a long night journey the trio arrived at
Meiningen on the morning of Thursday the 5th. As

the train approached the town they looked out with beating pulses till they caught sight of the Werra as it meandered in the distance through the plain of Meiningen; but their hearts failed on viewing the exiguity of that slender streak; and the thought that, even if their craft could float in the stream, she might yet not hold more than half the luggage they had brought, filled their breasts with dismay. For there were the tent, the poles, the bag of pegs and guys, the cooking-stove, waterproof sheet, blankets and yachting-bags for three, to say nothing of hampers of provisions, table, camp-stools, oars, sculls, mast, and sail! Here indeed were all the elements of a *fiasco* at the very outset. But for retreat it was now too late.

CHAPTER II

THE WERRA

"Οὐ γάρ πώ τις τῆδε παρήλασε νηΐ μελαίνῃ
Πρίν γ' ἡμέων."—ODYSSEY.

Meiningen—The start—First camp—Wading for four hours in
the dark—Wernshausen—Spring a bad leak—Camp at Salzungen—Trespassing—Vacha—Camp near Philippsthal—Swampy
camp at Berka—Herleshausen—Transformation scene in the
train—Visit to the Wartburg—Beautiful scenery near Falken
—Inn at Falken—Wanfried—Accident in mill-stream—
Eschwege, first lock—Allendorf—Lindewerra—Old scenes—
Witzenhausen—Cherry country—Munden.

MEININGEN, the largest town on the Werra, with a
population of 10,000 inhabitants, is pleasantly
situated in the midst of wooded heights at the head
of a small plain into which the valley of the Werra
here widens out. Its chief attractions are the Ducal
Theatre, the park, called the English Garden, and
the picture gallery in the palace of the Grand Duke
of Saxe-Meiningen. Its name is probably best
known in England through the famous performances
of Shakespearian plays by its theatrical company.

The Werra rises near Eisfeld, to the south of the

Thuringian Forest, thirty-five miles above Meiningen,
its total length to Münden, where it is joined by the
Fulda, being about one hundred and sixty miles.
Forming, as it does, the western boundary of the
Thuringian Forest, the scenery of its banks is almost
uniformly pretty, and rises to a high degree of beauty
in the regions of Falken, Treffurt, and Münden.

This river is best adapted for a camping voyage,
as there are but very few places on its banks where
it would be possible to obtain any but the most
primitive accommodation. There are twenty - one
obstructions in the shape of mills, but these can be
got over, as will be seen further on, with much less
difficulty than the impediments on the upper courses
of the Neckar, the Main, or the Danube.

Several hours of suspense were passed at the
Sächsische Hof till the arrival of the boat. At
length her future crew experienced the joy of seeing
her driven up on a waggon early in the afternoon,
and had the satisfaction of launching her under the
very windows of their hotel, situated on one of the
three branches into which the Werra divides at
Meiningen. The following day having been fixed
for the start, the remainder of the afternoon was
spent in visiting the Landsberg, a château belonging
to the Grand Dukes of Saxe-Meiningen, and commanding a fine prospect of the valley of the Werra
and of the Thuringian Forest. Early next morning
the party drove to the Dolmar, a basalt mountain,

from which a grand panoramic view of the Thuringian
Forest, including the Inselsberg, is obtained.   An
intelligent German, who turned out to be the burgomaster of Walldorf, a neighbouring village on the
Werra, reaching the summit about the same time,
was at great pains to draw the attention of the
strangers to distant points of historical interest
connected with the Thirty Years' War.   On their
return the friends spent some time in making a
number of necessary purchases and laying in a stock
of provisions for the voyage.   Before starting they
rowed to a beautiful smooth reach spanned by a
green iron bridge and flanked by a finely wooded hill
on the left, and the trees of the Ducal Park on the
right.   And there, with her crew on board, the boat
was photographed from the bank by the leading artist
of Meiningen.   This picture must have quite a historical value for the Meiningers, representing as it
does the first rowing-boat that has ever navigated
their waters.

There being a large weir across the river about
half a mile below the town, it was decided to send
the baggage down to this point by cart and to pack
below the dam.   On arriving at the spot with the
empty boat, the crew found their host and a crowd
of people waiting on the bank to witness their
departure.   The pile of luggage looked formidable
indeed; but by ingenious economy of space all was
made to fit in amazingly well, and the craft when

loaded for the start presented a remarkably ship-
shape appearance, much admired by the spectators.
But what was the most important thing, she
actually floated! All was now ready; and *without*
hoisting the British flag or raising a ringing cheer
(as the local papers stated them to have done), the
voyagers simply waved their farewells to their friends
on the bank, entered a rapid almost immediately,
and gliding swiftly round a bend of the stream, were
lost to view. What an intense relief it was not to
have stuck at the outset under the very eye of the
public! How humiliating to have had to leap out,
wade, drag the boat along, and possibly perform
other ignominious manœuvres! The naval prestige
of Great Britain was thus saved and perhaps even
locally increased for some time to come. There was
now a succession of rapids for upwards of three
miles, the channel being very narrow all the way.
The boat, however, grounded only twice, and easily
got off again. In nearly every rapid there is a
smooth tongue of water. A boat should always be
steered down to the point of this tongue—for the
water is invariably deepest here—and should then be
allowed to be carried along by the current, which
very often flows close under one of the banks. This,
of course, necessitates the frequent shipping of the
oars, and makes the handling of a rowing-boat rather
awkward. A Canadian canoe is for various reasons
much the handiest vessel in which to navigate the

upper courses of rivers. Its draught is very light,
the crew face frontways—an immense advantage,—a
channel of three feet in width is sufficient for its
passage, and there is no continual shortening of oars.

As the village of Walldorf is approached there
is a smooth reach nearly a mile long, which,
reflecting a fine wooded ridge and the rays of the
setting sun on its glassy surface, formed quite a
beautiful scene in the calm evening light. Just
above Walldorf there is a steep dam across the
river, with a kind of cutting in the middle, not quite
so steep and about six feet wide. Down this most
of the water rushes. As the banks here were high
it would have been a great labour to pull the boat
over; so it was decided to take most of the luggage
out and to risk shooting the lasher. Only one of
the crew remained on board and swept gaily down
without accident, to the great astonishment and
admiration of a railway official standing on the bank.

In the growing dusk a strip of meadow with a
wooded height for a background, a quarter of a mile
farther down, was selected for a camping ground.
There being a snug cove in the bank which seemed
made on purpose to receive the boat, that rather
formidable bark was soon turned into a little bight.
By a stupid mistake the two articles most essential
for preparing supper had been forgotten, viz. butter
and milk. Accordingly the Professor, who possessed
tolerable familiarity with classical German, and a

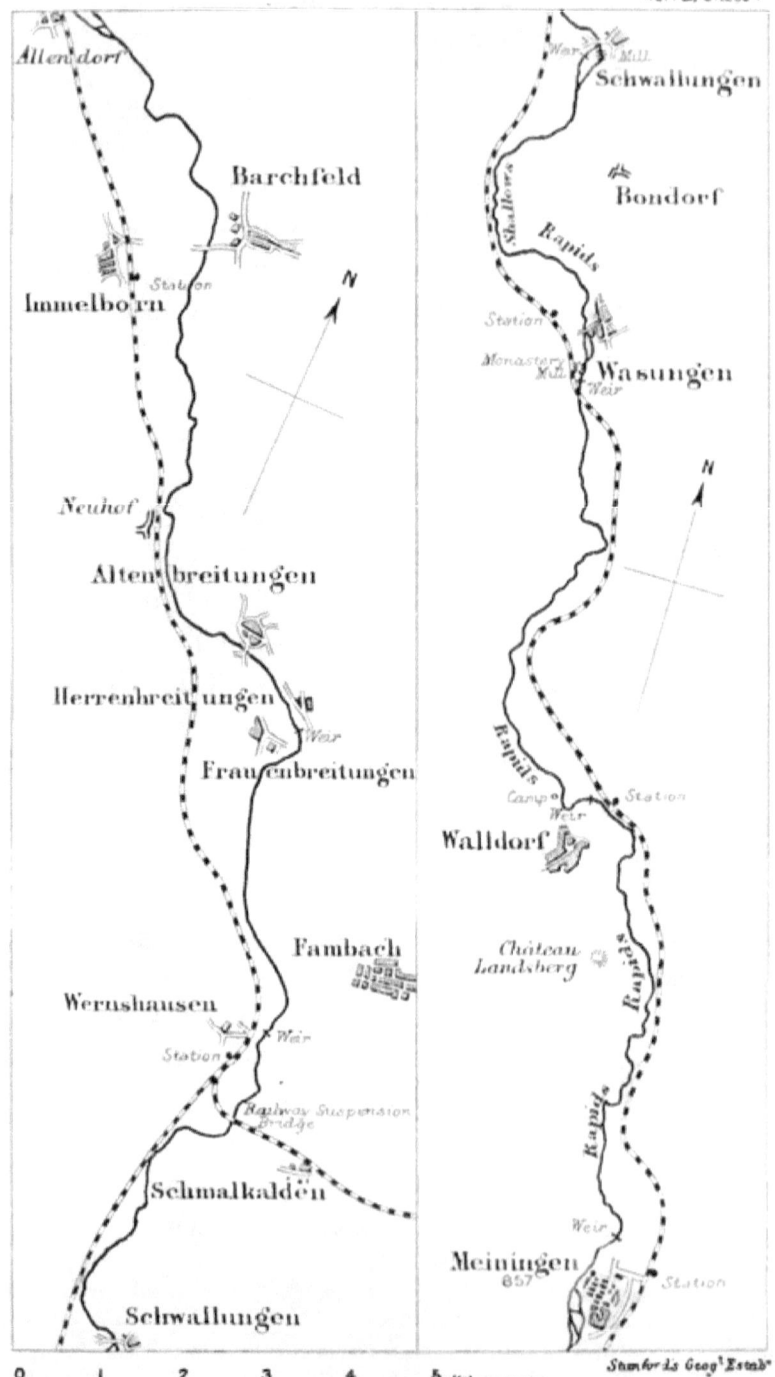

Allendorf

Barchfeld

Immelborn

Station

N

Neuhof

Altenbreitungen

Herrenbreitungen

Weir

Frauenbreitungen

Fambach

Wernshausen

Weir

Station

Railway Suspension Bridge

Schmalkalden

Schwallungen

Schwallungen

Wear Mill

Bondorf

Rapids

Shallows

Station

Monastery Mill

Wasungen

Weir

N

Rapids

Camp

Weir

Station

Walldorf

Château Landsberg

Rapids

Rapids

Weir

Meiningen
857

Station

0   1   2   3   4   5   Kilometres

considerable amount of self-confidence to make up
for defective knowledge of dialects, was despatched
to the neighbouring village in order to buy what was
needful. Meanwhile the Interpreter and Bow, as
practical men, remained on the spot to pitch the
camp. The tent was only just beginning to rise like
a magic fabric, when the Professor, clasping a large
bottle of milk to his bosom, and with chagrin visibly
displayed on his features, suddenly emerged from
the deepening gloom at the head of a procession of
some two hundred villagers. His phenomenal costume
consisting of white flannels, a blue "blazer," and a
large white-felt lawn-tennis hat, having very un-
mistakably aroused the curiosity of the unsophisticated rustics, he had soon found himself, in spite of
crafty doublings, marching at the head of an ever-
increasing battalion. His arrival at the scene of
operations resulted in the formation of a semi-circular
array of spectators, extending from a point on the
bank above to another below the encampment; and
from this moment onwards the most trivial actions of
the campers became the objects of wrapt observation.
By a beneficent dispensation of Providence the tent
had gone up under the public scrutiny without a
hitch. The table and stools were now unfolded and
set up on their legs, the lamps were lighted, the
kettle began to boil, buttered eggs were scraped in
the pan, and finally the supper-table was decked
with sundry luxuries and delicacies, all to the

intense delight of the encircling public. The Interpreter, in order to disarm criticism, now stepped
forth and proclaimed a general invitation to tea.
This invitation was pretty numerously responded to,
chiefly by young girls, one of whom was decidedly
pretty. Bow, in the pride of his heart, seized the
opportunity of displaying to these charmers the
marvels of his railway reading-lamp, when suddenly,
alas! the spring shot out into the darkness and was
no more seen. The enjoyment of the first supper on
the banks of the Werra was to some small extent
marred by the suicidal mania of swarms of midges
that would insist on drowning themselves in the tea
and inseparably associating their fate with that of the
scrambled eggs. By about eleven the last of the
visitors had departed, after bidding their hosts a
hearty good-night. The heavens were brilliant with
stars, and the three friends chatted and smoked
outside for a long time, enjoying the perfect stillness
and beauty of the night. They at last turned in and
were soon lulled by the murmur of the river into a
sound and dreamless sleep.

Early next morning the party were awakened by
the fisherman of the village, named König, who had
come to inspect Bow's trout-flies by daylight. On
expressing a wish to purchase some of these, he was
much pleased and surprised at being presented with
them. The Interpreter whispered that this was the
first kingfisher he had seen on the banks of the

Werra, but the other two pretended not to hear. Soon after the burgomaster (who had been on the Dolmar the day before), the doctor, and the magistrate (*Friedensrichter*), accompanied by many of the villagers, came down to see the preparations for the start. By half-past ten, when all was ready, a large crowd had assembled to bid the strangers farewell. Among them was a pretty girl, whose eyes one at least of the crew did not forget for many days.

Now began a succession of rapids, which alternated with reaches of smooth water. The left bank in this region consists chiefly of slopes clothed with larch and pine, there being occasional patches of wood on the right bank also. The railway comes pretty close to the river, a train now and then being, unlike model children, heard but never seen. This was a perfect summer's day. The surface of the water in the deep reaches was like a mirror, and the stillness was only broken by the song of the birds and the gentle plash of the oars. The only motions that caught the eye were the brilliant flash of an occasional kingfisher as it darted along, and the flittings of many dragon-flies lazily hovering in the hot midday air.

About four miles below Walldorf lies Wasungen, a small industrial town of about 3000 inhabitants. It is situated at the foot of a height crowned by a large building with a square tower, which was probably a monastery in former days. Here the first porterage

C

occurred, further progress being barred by a mill
and weir. The boat had to be dragged up a bank
about four feet high and carried down the other side,
a distance of about twenty-five yards, while a crowd
of admiring villagers looked on or lent a helping
hand.

Now followed, besides rapids, a number of shallows,
in which the heavily laden boat got rather badly
scraped, but fortunately without receiving any serious
damage. The scenery here began to improve, as
high hills crested with pine woods came into view,
the red cliffs at their base harmonising finely with
the bright green of the opposite bank.

Early in the afternoon the crew resigned themselves to the delights of a riverside lunch. This
was followed by revolver practice at a hock bottle
that had just been emptied; but though every
possible elevation was tried at the closest quarters,
the mark was only touched once. The friends
attributed their want of success to the fact that the
weapon had not cost more than five marks. It was
hardly the sort of shooter for the Western States of
America.

Bow now turned his attention to fishing, but with
no result. This was hardly surprising on so brilliant
and calm an afternoon, even with fish as completely
unsophisticated as those of the Werra. But, as is
sometimes said in Germany, Englishmen do not fish
in order to catch anything, but merely for the

pleasure of the thing. The other two meanwhile, lying on the grass, soon succumbed to the drowsy influence of the afternoon. When at last aroused by the empty-handed fisherman, they were shocked to find it was nearly seven o'clock. Starting off in a hurry, they soon arrived at a village named Schwallungen, with another weir and mill. The river here being evidently very low, it was decided, on the advice of some of the inhabitants, to send on all the baggage by waggon to the inn at Wernshausen, a village some four miles farther on. Embarking again with as little delay as possible, the voyagers experienced what was now the novel sensation of rowing in a perfectly empty boat. The whole population had by this time turned out to look on. This was rather unpleasant, as the water now became so extremely shallow that the crew had to get out and, wading in the river-bed, to drag the boat laboriously onward. The villagers kept accompanying them for some distance along the bank, but gradually dropping off, at length left them to their fate.

The experiences of the next four hours will never fade from the memory of any of the three friends. Darkness came on apace ; for the black clouds of an approaching thunderstorm rapidly covered the sky. A torrent of rain burst over the belated crew, and peal after peal of thunder began to reverberate among the hills, as the lightning-flashes grew more and

more vivid. Meanwhile the boat was being slowly
dragged along in water so shallow that in places
she would not even float, though absolutely empty.
The banks and the course of the river remained
hidden from view save when momentarily revealed
by the lightning. The entire bed of the stream was
bestrewn with rough stones, which rendered progress
extremely slow and exhausting. The Professor
suffered most, in consequence of the trust he had
been beguiled into placing in cheap wares. Before
starting he had bought for eight and sixpence in the
Strand a pair of boating-shoes quite equal, as he
boasted, to those for which his companions had paid
more than twice as much. Retribution was now no
longer delayed. The combined action of stones and
water wore completely away what proved to be
papier-maché soles, leaving to their owner the painful necessity of concluding that night's labours
barefoot, while his companions' shoes remained in-
tact. Yet even he, in spite of his wretched plight,
could not help admiring the beauty of the scenery
when lighted up ever and anon for an instant by the
forked flashes gleaming between the trunks of the
pines on the crest of the ridges that skirted the left
river bank. The storm at length passed away,
leaving the weary toilers drenched and blundering
onwards in complete darkness. It may have been
half-past ten, when having solemnly divided the
contents of their one bottle of soda-water to allay

their raging thirst, they in despair climbed the bank,
hoping to catch a glimpse of the lights of Wernshausen. None of course were to be seen; for there
are none at that hour in villages whose inhabitants in
summer rise and go to rest with the sun. One of the
friends proposed to spend the rest of the night on the
spot till daybreak. He was out-voted, and the heart-
breaking process of wading and dragging was
resumed. The river now luckily became deeper.
The crew scrambled in, but not before the man at
the bows had suddenly gone under, though fortunately
without letting go his hold of the painter. Now
came what must be a fine broad reach, which a train
suddenly rushing past proved to run parallel with
the railway at this point. As they were cautiously
rowing along, they were startled by voices on the
bank calling *Engländer! Engländer!* It was their
friends of the cart, who after hours of waiting at the
inn had come out to search for their belated em-
ployers. Cheerfully responding and guided by the
shouts, the three friends landed at about midnight
just above a weir, not, however, till more than one
rapid had sent them crashing into the bushes and
willows on the right bank. The distance to the inn
seemed a mile, but turned out next day to be but a
couple of hundred yards. The landlord had gone to
bed, but was soon aroused, and furnished a supper
which, like the luncheon at the cricket-match of the
Dingley Dellers, as described by Mr. Jingle, was

"cold, but capital." Turning in at about two, the crew rose late next morning, refreshed by a dreamless sleep. After laying in a stock of provisions, in the shape of bread, butter, eggs, and beer, they set off about noon on a cloudless midsummer's day. An hour's row brought them to a second weir. The porterage at this point was fraught with great difficulty and labour. The bottom of the boat having rested for a moment on an unobserved stake, gave an ominous crack. She had not been long afloat when she showed unmistakable signs of having sprung a bad leak. Soon after this, while passing a place named Alten-Breitungen, she was swept into the bushes by a rapid. The shock sent a number of rolls and hard-boiled eggs prepared for lunch flying into the fast-increasing bilge-water, to the infinite glee of the juvenile population assembled on the bridge.

The boat was now run ashore, the crack discovered, and the leak temporarily stopped with some tow and a strip of waterproof, which was cut from the tail of the Professor's mackintosh, and nailed on with some tin tacks that happened to be handy. No one should ever take a boat abroad without having a goodly supply of copper nails as well as strips of prepared wood to be fastened inside over any weak or damaged spot. It is also advisable to take, besides a bottle of varnish, a piece of soap, to be rubbed carefully all over the bottom of the boat before launching her. She is certain otherwise to leak for the first day or two, as is of course natural after a long railway journey in the heat of summer.

Above the town of Salzungen, which was reached soon after six, there are a number of broad stretches of water, with here and there an excellent gravel beach for a bathe. The view as you approach the first of the two weirs at this place is very pretty. While the other two remained behind to unload and pull the boat over, the Interpreter proceeded into the town (which has some 4000 inhabitants), and returned an hour later, laden with bread, ham, and bottles of beer, the object of general but unobtrusive curiosity. After a row of nearly a mile a camping ground was found on the right bank. The latter is here formed by a grassy slope, level at the top, which is about ten feet above the water and flanked by a ditch. The choice proved to be eminently judicious; for not only was the view excellent, but the camp remained absolutely undisturbed by visitors. The reason of this was discovered next morning. At about six o'clock were heard the footsteps of some one cautiously prowling round and round the tent. It turned out to be a little old peasant, apparently of the Hebrew persuasion. After a good deal of hesitation he summoned up enough courage to inform the intruders, with some show of sternness, that the land on which they had settled belonged to Herr Karl Israel, who allowed no one to trespass under any circumstances. On hearing that the strangers in-

tended departing at ten o'clock that same morning,
he was not only mollified, but showed signs of great
surprise, having evidently thought they meant to
take up their permanent quarters on Herr Karl
Israel's property.

During the night there had been a thunderstorm
with heavy rain, which, though lasting several hours,
did not penetrate the canvas. After dawn the clouds
and mists had rolled away, leaving a crisp and
brilliant morning.

Between Salzungen and Tiefenort the river winds
considerably, but after the latter place it straightens
out into splendid broad reaches. Particularly striking
is one which extends along the base of a finely
wooded conical hill, the apex of which is crowned by
an old ruin, while a narrow strip of green meadow
fringes the river. This proved an excellent spot for
a bathe and a midday rest. Resuming their oars, the
voyagers, a short way farther down, rowed past an old
fisherman standing on the bank. The expression of
blank amazement produced on his features by a vision
never seen before would have been a study well
worthy of an artist. No member of the crew, alas !
was equal to immortalising that look. His attitude,
too, as he was in the act of raising his net with both
hands, remained unaltered till the boat vanished for
ever from his sight. If a petrified figure with hanging jaw and protuberant eyes has since been discovered on that lonely shore, the solution of the

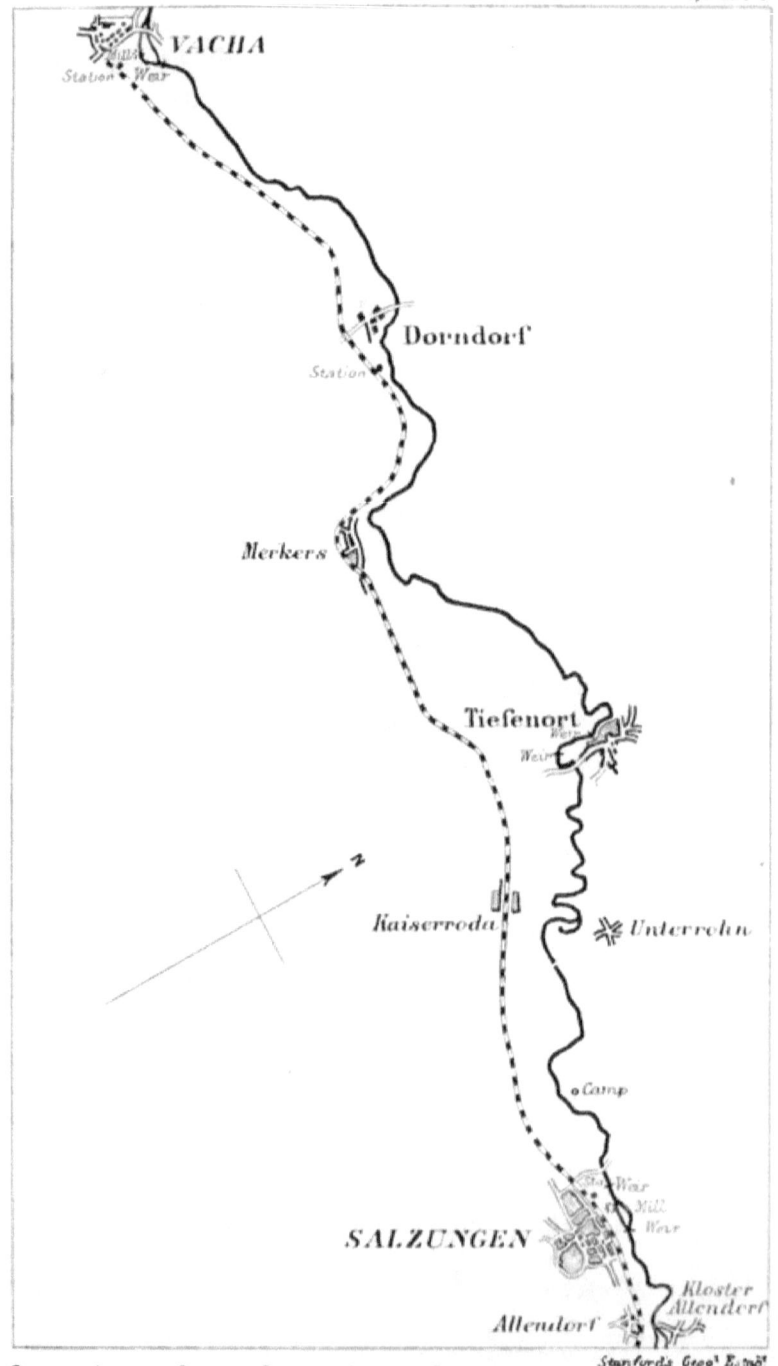

VACHA

Station *Weir*

Dorndorf

Station

Merkers

Tiefenort

Weir

Weir

N

Kaiserroda

Unterrohn

o Camp

SALZUNGEN

Weir

Mill

Weir

Kloster
Altendorf

Altendorf

0   1   2   3   4   5 *Kilometres*

mystery is now for the first time offered to the palæontologists of the Fatherland.

The system of fishing on the Werra is rather primitive. A sort of landing-net, about six feet in diameter, and attached to the end of a long thin pole, is immersed for some time and then suddenly raised by the operator. The guileless denizens of this stream have evidently not yet been much affected by the corrupting influences of civilisation.

Having rowed scathelessly through a roaring rapid on the site of a broken-down old weir, the voyagers passed along some fine reaches to Vacha. This little town must be very old, containing as it does several ancient walls and watch-towers. Its appearance is certainly more antique than that of any other place on the Werra. Landing at a restaurant on the bank for provisions, the crew had a glass of beer and a friendly chat with some of the natives. Then pulling the boat across at the weir, they rowed the "jolly miller" some way with them, greatly to his delight. For this, he said, was the first time he had ever seen, much less been on board, a rowing-boat on those waters. About three-quarters of a mile farther down a meadow with a fine view towards the river was selected for that night's camping ground. Owing to the deepening dusk it was not discovered till too late that a public road ran close behind the tent. Consoling themselves for this piece of ill-luck with a supper of buttered eggs, cutlets, and other

delicacies, the trio composed themselves at midnight
for a short but deep sleep. Passing carts awakened
them at a very early hour, but it was not till about
six that they heard footsteps cautiously encircling
the tent. At last a voice was heard to say: "Is
any one there" (*Ist Jemand da*)? The Interpreter
promptly responded in the affirmative from the
mysterious interior (the tent door being closed).
"I suppose this is a great fishing expedition" (*Das
ist wohl eine grosse Fischerei*)? continued the voice.
"No," replied the Interpreter monosyllabically.
"Ah," added the interrogator by way of explanation,
"I thought it was the Landgrave's fishing party
from Philippsthal" (*Ich dachte es wäre die land-
gräfliche Fischerei von Philippsthal*). "Then it must be
a land surveyor's tent" (*Ist es auch nicht ein geome-
trisches Häuschen*)? "No," continued the still hidden
inmate, "it is only a boating expedition" (*Wasser-
partie*), "undertaken by three Englishmen for pleasure;
but we do some fishing too." And forthwith tossing
aside the door-flaps the Interpreter displayed to the
astonished gaze of this inquisitive native the inside
of the tent, replete with Britons, clothes, appliances,
and luxuries of various kinds. "You will excuse me
for disturbing you," said the visitor apologetically,
"for a thing of this kind excites much curiosity here"
(*erregt viel Aufsehen hier*). "What an enterprising
race you English are," he continued; "no German
would ever think of undertaking an expedition like

this ; though he would not have to leave his own country to do so."

Having effected a comparatively early start at about half-past nine—for it never seemed possible to strike the camp and pack the boat in less than two hours—the crew reached, after scarcely a hundred yards' row, the most perfect camping ground it is possible to imagine. It was a small patch of meadow on the left bank, completely enclosed by trees and thick hedges on three sides, and apparently accessible from the river only. At sight of it the three friends stood up and with difficulty restrained themselves from wrecking the boat. The cheerfulness of Mark Tapley himself would have been put to a severe strain by such an opportunity lost. The chagrin naturally resulting from this discovery was increased on finding immediately beyond the ideal spot a mill, which necessitated unloading and packing again a few minutes after the start. The crossing too turned out to be a very difficult one, and occupied an unusually long time. The opportunity was here taken of patching up the leak more carefully than on the previous day. The appliances were the same, but proved sufficient to exclude the water till the last day of the voyage. After as much tow as could be inserted into the crack with the point of a knife had been forced in, a fresh strip of mackintosh was nailed over the weak spot.

The river is free from obstructions for about

five miles till a place named Lengers is reached.
Between that place and Meiningen, a distance of
thirty-five miles, there are eleven weirs, at each of
which the boat had to be unpacked, dragged over, and
reloaded. This process occupied at least half an hour
on each occasion, besides being very exhausting work.
For the first time the possibility of shooting the sluices
suggested itself. These are constructed at the side of
each mill for the passage of timber rafts. On the
movable paddles, with which the stream is dammed
across. being pulled out, there is a rush of water down
an inclined plane made of smooth boles. The drop is
between five and six feet, ending with large turbulent
waves at the bottom. After some deliberation it
was determined that the experiment should be made.
The boat was lightened by the removal of some of
the heavy baggage and two of the crew, while the
Interpreter, as having the best eyesight, remained in
charge to guide the trusty craft to her fateful plunge.
The miller undertook with alacrity to open the
sluice, and considered himself handsomely rewarded
for this service by the gratuity of a mark. Till the
rather slow process of withdrawing the paddles was
finished, the Interpreter kept the boat stationary in
mid-stream by backing. These were indeed minutes
of suspense, passed in speculating whether the boat
would be ripped up by iron nails, or stove in against
the stone wall at the side, or swamped in the waves
at the bottom of the fall. All was now ready; so

Station Gerstungen

Suhl

Camp

Untersuhl

Mill
Sluice BERKA

N

Dankmarshausen

Mill
Sluice

Widdershausen Mill
Sluice

Leimbach

Mill
Sluice Heringen

Wölfershausen

Lengers

Mill
Sluice

Philippsthal

Harnrode

Weir
Mill

Weir

VACHA

Heimboldshausen

Röhrigshöfe

Stanford's Geog¹ Estab¹

0   1   2   3   4   5   Kilometres

sculling her gently towards the gap, which was about
six feet in width, he had just time, as the boat was
caught by the swift current, to point her nose straight
with a pull of one hand and to ship the sculls in a
twinkling, when down she shot straight as an arrow,
and, plunging through the roaring waves below, was
brought to a standstill within fifty yards. The ex-
hilaration of these moments was great. As the prow
of the boat dived into the wave her keel at the stern
struck the edge of the last bole. This concussion
set tins, bottles, and everything movable rattling in
the most alarming fashion. No practical harm, however, resulted, except the shipping of some gallons of
water. The experiment having proved so successful
was repeated without mishap at all the ten following
mills, till the last at Wannfried, forty-five miles farther
down the river. At the very next mill, however,
where the shoot is very steep, and the waves in consequence are unusually rough, the boat narrowly
escaped foundering. Owing to this experience a
waterproof sheet was spread over the bows on subsequent occasions, and proved an efficient expedient
for keeping the water out.

In the afternoon a village of the name of Dankmarshausen was reached. The picturesquely situated
little church suggested the idea of a visit. The
strangers were directed to the precentor (*Cantor*),
who gladly admitted them, and allowed the Professor to play the organ. He assured the wander-

ing Britons that no Englishman had ever been in the
place before, much less had ever played on the organ
of the village church. The friends then betook themselves to the *Wirthshaus* (restaurant) for provisions
and a glass of beer. The landlady was a comely but
rather sad-looking widow of about thirty-five. The
Interpreter asked whether she knew Uhland's beautiful ballad about the three students of the Rhine,
beginning :—

> " Es zogen drei Bursche wohl über den Rhein,
> Bei einer Frau Wirthin da kehrten sie ein :
> Frau Wirthin hat sie gut Bier und Wein ?
> Wo hat sie ihr schönes Töchterlein ?"

Smiling at the analogy, she replied she knew it well ;
and answering the questions of the song, said her
beer and wine were fairly good, and that her little
daughter was hiding behind the stove. And sure
enough there she was, a pretty little girl of twelve,
too shy to show herself to the three students of
the Werra. Nearly the whole population turned
out to witness the embarkation ; but the *Wirthin*
and the *Cantor* were the most prominent in waving
their farewells.

As the evening began to close in the small town
of Berka was passed. It was noticeable as the first
place hitherto built immediately on the river. All
the previous towns and villages are situated at some
distance from the bank on rising ground. This fact is
doubtless due to floods in winter. The river at Berka

divided, as the voyagers imagined, into two arms. If
this is the case, the second branch apparently never
rejoins the first. What they took to be only the mill-
stream proved to be little better than a canal between
high banks, too narrow to admit of rowing, and seem-
ingly interminable. Owing to the approach of darkness a halt had to be made in this channel and a camp
pitched on wet ground little better than a swamp.
One member of the crew was terribly depressed; but
the Interpreter, in whom such circumstances almost
invariably brought on an attack of Mark Tapleyism,
received such an accession of cheerfulness that the
whole crew were soon as hilarious as possible over
their evening meal within the recesses of the tent.
This was all the more meritorious considering the
fact that a large number of slimy insects of more than
ordinary loathsomeness were beginning to crawl about
in all directions. The bursts of merriment at last died
away, and were doubtless followed by sounds of a more
sustained nature till long after the dawn of day.

Next morning an old peasant, the proprietor of
this swampy field, and his son, who attended the
grammar school (*Gymnasium*) at Eisenach, paid the
camp a visit. The boy, it appeared, was under a
form-master who was a friend of the Interpreter's.
Another instance of how small the world is! Having
shared a bottle of hock with their new acquaintances
the crew embarked at the rather late hour of eleven
o'clock. The map showed the river to be approach-

ing the region of Eisenach. The three friends had
for some time past entertained the project of visiting
the Wartburg from the nearest point on the Werra.
They were, however, still uncertain as to the feasi-
bility of this plan, no railroad being marked on the
chart. They had been proceeding very leisurely
with many delays and thoroughly enjoying the beauty
of the day, when suddenly a railway station became
visible on the bank. It was so near that the name
could easily be made out from the boat to be Herleshausen. On inquiry it proved that Eisenach was
distant only a quarter of an hour by rail, and that
the next train was due in ten minutes. It was
decided to take this, the bags being accordingly
carried up to the tiny station. When about to take
their tickets the friends discovered to their dismay
that they had absolutely no German money left,
having parted with their last mark to the miller who
had opened the previous sluice for them. They had
nothing but one Bank of England five-pound note.
This the station-master naturally declined to change.
At the very last moment, however, as the train
steamed in, he was induced, after much expostula-
tion, to the step—unprecedented in German railway
annals—of supplying return tickets on the security
of a boat. The latter was tied up to the bank exactly
opposite the station and left in charge of the points-
man, and under the very eye of the station authori-
ties. There was just time to dash, regardless of an

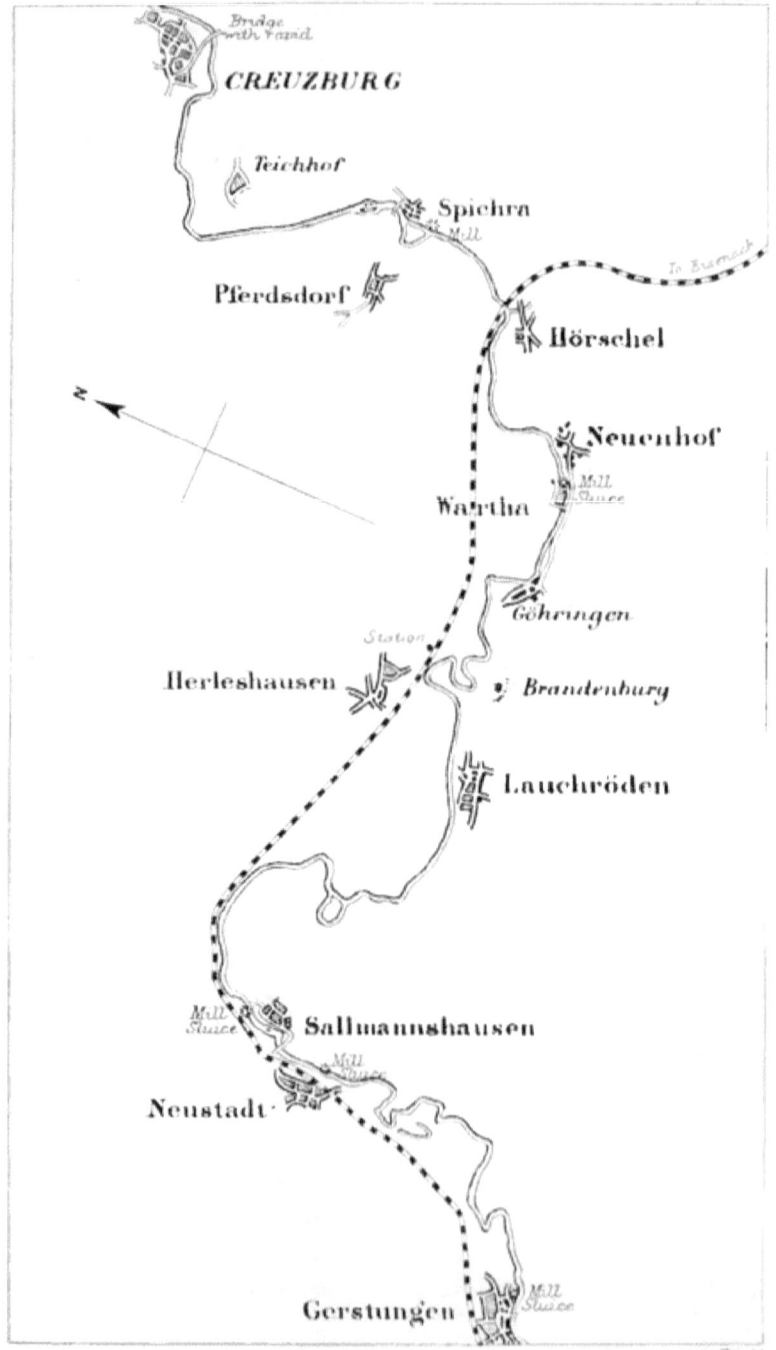

CREUZBURG

Bridge with Fond.

Teichhof

Spichra
Mill

Pferdsdorf

Hörschel

To Bismach

Neuenhof

Mill
Sluice

Wartha

Göhringen

Station

Brandenburg

Herleshausen

Lauchröden

Mill
Sluice

Sallmannshausen

Mill
Sluice

Neustadt

Gerstungen

Mill
Sluice

0   1   2   3   4   5 Kilometres

obstructive guard, into a ladies' compartment, the
only unoccupied one in the train. This forcible
seizure of an empty carriage was, be it noted,
perpetrated in malice prepense. For though not
altogether cowards, the voyagers felt unable to face
the population of Eisenach in the never-before-beheld
English blazers, and flannels white only in the
remote past. For the next few minutes the air of
that small *Frauen - Coupé* was thick with coats,
trousers, shirts, brushes, toothpicks, combs, boots,
ties, shoe-horns, vaseline pots that flew promiscu-
ously from the profound depths of the respective
yachting-bags. Never assuredly had that *Frauen-
Coupé* been the scene of such frantic haste or of
the transformation of three weather-beaten boating
men into civilised-looking mortals of ordinary appearance, such as emerged on the platform at Eisenach.
The remaining passengers, with whose heads the
windows of the train were densely crowded, showed
pretty plainly their amazement at the sudden altera-
tion. As the friends, having thus rapidly changed
their clothes, were doing the same with their five-
pound note at the buffet, a gentleman hurried up to
greet them and inquire with keen interest after their
welfare. He introduced himself as a member of the
crowd which had seen them off at Meiningen. After
a night on the Wartburg and a delightful morning
spent in the Drachenschlucht and Annathal, the crew
returned to Herleshausen in time to start about noon.

A short way farther down on the right bank there
is a fine old ruin called, as they were informed, the
Brandenburg, and perched on a height above the river.
Later on in the afternoon an old man standing on
the bank inquired as to the destination of the voyage.
It was Bremen, he was told. "Ah!" he said, "I
thought this river came out at Hamburg; but I have
a son near Bremen; if you see him, greet him from
me." It did not occur to him to mention his own
name or his son's address; but the voyagers undertook to convey the message. They stopped for lunch
near a place named Neuenhof, under a modern château,
the first they had as yet seen on the banks of the
Werra. Going up to the inn for provisions and beer,
they there met a son of the burgomaster, who said
he had read about them in the papers and had
been on the look-out for them during the last two
days.

The river now for a distance of about sixteen
miles is (except at Ebenshausen) without obstructions from Spichra to Falken. The scenery after
Kreuzburg, about three miles below the former
place, becomes very beautiful. The stream winds
in a north-easterly direction for five miles to Mihla,
after that flowing in two great bends north-west
to Falken. Below Kreuzburg there are some fine
bare cliffs with buttresses of rock jutting out, followed by charmingly wooded ridges alternating on
the right and the left bank. Especially striking is a

hill near Mihla, overgrown with beech, ash, and fir,
while a splendid broad reach of river flows past,
reminding one of the Clevedon woods on the Thames.
The appearance of the boat on the scene some way
farther down became the signal for all the agriculture
on the right bank, which was flat, stopping dead, and
the horses and peasants assuming that statuesque
attitude which was so characteristic of these riparians
when that trusty craft came within their ken. The
last two and a half miles above Falken are a fine
stretch of water for rowing. The memory of the
writer reverts to this wide and crescent-shaped reach
as one of the loveliest bits of river scenery he has
ever beheld. Its charm was heightened by the
rare beauty of the evening. The half-moon hung
in a perfectly cloudless sky over the dark crest
of a wooded ridge and was mirrored in the placid
stream below, while the stillness of the deepening
twilight was unbroken save by the plash of
the oars and the song of the rowers as they
slowly glided down. In the growing darkness they
paddled down to the mill, intending to leave
the boat in charge of the miller; but finding
it deserted, they disembarked, and the Interpreter
made for a light gleaming in the distance between the trees. It turned out to proceed from
a cottage in which a family of peasants were assembled round their evening meal. On the Interpreter explaining the situation and his wish to find

an inn if possible, two of the men of the family
volunteered to convey the hand-luggage to the
Wirthshaus of Herr Schmidt.   Being shown the way
down to the boat for this purpose, they were much
startled at beholding the nude form of Bow suddenly emerging from the waters of the Werra in the
gloom of night.   As there was only one bed and one
sofa available, the Interpreter was obliged in consequence of the adverse toss of a coin to pass the
night on a table.   The landlord, a most obliging and
intelligent man, informed his guests that he had
served as a private in the wars of '66 and '70, and
was in the habit of going to Berlin every year for a
holiday.   The bill, which included the night's lodging, supper, breakfast, and provisions for the following
day, and was made out in the name of *Die drei
Herren aus England* (the three gentlemen from England), amounted to the surprisingly small sum of
eight marks.

Next morning the mill-sluice was shot in view of
a large public, and for some distance down the bank
there was quite a stampede of enthusiastic well-
wishers.   About two miles lower down lies the picturesque little town of Treffurt, nestling in a valley,
with the ruin of the Normanstein crowning the
hill above.   Near this point there are some fine red
slate cliffs with overhanging foliage, while the Heldrastein towers to a height of 1100 feet above the
valley.   This hill would well repay a visit, as it is

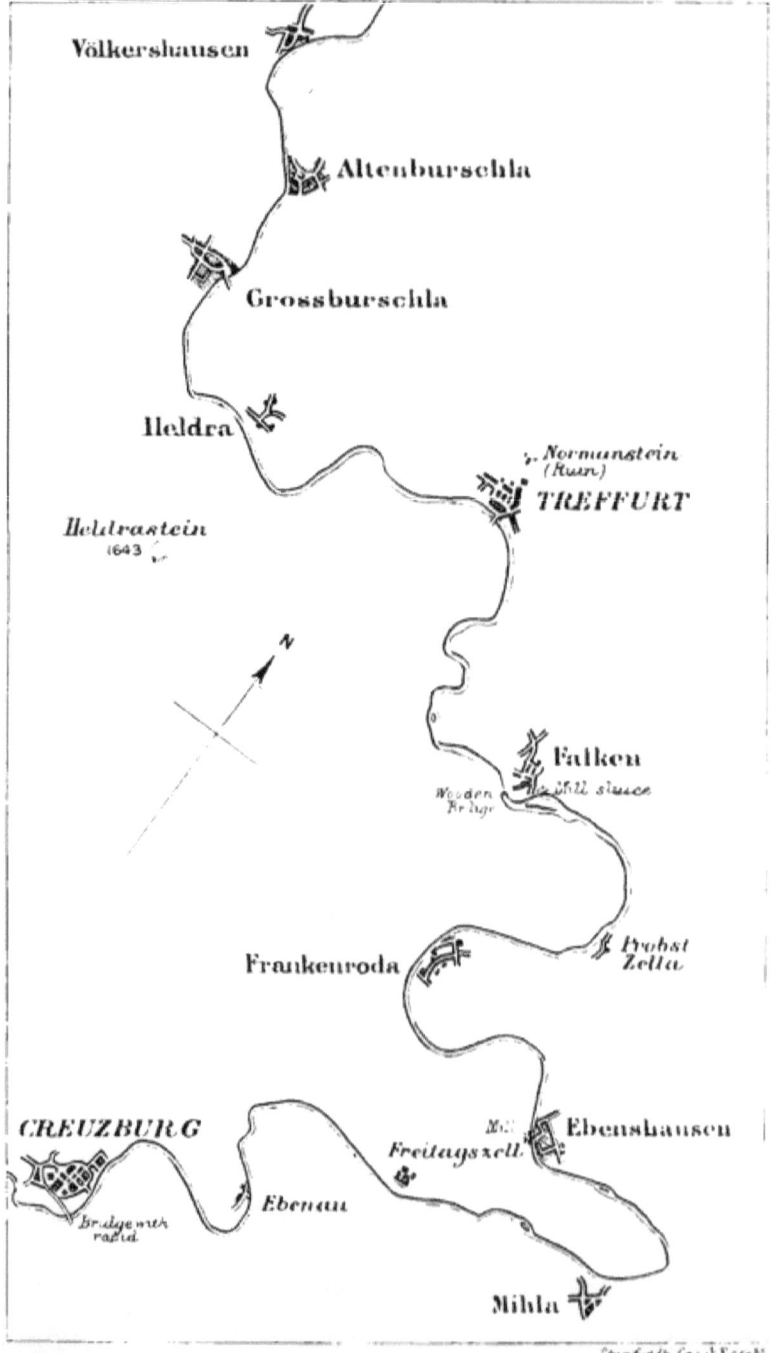

Völkershausen

Altenburschla

Grossburschla

Heldra

Normanstein
(Ruin)
TREFFURT

Heldrastein
1643

N

Falken
Mill sluice

Wooden
Bridge

Frankenroda

Probst
Zella

CREUZBURG

Ebenshausen

Freitagszell

Ebenau

Bridge with
rapid

Mihla

0 1 2 3 4 5 Kilometres

Stanfords Geogl Estab

said to command a magnificent view of the Werra and
of the surrounding country. After a row of two
hours Wannfried was reached, the last place on the
river with a mill-sluice, and the first to boast a
clinker-built boat. As the miller was unusually long
about pulling up the paddles and the stream was strong,
the Interpreter became too exhausted to back against
the current. A night passed on even the best of
tables tends to diminish a man's powers of endurance
on the following day. In order to save himself from
coming to complete grief in the partially open sluice
he was compelled to let himself drive against a wooden
partition in front of the mill-wheel. A calamity
might thus have occurred on the very last occasion ;
fortunately, however, no further damage was done
than the partial breaking at the blade of an oar and
a scull that protruded from the bows. After frantic
exertions to pull the boat against the stream (which
was now running with its full force) by means of
bushes and stakes, he got her round only just in time
to shoot the lasher successfully.

Five miles farther lies Eschwege, a town of 8000
inhabitants, situated on both sides of the river. It
is a very old place, being said to date from the time
of Charlemagne. The first lock on the river occurring here ought to have facilitated the boat's progress ; but as it was unluckily undergoing repairs,
a very difficult and toilsome porterage was rendered
necessary. The scenery after Eschwege falls off con-

siderably, being tamer, owing to the increase of
cultivation and the corresponding decrease of wood.

In consequence of a rather fatiguing day of
twenty-seven miles, following on a bad night's rest, the
crew felt very tired, and resolved to put up at Allendorf. This is a town of from 3000 to 4000 inhabitants, with a railway station and a *Kursaal* for the
benefit of some 400 invalids who frequent the place
for its salt baths. Allendorf made rather an inhos-
pitable impression, as the only two hotels in the
place could not take the weary wayfarers in. So
they were ultimately reduced to lodging for the night
above a butcher's shop.

The second lock on the Werra, which is a very
good one, occurs here. Some rafts went through at
the same time next morning, two of the men
turning out to be natives of Wernshausen, where
the nocturnal adventure previously related had
ended. An hour's row brings one to Lindewerra, a
small village overhung by a projecting rock, called
the Devil's Pulpit. This was the spot from which
the Interpreter in his boyhood used to start on his
boating expeditions with his German friends. After
three or four winds of the river in a north-westerly
direction, there comes into view the picturesque old
castle of Hanstein, a favourite excursion by rail from
Göttingen. Here begins a famous cherry country,
often visited by the Interpreter and his friends in
their schoolboy days. The crew landed some way

Unterrieden

Wellingerode

Wendershausen

Albungen

Werleshausen

Jestädt

Oberrieden

Station

Lindewerra

Station

N

ESCHWEGE

Ellershausen

Lock

Wahlhausen

Gr.
Leuchtberg

Station

Sooden

Schwebda

Station
Lock

Tunnel

ALLENDORF

Frieda

Weiden Hofe

E

Klein Vach

WANNFRIED

Mill sluice

Albungen

Völkershausen

0   1   2   3   4   5   Kilometres

above Witzenhausen to buy five pounds of cherries, the produce of trees growing close to the river bank. This purchase produced a visible deterioration in the speed of the boat as well as in the quality of the steering. The crew suddenly found themselves drifting past the picturesque little town of Witzenhausen and close upon a rather ugly rapid under the stone bridge which here spans the river. This was, however, successfully shot by taking the arch next to the left bank.

The scenery in the last six miles, as Münden is approached, grows remarkably fine, the river now flowing through a defile of high, dark pine-clad hills. Immediately above the town the stream divides, the left and more rapid branch flowing to the lock. Münden, a pleasant town of about 6000 inhabitants, is charmingly situated in a richly wooded country on the tongue of land formed by the confluence of the Fulda and Werra, to which fact it owes its name (derived from *Mund*, mouth). The combined waters from this point onwards bear the name of the Weser. Münden is well-known as the seat of a first-class academy of forestry, and is much visited by the inhabitants of neighbouring places for the beauty of its scenery. The town of Cassel, where, at the Palace of Wilhelmshöhe, Napoleon III. resided as a prisoner during the latter part of the Franco-German war, is distant only fifteen miles, less than an hour by train, and would

well repay a visit, if only for the sake of the
magnificent picture gallery there. The boat being
left in charge of the lock-keeper, the crew drove
up to the *Hessische Hof* in the hotel omnibus
to avoid publicity. Their funds were by this time
pretty nearly exhausted, but a registered letter containing money (which a Göttingen banker had most
obligingly sent in exchange for a cheque) was awaiting the Interpreter at the post-office. This he was,
however, unable to obtain possession of, having
stupidly omitted to bring a passport with him from
England. Fortunately remembering some former acquaintances who lived in the country a few miles from
Münden, he lost no time in taking a fly and driving
out to their place. After a kind reception he returned with the estate manager, who furnished the
guarantee required by the rules of the post-office.
Some young officers from the riding-school at Han-
over were staying at the hotel, and had spent the
evening carousing pretty freely. When the crew
retired at about midnight two of these young sons of
Mars were discovered seated on the box of an empty
coach in the yard, urging on imaginary steeds with
cracking whips and loud yells of encouragement.

Owing to the numerous and unforeseen obstructions on the Werra the progress made had fallen
very far short of anticipation. The Interpreter was
unfortunately obliged to be back in England by a
certain date. In order, therefore, to reach Bremen

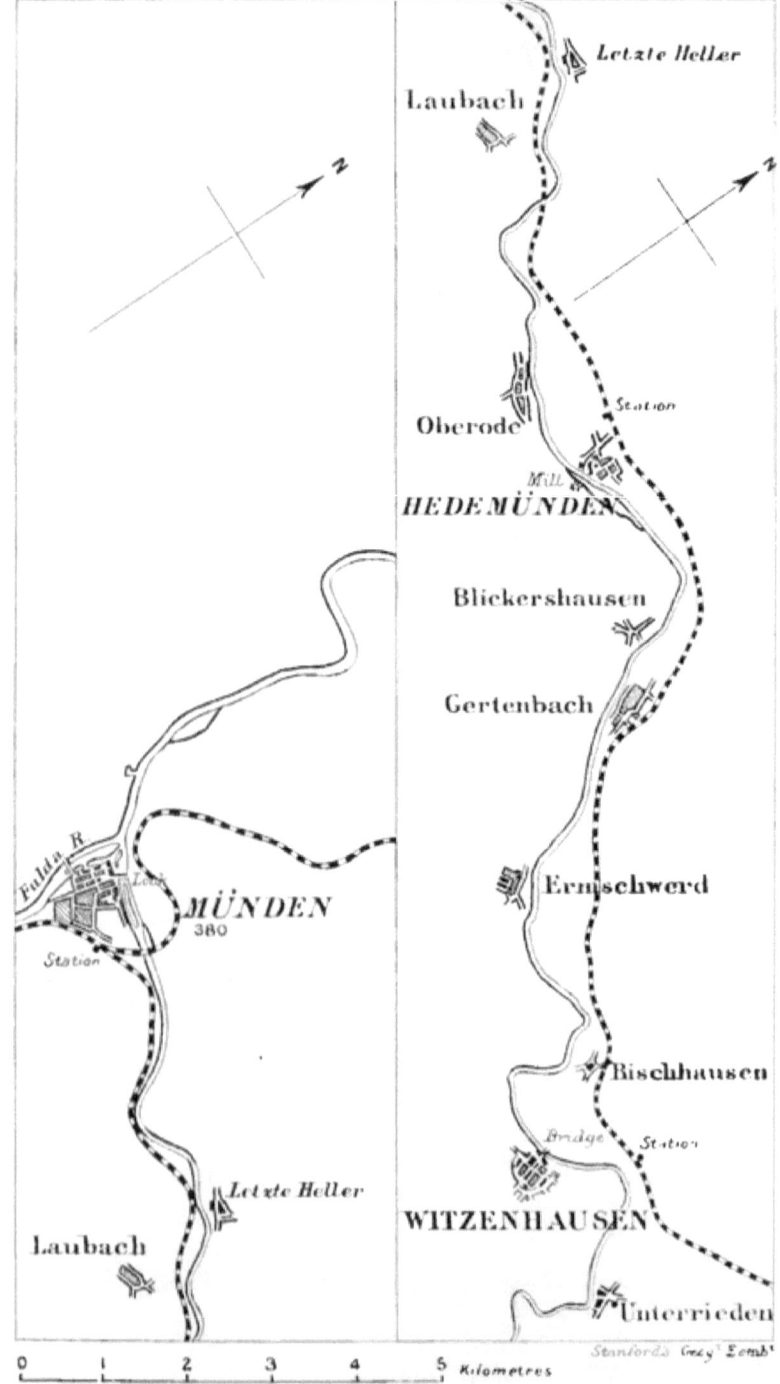

Letzte Heller

Laubach

Oberode

Station

HEDEMÜNDEN

Mill

Blickershausen

Gertenbach

Ermschwerd

Fulda R.

Lock

MÜNDEN
380

Station

Bischhausen

Bridge   Station

Letzte Heller

WITZENHAUSEN

Laubach

Unterrieden

0   1   2   3   4   5   Kilometres

in time, all thought of further camping had now to be finally abandoned. As the steamer leaving Bremerhafen on the following Thursday morning had to be caught, only four clear days were left for finishing the remaining distance, 232 miles (372 kilometres), the previous 125 miles having taken eight days. This was indeed a formidable prospect. Though there was but one more obstruction between Münden and the sea—the lock at Hameln—eleven hours a day of hard rowing would certainly be necessary to accomplish the feat. An average speed of five miles an hour was the utmost that could be expected, with a stream, the fall of which could easily be calculated—Münden being but 380 feet above the level of the sea—to be only twenty inches per mile. In spite, however, of faint-hearted counsels, it was at last resolved to make the attempt. The result remained to be seen.

CHAPTER III

THE WESER

"Tu, nisi ventis
Debes ludibrium, cave."—HORACE.

SUNDAY began inauspiciously with rain. This, it is true, soon cleared away, and was followed by bright sunshine interrupted only by a sharp thunder-shower in the early afternoon. But a strong wind springing up rendered the water so rough that the heavy oak boat, unable to rise to the waves, shipped several seas. One of the crew, moreover, lay prostrate, owing to over-indulgence in cherries on the previous day. The scenery during the whole of this day's voyage was uninteresting save a fine steep cliff below Carlshafen, where the river takes a sharp bend towards the north. The most rapid fall in the Weser is

between this place and Holzminden, for here it
descends seventy feet in twenty miles. Quite a
flotilla of punt-like boats was noticed near Carlshafen, drawn up on the shore, presumably for the
use of fishermen. Some rope-ferries also occur on
this part of the river.

The only place with any interest attaching to it
passed that day was Corvey, on the left bank about
a mile below Höxter. It was once the most famous
Benedictine abbey in North Germany, having been
founded as early as 816 by Louis the Pious. In the
year 1514 a manuscript of the first five books of the
Annals of Tacitus, which were till then supposed to
be irrecoverably lost, was found in the library. The
story of its discovery suggested to Gustav Freytag
the plot of his well-known novel, *Die verlorene Hand-
schrift* (the lost manuscript).

A steady row from 10.30 A.M. to 9.15 P.M. was
only interrupted by a brief lunch and a short sail.
Now the mast was rigged up for the first time in
order to utilise a wind blowing so strong abaft that
the boat, heavy though she was, tore along at the
rate of six miles an hour. So rapidly, indeed, did
the kilometre stones (which mark the distance on
the bank from Münden to Bremen) seem to fly past,
that an American observer would no doubt have
described them as producing the impression of a
riverside cemetery.

Holzminden, the place of that night's sojourn,

was reached some time after sunset, the boat being
left in charge of a ferryman. During the course of
dinner the Interpreter, entering into conversation
with a stranger sitting next to him, related some of
the incidents of what he described as a *Lustfahrt*
(pleasure trip) on the Werra and the Weser. The
Teuton, adopting the usual attitude of foreigners
towards enterprises which involve hardship and
strenuous physical exercise, and plainly showing his
commiseration, strongly recommended the misguided
Britons to conclude the voyage in tow of a barge.
The improvement in the hotel accommodation as the
river increases in size may be judged by comparing
the amount of the bill—thirty-two marks—with
that of the little village inn of Falken ; but whether
it represented four times the value is a question not
so easy to decide.

A start having been made soon after eight o'clock,
the first six miles were rowed in exactly one hour.
As a stiff breeze was following straight astern, nearly
the same pace was kept up sailing till Bodenwerder
was reached—a distance of twenty miles. This place
deserves to be mentioned as the birthplace and home
of the most famous liar known to literary history—
Baron von Münchausen. It is interesting to note
that the incredible adventures which that mendacious
nobleman was in the habit of relating in the circle
of his friends were first published in English by a
German named Raspe, who had fled to London to

escape the consequences of stealing coins from the collection under his charge at Cassel. This English edition was anonymously translated into German by the poet Bürger in 1787.

At Bodenwerder the river, hitherto so accommodating, made an uncompromising bend towards the west, keeping a westerly or north-westerly direction for the rest of the day. The next eight hours were consequently spent in a strenuous struggle with a gale blowing steadily on the fore-quarter or beam, and raising quite a sea on the ever-broadening expanse of the Weser. The rain, too, beat relentlessly during all those leaden-footed hours in slanting torrents on the toilers at the oar. Despair began to gather black on the brow of at least one of the mariners. The hard-boiled egg and bottle of German beer were with the utmost difficulty consumed under the sheltering umbrella amid the pitiless downpour. Mark Tapley might well have taken some credit to himself for keeping his spirits up on such a day. The one ray of consolation that lightened the mental gloom of the voyagers was the conviction that their German friend of the previous night could not possibly have taken his stand on any point of the bank that day to witness their miseries.

By four in the afternoon they had made the town of Hameln, known to fame chiefly as the home of the Pied Piper—

> " Hamelin town's in Brunswick,
>   By famous Hanover city ;
>   The river Weser deep and wide,
>   Washes its walls on the southern side."

Though Browning had probably no personal experience of the inhabitants of the Weser valley, he saw, with true poetical insight, the importance of clothes in the legend; for he says of the Piper that

> " His queer long coat from heel to head
>   Was half of yellow and half of red."

Had the ancient musician but worn an English " blazer," there can be no doubt that he would have drawn after him to their doom not only the youth, but also the greater part of the adult population of Hameln.

While passing through the magnificent lock the three friends telegraphed to the hotel at Minden announcing their expected arrival about midnight. But when they got off again it blew such a gale that all hope of accomplishing this project was given up. One of the crew was now almost a corpse, while the Professor complained of being completely worn away. The latter, however, retained a sufficient amount of energy to give vent to his feelings in tolerably strong language for most of the afternoon. Some consolation he derived from a pipe, which, after a prolonged struggle with wind and rain, he managed to light with matches obtained from a passing barge. The last two hours of that day's row he described as " simple h—l,"

expressing a conviction that a *Lustfahrt* on the Weser
would be one of the torments of the damned.

The town of Rinteln, about fifty-two miles and
a half from Holzminden, and now the utmost goal of
their ambition, seemed never to be coming in sight,
so interminable did the convolutions of the river
appear to the jaded mind. Like everything else the
weary distance came to an end at last. The exhausted trio trudged up to the chief inn, the *Stadt
Bremen*, carrying their oars with them for security.
They were unconscious of the disreputable appearance
they must have presented in their soiled and soaking
flannels. When the Interpreter inquired as to rooms,
the landlord suggested in reply that the inn over the
way—a wretched little place—might suit them better.
This advice was more than the nerves of the Professor,
already worked up to the highest pitch of irritation,
could endure, and the vials of his wrath were poured
forth in a formula, extemporised in the heat of
the moment, which though unheard before in the
Fatherland, was yet perfectly intelligible to the object
of the outburst—*Potzteufel, Götterdämmerung und
Höllerei, ist dies Stadt Bremen oder nicht?* Their
language evidently proved the strangers to be gentlemen ; for they were now welcomed with the utmost
humility by their host, who afterwards even undertook the menial office of carrying down their boots
with his own hand. Such is the magical effect of
appropriate diction.

Rinteln, the seat of a university in former days,
was known to the Interpreter from a visit during the
summer vacation some years previously. The landlord, who was a great gossip, rattled off in answer to
interrogatories a vast amount of information about
the leading inhabitants. The fate of a large and
well-known family of daughters he reeled off with
great volubility, winding up with the remark:
Anna, die dicke, ist noch zu haben (Anna, the fat one,
is still eligible).

One hundred and two miles had now been accomplished in two days, and one hundred and thirty still
remained to be done in the next two. The river for
some distance below Rinteln is in parts, owing to its
breadth, rather shallow and requires careful steering
in order to avoid running on sunken rocks. Soon
after starting the first windmill was observed, a sure
indication of the approach of a flat country. The
course of the river from Münden to Minden lies
through a series of picturesque valleys formed by
the irregular range of the Weser hills; but after it
issues into the plain through the narrow pass called
the Porta Westphalica the banks become perfectly
flat and uninteresting. The level strip of land between the hills and the river above the Porta was
the scene of the battle of Idistaviso, fought between
Germanicus and Arminius and described in the
Annals of Tacitus. The Professor was with great
difficulty restrained from landing here in order to

test the credibility of the historian, who relates how Arminius and his brother carried on a colloquy from opposite sides of the Weser. The Professor was very sceptical as to the width of the river—about two hundred yards—admitting of a conversation being conducted from one bank to the other. Perhaps he will be found on some future occasion undertaking a special journey for the purpose of prosecuting on the spot researches which will settle this very important question.

The first part of this day's voyage was rowed; but from Vlotho, where the river turns northwards after flowing twenty miles due west, the sail was used with great effect till within two or three miles' distance of Minden. The rain came down all the morning, and the beautiful scenery of the Porta, where the Weser hills closing in on the river form a defile, was passed in a perfect torrent. Minden was reached at about two o'clock, in five hours' time from the start. It was unfortunately necessary to land here, as Bow had a money-letter awaiting him at the post-office. The strength of the stream renders it difficult to effect a landing at Minden. This was at length managed, the boat being left in charge of a bargee. The landlord of the *Stadt London* most obligingly consented to be surety for the strangers at the post-office. Feeling bound in return to do something for the good of the house, especially as they had wired for rooms the day before, they ordered a sumptuous dinner. On its

E

conclusion they invited their genial host to join them
in a bottle of champagne, to which he replied with
another. He too had served in the Franco-Prussian
war, and that under an officer well known to the
Interpreter.

It was already seven in the evening before a
start was made, and 105 miles remained to be accomplished before nightfall on the following day. The
only possibility of performing this *tour de force* was
by going on continuously all night and the whole of
the next day. Even thus an average speed of four
miles would have to be kept up for twenty-six hours.
However, the inspiration of generous liquor filled the
souls of the crew with rosy hopes. It was a beautiful
evening, the water being perfectly calm and the sky
without a cloud. The moon, now nearly full, rose
red and cast her sheen on the tranquil waters. Thus
began the novel and hazardous experiment of navigating an unknown river by night. A four hours'
steady row had accomplished twenty miles by eleven
o'clock. Cox had meanwhile prepared supper and
made tea (with filtered Weser water) in the stern.
The voyagers then enjoyed a short rest as they
partook of their evening meal, floating down the
moonlit stream. By this time a good wind had
sprung up behind; and as the map showed the
river to flow in the same direction for twenty
miles, while the current ran fairly fast, the crew
determined on reserving their energies as far as

possible by sailing during the remainder of the night.
The Interpreter taking the helm, Bow assumed the
office of look-out, while the Professor composed himself to sleep amidships. The moon having disappeared behind thick clouds for the rest of the night,
it became extremely difficult to descry anything
ahead, even at a short distance. The boat was now
scudding along before the wind at a fine pace.
Suddenly Bow shouted, " Look out, mind your heads !"
and in an instant down came the mast and sail with
a splash in the water. He had fortunately seen,
when only a few feet off, a ferry-cable which extended across the river, and had managed to hitch
out the mast in the very nick of time, thus saving it,
as well as the heads of his friends. The rope was so
low that it grazed the Interpreter's arm, though he
was lying down flat on the stern seat. This little
incident effectually banished any further thoughts of
sleep. The excitement had hardly subsided when
the boat ran straight into a snag embedded in the
very middle of the stream. The bows stuck fast,
while the stern was swung rapidly round by the
current. For a moment the crew expected to be
emptied into the water with all their belongings, and
to find a watery grave far from their native shores.
But by good luck the impetus of the boat caused her
to slide off stern foremost without having sustained
any injury. Bow's vision after these mishaps became
so preternaturally acute that he distinctly made out

imaginary ferry-ropes as the villages were passed,
and hoisted out the mast with feverish haste to
avoid the impact. Curiously enough no real ones re-
curred till some time after daybreak. All this distance the banks are low, while the river, being upwards of two hundred yards in breadth, is generally
shallow on one side or the other. For these two
reasons steering in the dark was a sufficiently hazardous undertaking, quite irrespective of any obstacles
that might at any moment present themselves.
Sailing at night is, moreover, much more risky than
rowing, as it is impossible to stop the way of the
boat at short notice. To unship the mast and get
out the oars would occupy too much time for many
an emergency, especially when the crew is bound to
have fallen into a semi-somnolent condition. However, this particular crew was now so wide-awake that
they determined to light their pipes, which they succeeded in doing only after many vain efforts. Rain
soon began to fall, and umbrellas were put up. The
notion of sailing down an unknown river at midnight,
smoking pipes and under the shelter of umbrellas,
struck the voyagers as so grotesque that many a
peal of laughter, never heard before at that hour on
those lonely shores, rang out over the waters. The
boat had been gliding along noiselessly through the
darkness for some miles, when Cox was aroused by
a shout from Bow to pull the left rudder-string
hard. A steam-dredger (*Dampfbagger*), moored in

mid-stream at a bend in the river, had suddenly
loomed out of the night, and a collision was only
just avoided by steering through the narrow passage
between the vessel and the bank. There turned out
to be a chain under the surface of the water attaching the dredger to the shore. This chain scraped
the bottom of the boat, unshipping the rudder; she
consequently swung round and ran into a pile, but
again got off without damage. Had it not been for
her extraordinarily strong build, the skiff would undoubtedly have come to grief that night. As it was,
the only injury she had apparently sustained was the
loss of the strip of waterproof tacked on to stop a
leak soon after the commencement of the voyage.
She was soon found to be letting in water rather
badly, and the crew spent most of the rest of the
voyage with their feet steeped in bilge-water, which
was kept within bounds only by repeated baling.
To run ashore and stop the leak there was no time
on the day which was now going to break. When
the first signs of dawn began to appear, the moon,
about to set, emerged from behind a black mass of
cloud, and as she hung full-orbed like a golden lamp
on the horizon illuminating the dark canopy above,
presented a striking and beautiful sight. It was
curious to note how, as morning broke, the concert of
the birds seemed to strike up in a moment all along
the banks. The contrast between the sudden volume
of sound and the preceding stillness, unbroken save

by the gentle lapping of the water, produced quite
a startling effect. The sleepless voyagers were, perhaps, all the more impressed, as they themselves
were by no means in a singing mood.

Nienburg was reached at about half-past five, the
last twenty miles having been done under sail alone.
The performance of forty-one miles during the night,
though not bad under ordinary circumstances, did
not contribute much to raise the spirits of the jaded
trio; for had they not still the prospect of sixty-four
miles more of unremitting toil before their labours
were over? That such a distance, formidable enough
after a good night's rest, could be accomplished by
nightfall, seemed all but hopeless even with a favourable wind. A short halt was made for breakfast on a
strip of sandy beach some little distance below Nienburg. The energies of the crew were somewhat revived
by a copious draught of warm tinned soup, but their
complexions still remained very green in the bright
morning light. When again afloat they had gradually
to realise the disheartening fact that the wind, which
had favoured them all night and was now increasing
in strength, would be their enemy for the rest of the
voyage. The general trend here taken by the Weser
towards the north by north-west for about thirty
miles was just sufficient to render the wind worse
than useless for sailing purposes. But the cup of
their misery was not yet full. Heavy showers began to fall and continued till evening, keeping the

crew drenched to the skin all the time. In addition
to this, Stroke at least always had his feet immersed
in bilge-water. Could even the just man have been
perfectly happy under these circumstances?

The Professor, who was the most exhausted, would,
when his turn to row came—two out of every three
hours—insist on hoisting the sail on the plea that the
wind was decidedly growing more favourable. When
the futility of the manœuvre had been repeatedly
proved by the boat running ashore broadside in half a
minute, he at length gloomily resigned himself to the
oar, swearing solemnly that he would never, never
again, during the remainder of his natural life, enter a
boat for the purpose of undertaking a *Lustfahrt!* It
is almost superfluous to add that this vow was egregi-
ously broken before a full month had elapsed. Most
of his strokes, it will easily be believed, were not very
energetic; but now and again he would plunge his
oar deep into the river with a malignant dig, invariably to the accompaniment of a very audible mono-
syllable. In some reaches the wind blew straight
up stream, and raised quite a sea. Thus a considerable amount of water was shipped, in addition to the
contributions of the leak and of the driving rain. By
4 P.M. thirty-six miles had been done by unceasing
labour, and twenty-eight were still left to accomplish
in the remaining five hours of daylight. The task
seemed perfectly hopeless. For the river not only
became extremely broad by the accession of the waters

of a large tributary, the Aller, but now took a final
bend towards the west in the very teeth of the wind.
The waves in mid-stream were too large for the
heavily laden boat to stand, so that she had to coast
along the bank at the rate of hardly two miles an
hour. At this pace Bremen could not have been
reached till six o'clock next morning. The result of
such an experience would probably have been a prolonged stay in a hospital for at least one member of the
crew. Fortunately, as on the previous days, the wind
died away towards evening. By seven o'clock the
water became as smooth as a glass, and the sky grew
perfectly clear. The moon rose full and was reflected
in the broad expanse of the river. The force of the
stream now made itself felt, and the energies of the
rowers revived for a final effort. The towers of
Bremen became visible over the low-lying plain
while yet a long way off, but never seemed to come
any nearer. However, the mere sight of them gave
strength to the toilers, who rowed into Bremen in quite
fine style at half-past nine, as the shades of night
were beginning to fall. Thus the feat of doing 105
miles in twenty-six consecutive hours was an accomplished fact, in spite of adverse fate. The satisfaction
of having carried out their purpose was quite an
adequate reward for the hardships of the voyage. A
boatbuilder was found, who undertook to convey the
skiff to the station in time to get her off by the eight
o'clock train next morning. The friends then drove

off in a cab to the Hôtel de l'Europe, and, profiting
by previous experiences, at once explained to one of
the waiters that flocked down the steps the cause of
their disreputable appearance. They were received
with open arms, the explanation having apparently
been unnecessary. This difference of treatment is
probably to be explained by the fact that the inhabitants of large cities are keener observers of men.
A luxurious dinner rewarded the toils of the preceding night and day ; but it did not, perhaps, receive
the keen appreciation which its excellence deserved.
To the amazement of the attendant waiter, two of the
crew now and again allowed their heads to drop on
one side and broke out into the most uncompromising snore. Had they not been aroused on each
occasion in order to resume operations, there is no
telling how long this rare kind of table-music would
have continued.

Next morning the Interpreter, after passing
through the painful ordeal of rising at five, saw the
boat and all the luggage safely packed on a truck ;
but no officer was present to pass them through the
custom-house. When the crew turned up at the
station in good time for the eight o'clock train to
Bremerhafen, it was announced that the custom-house
would not open till the exact moment of the train's
departure. The Interpreter was accordingly compelled to leave his friends behind to arrange about
the boat. The last thing he saw, as the train steamed

out, was the Professor standing on the platform
engaged single-handed in a hot altercation with a
knot of officials. The latter looked as if under the
circumstances they would have preferred to pass the
boat before the regulation time.

The Interpreter, having despatched a telegram
from Bremerhafen to the old gentleman at Heidelberg and to the hotel-keeper at Meiningen, went
on board the steamer, vexed at the prospect of
having to cross alone. The hour of departure having
long passed by, the captain at length announced
that he had received instructions by telegram from
the office of the German Lloyd's Company to wait
out in the harbour till two o'clock for the arrival
of two other passengers from Bremen. Shortly
before that hour a tender was seen approaching,
and soon the white lawn-tennis hat of the Professor
became visible on its deck. Such is the reward
of dogged pertinacity! The captain swore that no
steamer of that line had ever in his experience been
delayed four hours for the sake of passengers.

The greater part of the voyage was spent in taking
out arrears of sleep, while most of the remaining
hours were devoted to dividing the common camping
property by the arbitrament of cards. The boat
had after all to be left behind, as no truck was pro-
curable at short notice to convey her from the station
to the quay. She came on by the next steamer;
and all the belongings of the crew were safely

delivered at Bow's abode, with the exception of the
hock bottles, which arrived empty. This slight
deficiency was, however, made up for by the con-
scientious delivery of a good-sized piece of bacon.
The latter fact compelled Bow to avail himself of the
hospitality of his friends for several days. He was
only enabled to return after his rooms had undergone
a thorough course of fumigation. Thus ended one of
the more far-reaching results of this the first voyage
on German waters.

CHAPTER IV

THE NECKAR

' Qualis in aerii pellucens vertice montis
    Rivus muscoso prosilit e lapide
Qui cum de prona praeceps est valle volutus
    Per medium densi transit iter populi,
Dulce viatori lasso in sudore levamen
    Cum gravis exustos aestus hinleat agros."—CATULLUS.

The Crew—Preparations—Strange influence of curry-powder—The
Neckar *gradus*—Start from Cannstatt—Camp near Münster—
Sleeplessness—Merry jests—Bad leak—The Neckar a great
bathing river—Hoheneck—Camp above Marbach, Schiller's
birthplace—Mundelsheimer wine—Its effects—Third camp—
The miller's erroneous views about Englishmen corrected—The
sentimental singer—An outrageous snorer—Heron Reach—
Besigheim—Dangerous rapid at Kirchheim—Camp above
Lauffen—Heilbronn—The Captain's oratory—Würtemberg *v.*
Imperial post-cards—Camp near Neckarsulm—Chain-steamers
—Their diabolical nature—Repairing boat—Stay at Wimpfen—
Fine scenery steadily increasing in beauty—Woods near Binau—
Eberbach—First Officer's illness—Row on in the dark—Stop at
Neckarsteinach—Magnificent scenery—Heidelberg—First
Officer rests there for a day—Camp below Heidelberg—Dangers
from towing-ropes—Return to Heidelberg—Start again—Rain
—Camp below Ladenburg—Mannheim—Confluence of the
Neckar and the Rhine.

THE complete success of the experimental voyage on
the Werra and the Weser led to the organisation on

a larger scale of a similar trip to Germany in the summer of the following year. Owing both to the obvious ease with which they could be combined for a single expedition and to the beauty of their scenery, the rivers fixed upon were the Neckar and the Moselle, together with that part of the Rhine which lies between the mouths of those two tributaries, the total distance being some 350 miles. The boat selected was an in-rigged four-oar, which was despatched to Cannstatt on the Neckar about the middle of July, three weeks before the day chosen for the start.

Two of the crew, the Interpreter and Bow of the previous voyage, are already known to the reader. The three new members all belonged to one Oxford college, which was, however, not the same as that of the other two. The height of these three, averaging as it did six feet two inches, was calculated to impress the inhabitants of the river valleys about to be visited rather deeply with the physique of British oarsmen.

The tallest was the most famous oar Oxford had known for many years. He had not only three times rowed victoriously in the Inter-University Boat-race, but had also won in his college eight the Grand Challenge cup at Henley Regatta two years before. Besides having been president of the University Boat-club, he was one of the most distinguished representatives of All England in the football field.

He was of course unanimously elected Captain of the
present crew. Throughout the voyages about to be
described he invariably displayed that vigilance and
promptitude of action which are characteristic of a
born leader of men.

The second addition was also an oarsman of no
mean prowess. He had both rowed head of the river
at Oxford and occupied the thwart behind the
Captain in the crew which won the Grand Challenge
at Henley. He was appointed First Officer. To him
and to Bow were assigned the special duty of pitching the tent and striking the camp.

The third newcomer was a distinguished member
of his college and the most energetic of oarsmen.
His offer to officiate as Chaplain to the crew was at
once accepted. As his duties in this capacity did not
promise to be very heavy, he undertook, with the
greatest self-effacement, to combine with his spiritual
post that of bottle-washer-in-general and under-cook.
He had recently acquired an elementary knowledge
of the higher cookery ; but neither the appliances
at hand nor the provisions obtainable on the Neckar
and the Moselle allowed much scope for the develop-
ment of his talents in this direction. In addition to
his other functions he frequently acted as sub-inter-
preter, a post he was very well qualified to fill.

On the Interpreter himself, besides the duty of
conversing and negotiating with the natives, devolved
the appointment of head-cook, and, in spite of his

lack of business capacity, that of purser, the latter
post being considered naturally inseparable from that
of Interpreter. Thus were their various functions
assigned to each member of the crew before the
expedition started from England.

The equipment was much the same as in the
previous year, but of course on a larger scale in proportion to the increase in numbers. A gipsy tent,
thirteen feet by seven, was purchased, and proved in
practice to accommodate five sleepers with great
comfort. A large but very compact cooking-stove
was also bought, and was afterwards found to be
fully equal to all the requirements—which were considerable—of a crew of five. On one occasion, for
instance, twenty-five buttered eggs were prepared at
one time in a pan which it contained.

As in the previous year, the Interpreter made,
from the maps of the German Ordnance Survey
(*Generalstabskarten*), a chart in sections which folded
double and fitted conveniently into a pocket-case.

All arrangements being now in readiness, the
crew converged from various quarters at Victoria
Station half an hour before the departure of the Continental express on the evening of 4th August ; and
having successfully collected and registered their
multifarious paraphernalia, set off with many cheerful anticipations of their coming holiday tour.

The sea during the crossing to Flushing being as
smooth as a mirror and the night one of brilliant

starlight, nearly all the crew remained on deck.
The other four having been aroused by the bright
sunshine of the early morning, were somewhat
alarmed at being unable to find the Interpreter anywhere, but after a renewed search they discovered
him curled up in the hollow of a large coil of rope on
deck. Their laughter sufficed to wake him from his
sound slumbers.

The second night they spent at Heidelberg. The
Interpreter, on opening his bag at the hotel, found
that a bottle of curry-powder, which he had crammed
in at the last moment before starting, in the expecta-
tion that it would prove useful for cooking purposes,
had been completely smashed. The consequence was
that not only were he and the rest of the crew seized
with a violent fit of sneezing—the others for some
time without knowing the reason why—but that
parts of several of his garments long retained the
unattractive hue of that well-known spice. This
little incident laid the foundation of a *gradus* elab-
orated by Bow in the course of the trip, with a view
to assist him in the composition of a heroic poem in
hexameters, which was to describe the voyage on the
Neckar in a manner worthy of his poetic talent.
The poem was subsequently half completed, and
would probably have been incorporated with these
pages had it not been temporarily lost. From the
vocabulary in question the following are a few
extracts, all of which have reference to some incident

or other of the voyage: Chaplain—"irreverend"; drawers—"Damoclean"; river—"hell-deep"; shirt—"curried"; toothpick, etc.—"second-hand."

Before quitting Heidelberg Bow and the Interpreter made inquiries for the old gentleman who had taken such an interest in them the year before. They learned, much to their disappointment, that he had left and was now living at Frankfort-on-the-Main. They were, however, glad to be told that he was still in the enjoyment of perfect health.

The five friends reached Cannstatt on a blazing afternoon at about four o'clock on 6th August. At once making their way to the goods station, they, to their great joy, saw while yet a good way off, the bows of an English four-oar protruding from the end of a covered truck. It proved to be their boat, which had arrived two days before. They lost no time in making arrangements for her being conveyed in a cart to the left bank of the Neckar, just below the town. In the meantime they dined comfortably at the Hotel *Hermann*, arriving at the starting-point about seven o'clock. The spot was by no means a good one for launching and packing the boat, not only owing to the mighty stench prevailing there, but also because of the shallowness of the water near the stony shore. The slowness in loading which resulted from the latter drawback was rendered well-nigh unendurable by the former.

At last everything was on board, all the luggage

fitting in wonderfully well. It was a little after
eight o'clock when they pushed off, rowing away
rapidly into the deepening dusk. Owing to the
lateness of the evening their departure took place
without causing the sensation it otherwise would
have done. To have got off within four hours of
their arrival was tolerably expeditious work, especially as it was managed altogether without hurry.

In the meantime there was plenty of water in the
channel; but the crew wished only to row far
enough to find a suitable camping ground beyond
the reach of the town. This plan seemed in every
way preferable to sleeping at a stifling hotel in
weather as sultry as it then was. They soon discovered an excellent spot on the left bank about a
mile from Cannstatt, and situated in a very pretty
orchard a short distance above the village of Münster.
They had selected their ground so well, as far as
privacy was concerned, that though not afloat till
ten o'clock next morning they were not disturbed
by a single visitor. In spite of its being now almost
quite dark, the tent was pitched without difficulty ;
for one of the crew had already put it up in a back-
garden and slept in it for several nights by way of
practice before leaving England.

When the encampment was ready the friends
foolishly thought it advisable to brew some tea to
wash down their light evening meal. Partly owing
to the potency of that beverage, and partly, no doubt,

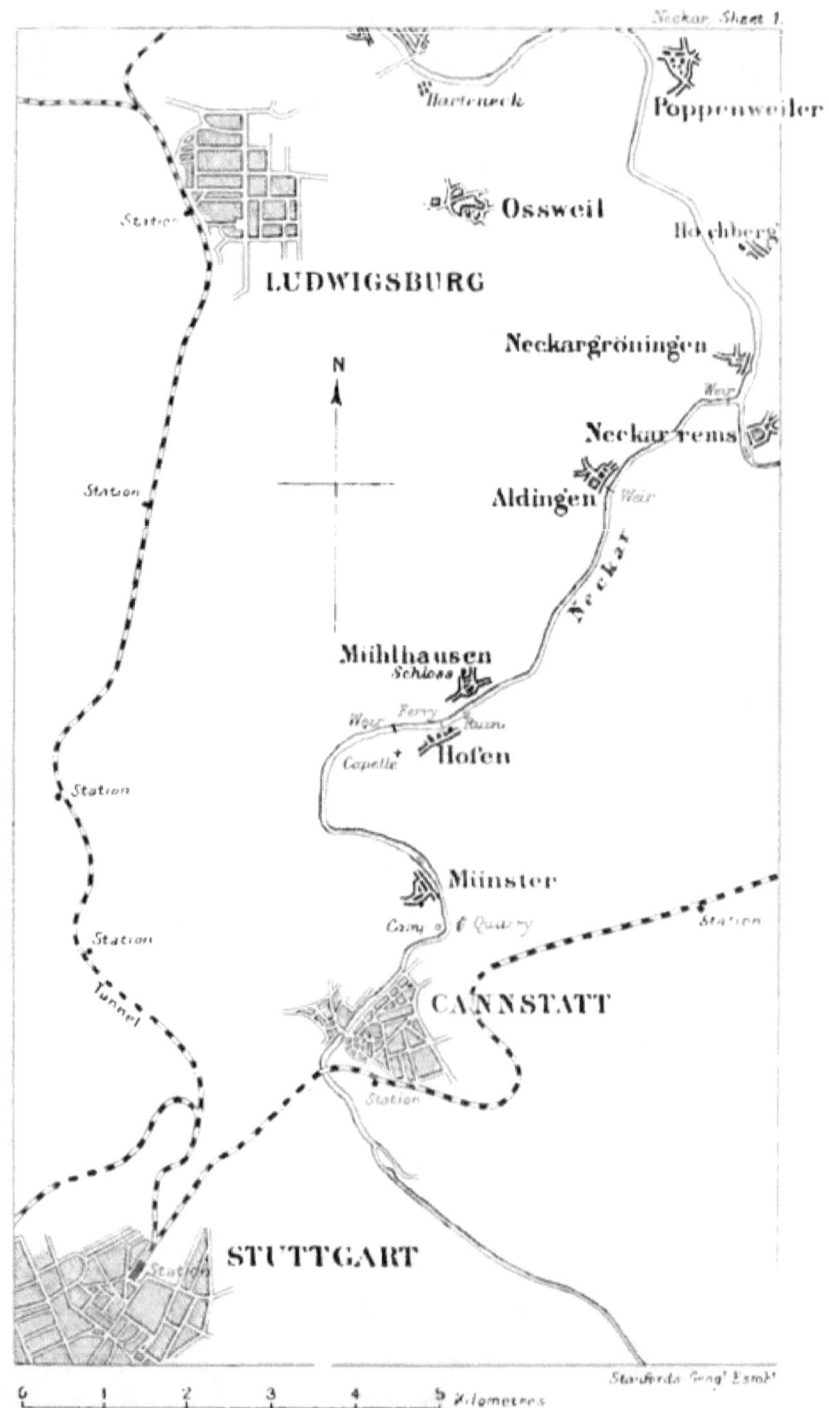

Harteneck

Poppenweiler

Ossweil

Hochberg

LUDWIGSBURG

Neckargröningen

Weir

Neckar rems

N

Aldingen   Weir

Station

Neckar

Mühlhausen
Schloss

Weir   Ferry

Capelle   Hofen

Station

Münster

Quarry

Station

Station

Tunnel

CANNSTATT

Station

STUTTGART

Station

0   1   2   3   4   5 Kilometres

to the extraordinary hardness of the ground, which
had been baked for weeks by a scorching sun, sleep
refused to be wooed by patient waiting. The whole
crew lay outstretched in silence for perhaps two
hours, looking out through the open tent-door on the
bright moonlit scene, or with closed eyes imagining
now and again that they heard under them the scrap-
ings of moles or mice endeavouring in vain to emerge
from their burrows beneath the waterproof sheet
which covered the floor of the tent. At last, about
midnight, they cast off all pretence and simultaneously
burst out laughing at their attempts, equally futile in
each case. Having by this time attained to a pre-
ternatural pitch of wakefulness, they now devoted
themselves to beguiling the slow-paced hours with
merry jests and sallies of repartee. The scintillations
of wit then struck out probably seemed far more
dazzling in the dead of night than they would appear
in the broad light of day. It is therefore no doubt
fortunate that most of them were wasted on the midnight air, having passed into the darkness of oblivion
for ever. Unless, indeed, the stream of time has, as
Bacon says, brought down what was lightest, allowing
weightier things to sink to the bottom. Thus one
unblushing watcher is still remembered to have made
some remark about " Cannstatt, but can't sleep" ; and
when the Captain, unable any longer to endure the
strain of inactivity, sallied forth in his nightshirt to
try the effect of fishing by moonlight from the bank

in front of the tent, another made the unabashed
statement that he had never seen so fine a *chemise en
scène* before.   It is only due to the other three to
assure the reader that this observation was followed
by a stillness so deathlike that the Captain hastily
returned to find out the cause.

Just about the time in the early morning when
they had at last dropped off through sheer weariness,
they were suddenly awakened by the commencement
of operations of the most noisy and exasperating
nature in a quarry on the opposite bank.   They
accordingly rose betimes, but, strange to say, not
altogether unrefreshed.

As breakfasting, washing up, striking the camp,
and packing the boat took up about three hours,
they did not get off till ten, glad at last to escape
from the gratings, sawings, hammerings, and other
disagreeable sounds proceeding from across the river.
They were, however, not to get away from them as
quickly as they expected, for they almost immediately
stuck in some shallow rapids, from which they took
a considerable time in getting clear.   The river was
no doubt lower this year than usual, owing to the
drought that had prevailed for weeks past.   Ordin-
arily little difficulty would be experienced in rowing
down this reach.

The first weir was reached near a village about
four miles from Cannstatt.   This necessitated unloading and carrying the baggage some distance,

but the pull-over for the boat was easy and straight.
The channel below being rather long and dangerous
till it joined the main branch of the river, the Captain,
with the solicitude which he always showed, leapt
out, and wading in front conducted the boat to
safety.

She was now found to be leaking rather badly,
and was accordingly run ashore to be examined.
After well soaping the seams which appeared to let
in the water, the crew resumed their oars and soon
came to a fine reach below the village of Aldingen.
Here they stopped to have a glorious bathe in the hot
sunshine of a cloudless forenoon. At the third obstruction, a weir near the mouth of a tributary which
flows into the Neckar on the right, and close to a
fine château rising on an eminence, the porterage
was long and tedious. Below this they passed under
one of those covered bridges of which there are
several on the Neckar, and which also frequently
occur on the Danube above Sigmaringen.

A short way below Hochberg, and about ten miles
from Cannstatt, there begins a fine crescent-shaped
reach, the banks consisting partly of wooded slopes
and partly of cliffs or vine-terraced hills.

As Hoheneck was approached the river appeared
alive with soldiers bathing in companies. These, no
doubt, came from Ludwigsburg, the military depôt
of Würtemberg, situated about a mile and a half
from the left bank. The inhabitants of the Neckar

valley certainly make full use of their opportunities
for bathing. Boys especially were seen in large
numbers nearly all the way to Heidelberg not only
disporting themselves at the many swimming-baths,
but also about the unfrequented banks. Though the
Germans in general derive so little advantage from
their rivers for boating, they certainly utilise them
to the full in the matter of bathing during the summer months. This is no doubt owing to the great
heat, and partly makes up for the total absence of
the practice of tubbing.

Hoheneck is a little place, with an open-air
restaurant overlooking the Neckar. Stopping here
at half-past three, the friends dined very comfortably
in a shady corner immediately above the river. The
place is, doubtless, a favourite resort for the citizens
of Ludwigsburg. Though this was an ordinary week-
day, there were a number of visitors who had come to
spend the afternoon there, and drink their coffee or
beer in their sociable and contented German way.
On Sundays or other holidays open-air concerts probably take place here during the summer months.

After dinner the crew rowed on for two miles, and
as the evening was drawing in decided to camp
before reaching Marbach. There was, however, a
good deal of indecision as to the exact spot to be
selected, a hot controversy raging for some time between the advocates of the right and of the left bank.
The latter was high and sheltered by trees, whereas

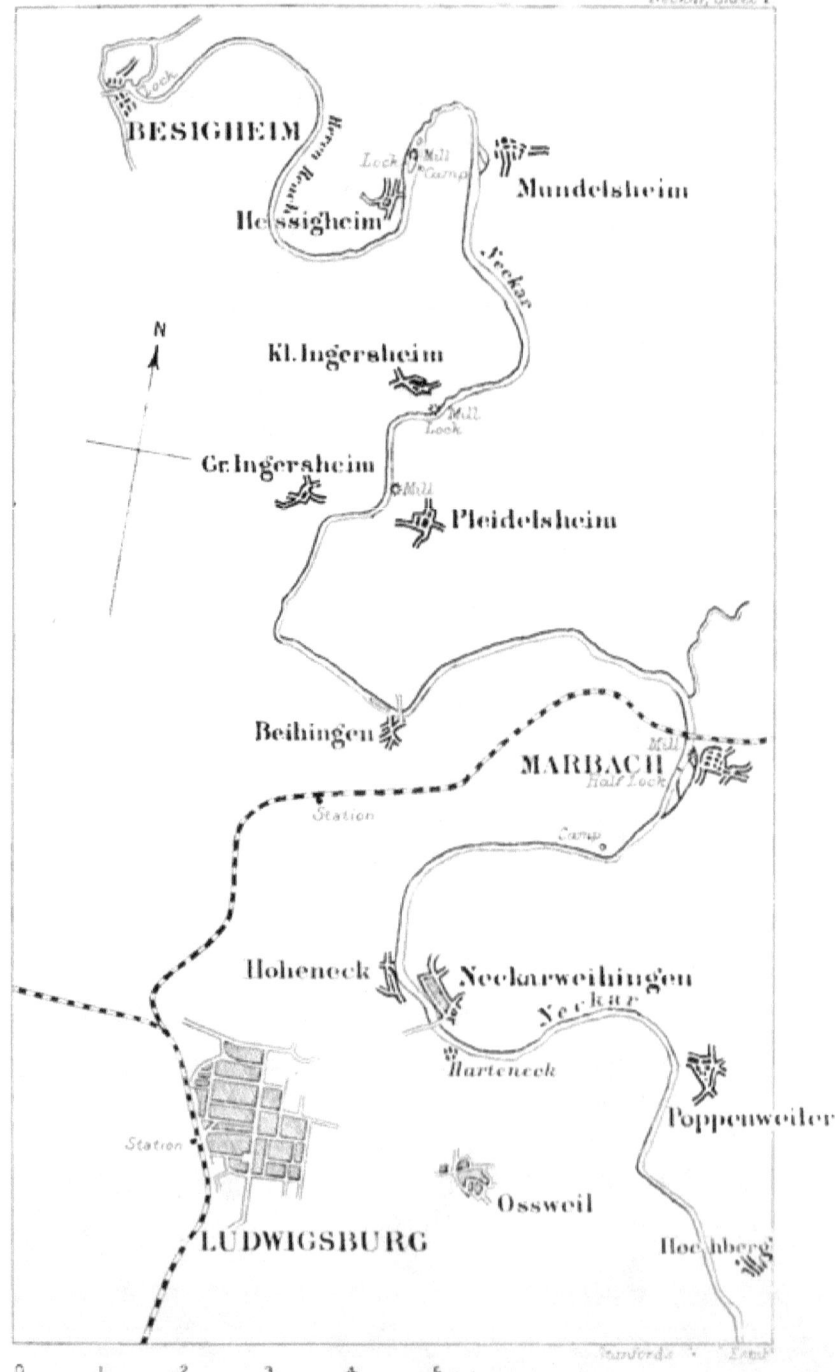

BESIGHEIM

Lock

Herrn Mühl

Lock Mill Camp

Hessigheim

Mundelsheim

Neckar

N

Kl. Ingersheim

Mill Lock

Gr. Ingersheim

Mill

Pleidelsheim

Beihingen

MARBACH

Mill

Half Lock

Station

Camp

Hoheneck

Neckarweihingen

Neckar

Harteneck

Poppenweiler

Station

Ossweil

Hochberg

LUDWIGSBURG

0   1   2   3   4   5 Kilometres

the right was low and open. At last a place on the
left was fixed on about a mile above Marbach. The
supporters of the right bank could not, of course, be
got to admit the superiority of the site chosen, it
being impossible to disprove the unknown virtues of
their ground, and the present site certainly having its
drawbacks. For the bank was abrupt and high,
while the narrow strip of level ground at the top,
flanked by vineyards, was only just broad enough to
admit of the tent being pitched there. Later on
it proved to possess the additional disadvantage of
being pretty numerously inhabited by ants. The
landing being so steep, it was only possible to drag
the heavy luggage up by forming a chain, and thus
handing it from one to the other. The spot had,
however, the merit of being perfectly private, as
well as of being situated in the middle of a fine
reach of the river. The crew were thus enabled to
have a splendid bathe in the bright moonlight before
turning in to rest.

Though up by six next morning, they did not
manage to be afloat till ten o'clock. Having rowed
but a very short way, they came in sight of a
spot with such irresistible attractions for bathing
that they stopped and enjoyed a most refreshing
swim, while the rays of the morning sun, already
very hot, beat down on their heads.

Half a mile farther down lay Marbach, a little
town very prettily situated on the right bank. This

was Schiller's native place, and the house in which the famous poet was born is still preserved very much in the condition it then was in, now more than 130 years ago. The Swabians are justly proud of their country having produced so many great writers ; for, perhaps, no other part of Germany can claim so large a proportion of the names renowned in German literature. The Swabian dialect, too, was the literary language of Germany in the most brilliant period of the poetic activity of the Middle Ages—the epoch of the *Nibelungenlied* and of the chivalrous lays of the Minnesingers.

From a height above the town, the Schillerhöhe, a beautiful view of the valley of the Neckar may be obtained. As the voyagers looked back while rowing away they could not help being struck by the picturesque effect of the mill and its surroundings. Just below Marbach the railway crosses the river by a viaduct which is 100 feet high, and commands a fine view. In the reach after this, where the stream bends round to the west, there was a great rapid, which the boat, however, passed through without injury.

About noon the crew put ashore in the neighbourhood of a village, to which the two interpreters repaired for the purpose of purchasing provisions for lunch. The Captain and Bow meanwhile devoted themselves to fishing, and were successful in catching six dace of various sizes.

Leisurely rowing on they put in just below Mundelsheim, while the Interpreter and the Chaplain went up into the village to buy meat and wine. Having tasted the local Neckar wine, red Mundelsheimer, at the inn, they found it so excellent that they returned with a large quantity of it in a most picturesque blue jar, for which they paid only a mark. This jar, closely resembling a Greek amphora in shape, appealed so strongly to the archæological tastes of the Chaplain that he vowed he would take it back with him to England as a memento. It was, however, hopelessly fractured on the following morning, possibly in consequence of a slight *tremor alcoholicus* induced by what it had contained on the previous day.

When they had returned with their treasure to their expectant companions, the crew resumed their oars for another mile until a mill came into view. Here, as it was now beginning to grow dark, they resolved to encamp for the night. It was an ideal place for this purpose, being an island above the lock, with a small piece of greensward backed by a clump of trees. No human habitation was anywhere in sight save the solitary mill. In this charming spot they pitched their tent. A most luxurious supper, the *menu* of which included fish of their own catching and veal cutlets, was rendered additionally festive by copious draughts of the delicious Mundelsheimer.

The miller and his men, who came down to visit

the encampment, were greatly delighted with the
hospitality which was extended to them. The former
seemed much impressed with the height of the three
tall members of the crew, saying he had till then
thought that all Englishmen were short. The Interpreter, however, intent on maintaining or even
increasing the prestige of his country, assured the
miller that these three more or less represented the
average male growth of the British isles, while his
own and Bow's shorter stature was to be accounted
for by the fact that they had not yet quite finished
growing ("laterally" being the mental reservation).
To such lengths of prevarication may national vanity
impel even the most veracious of men.

When it was beginning to grow late, one of the
crew, under the inspiration of the generous Neckar
wine, retired to a plank which crossed the mill-race
by way of a bridge. Upon this he sat himself down,
and, dangling his legs over the rushing waters, poured
forth his soul in song. A melody faintly resembling
the *Lorelei* was borne on the evening breeze to the ears
of the other four, who already lay stretched on the
floor of the tent; but it was audible to three only.
For the Interpreter had already started an opposition
tune of his own, which was, perhaps, more unmusical
and certainly less poetical in its character. He, like
so many other mortals, had, until the present voyage,
imagined himself to be entirely exempted from any
frailty in the matter of snoring. But the earnest re-

monstrances of his friends next morning led him to
believe that there must be a substratum of fact in
what they said. In order that the rest of the crew
might not be kept awake indefinitely, one of the
remaining four was on subsequent nights told off to
engage him in conversation on some plausible topic
till the milder pipings of the others began to be
heard. For otherwise tent-shaking and sleep-dispel-
ling reverberations would roll forth the instant the
Interpreter felt the magic touch of mother earth. It
is greatly to the credit of the others that they re-
frained from the unkind remedy so much in vogue
at public schools—a lump of soap.

One of the crew having a hungry nature was
regularly stirred to activity at a very early hour by
the craving for breakfast; but his persistent admoni-
tions to the four sluggards probably only resulted in
making things about half an hour later than they
otherwise would have been. In any case, the voyagers
never managed to get off from an encampment before
ten o'clock, the amount of work to be done being
really very considerable.

Passing through the lock, they soon came to a
charming semicircular bend, about a mile in length,
formed by a beautifully wooded hill, and abounding
in herons. This is certainly the most beautiful bit
of scenery between Cannstatt and Heilbronn. It is
marked as Heron Reach on the map. Then followed
a series of rocky and vine-clad hills. At Besigheim

the river divides into two arms, forming an island
half a mile long, and nearly as broad. Taking the
right branch, and leaving the town with its striking
mediæval towers on the left, the voyagers went
through the lock. After buying provisions at the
next village, they stopped at the following lock, and
lunched by a spring below the railway.

From Besigheim onwards the line more or less
closely follows the left bank of the Neckar till
Heilbronn, and the right from there to Heidelberg.

At Kirchheim, where the lock was being mended,
it was resolved, in order to save a very exhausting
porterage, to risk taking the boat down a narrow
channel containing a very turbulent rush of water.
She was accordingly unloaded and guided down the
roaring and dangerous rapid with great skill by the
Captain and Bow. During her swift passage she
shipped a quantity of water, notwithstanding the
tarpaulin stretched across her bows; and it was only
with great difficulty that the two, by swimming
alongside for some distance, were at length able to
pull her up. Much time having been lost one way
or the other over this transit, the voyagers soon had
to think of choosing a camping ground. So after less
than an hour's row they landed at a good place on
the left bank, a mile above Lauffen, in time to pitch
the tent conveniently before it grew dark.

The site selected was an excellent one, being a
level grassy spot between two rows of poplars. It

Heinsheim

Offenau

Jagstfeld

Friedrichshall

Wimpfen (am Berg)

Wimpfen (im Thale)

Kochendorf

Neckar

N

Camp

Unter Eisisheim

Station

Neckarsulm

Neckargartach

Wartberg 366

West Station

Heilbronn

Böckingen

Klingenberg

Sontheim

Schweinsberg

Horkheim

Half Lock

Lauffen
Stadt & Schloss

Dorf Lauffen

Camp

Neckar

Kirchheim

Lock

Half Lock

Gemmrigheim

Ferry

Lock

Mill Lock

Besigheim
Station

Hessigheim

Camp

Mundelsheim

Stanford's Geog.¹ Estab.

0 1 2 3 4 5 6 7 8 9 10 kilometres

proved to be private property—not common-land, as was often the case—for the owner turned up early next morning. The retrospective permission to use his land, which he hinted at as necessary, was soon acquired by a gift of two marks. The amount of the compensation evidently appeared a considerable sum to him, as he returned after a short absence with a large can of milk to show his gratitude.

Starting off under a blazing sun, as on the two previous mornings, the crew soon reached the weir of Lauffen, where they had to unload and drag the boat across. Now came a fine view of the village on the left, and the walled town of Lauffen on the right, with their church and castle picturesquely rising from two rocks on opposite sides of the river. The stream after this place sweeping round to the east brings the voyager to a fine reach a mile long and bordered with poplars. Then follows an uninteresting tract until Heilbronn comes into view. This prosperous manufacturing town is, with the exception of Mannheim, the largest place on the Neckar, having a population of 25,000. It is beautifully situated on both sides of the river, though the greater portion of it lies on the right bank.

Mainly in deference to the wishes of the hungry member of the crew, who wished to have a square meal once in a way, they landed here and enjoyed a sumptuous *table d'hôte* dinner in the garden of the *Eisenbahn* Hotel, with a bottle each of the very

excellent Neckar wine of the neighbourhood. The
table at which they were sitting happened to be
close to the broad road which runs along the left
river-bank. As there was only a low railing between them and the street, a crowd of boys had
assembled to see the lions feed. The Captain at
length arose, feeling himself called upon to deliver a
harangue to the expectant youth. If the primary
object of oratory be persuasion, he certainly fell
lamentably short of that result. For his very first
words, accompanied by a dramatic gesture : *Ich bin
Schulmeister*, were received with shouts of incredulity. That a form so gigantic, encased in flannels,
and finished off with a large, soft, white-felt hat,
should represent a schoolmaster, struck the mind of
the German boy as a statement passing the bounds
of belief. After he had with great eloquence addressed to them various other observations, all of
which were received with enthusiasm, the Captain
resumed his seat, having no doubt established an un-
dying popularity in the boyish tradition of Heilbronn. This feat was all the more remarkable as he
had left England only a week before entirely innocent
of any knowledge of the German language. Owing,
however, to the influence of his recent surroundings,
his conversation had in a few days become so highly
coloured with German nouns that hardly anything
but its grammatical framework still remained English.

At Heilbronn one member of the crew picked up

a piece of experience which may prove of use to
other travellers in Germany. Having some post-
cards of the German Empire in his possession, he
addressed one of them to England, with directions
about forwarding letters, and dropped it into the
letter-box, deaf to the warnings of the waiter, who
affirmed that a card of the kingdom of Würtemberg must be employed. The result was that the
Imperial post-card never reached its destination, and
the sender very nearly lost an important appointment in consequence of his whereabouts being unknown.

There are two heights near Heilbronn, the
Wartberg and the Schweinsberg, from which magnificent views of the Neckar valley and of the
surrounding mountain ranges may be obtained. But
the voyagers did not attempt to ascend them owing
to the broiling heat, as well as the lateness of the
afternoon.

They resumed their navigating labours by transporting the boat over the weir below the bridge amid
a crowd of spectators; for not only was it Sunday
afternoon, but the scene of operations lay almost in the
centre of the town. When launched below the weir, the
boat would not move because of the shallowness of
the channel, which was bestrewn with large stones.
So the Captain sprang out, and wading along in front,
cleared a course by tossing aside right and left the
boulders barring her progress. This performance

must have confirmed the incredulity of the boys who
had listened to his speech, and now swelled the
throng of onlookers.

Having overcome these initial difficulties, the
crew rowed on without further obstructions past long
lines of anchored rafts, till they reached Neckarsulm,
a small town about a quarter of a mile distant from
the right bank. The two interpreters landed here
to buy provisions for supper and next morning's
breakfast, while the other three rowed on to select
a suitable spot for pitching the tent before darkness
came on.

The boat, which was rather an old one, had been
leaking rather seriously ; for though only an hour
had elapsed since the start from Heilbronn, the water
was already beginning to encroach on the feet of
the rowers. This was in the meantime assumed to
be due to the general flabbiness of age ; for no actual
hole had as yet been discovered.

The encampment was ready when the catering
contingent arrived—*minus* a considerable proportion
of the beer and milk procured at Neckarsulm. They
had trudged a good distance across the sultry plain
and were approaching the tent, when to their re-
ciprocal wrath the handle of the basket they were
carrying between them suddenly gave way, and the
loosely corked bottles it held were dashed to the
ground. It is a curious trait of human nature, that
when a man suffers from an accident brought on

by his own want of foresight, he almost invariably throws the blame on some one else.

The Captain did not get much sleep owing to the number of huge rafts that passed during the night. Had he not on one occasion rushed out of the tent and staved off one of these, the boat would probably have been crushed between it and the bank to which she was moored.

A good deal of general sleeplessness was caused in the early hours of the morning by passing chain-steamers (*Kettendampfer*). They produced large waves which dashed against the banks and endangered the safety of the boat. It was, however, by no means on anxiety that the wakefulness of the whole crew now depended. These vessels, which are a kind of tug of surpassing ugliness, ply between Heilbronn and Mannheim, being similar to those employed on the Moldau and Elbe between Prague and Hamburg. From both ends, which are shaped alike and are flush with the water, they gradually rise to the centre, where the funnel and the machinery are situated. Along a groove running down the middle, from stem to stern, passes a thick iron chain, which otherwise rests in the bed of the river and the ends of which are fastened at Heilbronn and Mannheim. An arrangement of cogwheels drags the monster slowly upstream by clutching and passing down the chain. There is nearly always a long string of barges behind. The rattling, grating,

G

rasping, panting, and whistling called forth by the
process is probably the most diabolical combination of
sounds hitherto invented by the human mind. Any
one hearing it for the first time feels an almost
irresistible impulse to firmly fix a finger in each ear
and make a bee-line at the top of his speed straight
across country regardless of obstacles. Fortunately
the human ear seems to grow accustomed to anything
in time. What other theory could explain the fact
that these vessels have crews? Possibly, however,
only those who have been born deaf take employment on them.

For the information of the curious it may be
added that the chain can be got rid of at certain
points where the links may be unlocked.

The morning was spent in idleness by four of the
campers, while the Captain brought his knowledge of
carpentry to bear on the problem of repairing the boat.
Every drop of water was emptied out and the boards
all removed; but there was absolutely no sign of a leak.
As the hole was, therefore, obviously somewhere above
her present water-line, she was first deeply loaded in
the stern and then in the fore-part. Now at last a little
jet of water becoming visible in the extreme bows betrayed the weak spot. This had hitherto been concealed by the luggage. The ends of the planks in
that quarter were when pressed found to be almost as
pliant as *papier-maché*. To repair this kind of damage
successfully required no small amount of skill.

As the inside of the tent was all this time like an oven, while there was no other shelter from the scorching sun, the four unoccupied hands spent most of the forenoon in the water. Stopping the leak occupied so many hours that a start was not made till three o'clock. In order to save time it was determined to spend the night at Wimpfen, though that place was hardly five miles farther on. Having after a very easy row reached the town, which is beautifully situated on a hill to the left, they landed almost below their hotel. This lies some way up the wooded slope and commands a charming view of the Neckar. In the village below (Wimpfen im Thal), about half a mile farther up the left bank, there is a fine Gothic church, more than 600 years old, which well deserves a visit. The town on the hill is supposed to occupy the site of a Roman settlement known to have been destroyed by the Huns, numerous Roman remains having been found in the salt mines there.

As the voyagers had no cooking or packing to do next morning they were afloat by the unusually early hour of eight. Rowing slowly away they enjoyed a fine view of the picturesque town set on the hill, with its ancient tower rising tall and square at the top. They had hardly proceeded an hour when the water was found, in spite of all the previous day's tinkering, to be coming in so fast as to oblige them to land and bale. The Captain then resumed his

carpentering, while the rest, more fortunate, were
able to mitigate the burning heat by bathing. A
picturesque castle rising almost opposite on the left
bank lent a kind of romance to the scene as they
swam about in the stream below.

The delay of two hours was well utilised by the
Captain; for the leak was so effectually stopped as
to give no more trouble for the rest of the voyage.

They now rowed on through delightful lonely
reaches, rendered still more charming by an old ruin
here and there crowning the heights, past a beautiful bend after Gundelsheim, till they arrived at
Neckarzimmern. Here they disembarked, and after
procuring some beer at the inn from a sprightly and
pretty *Kellnerin*, returned to the boat, in which they
lunched. Half a mile above this town rises the ruin
of Hornberg, where the hero of Goethe's play, Götz
von Berlichingen, ended his days in 1562.

The scenery of the Neckar valley had been pretty
all the way from Wimpfen, but after Neckarelz it
noticeably increased in beauty, the river now winding among rounded and magnificently wooded hills.
Farther on the banks grow still grander till they
reach their climax in the region of Heidelberg.

The heat of the past two days had begun to tell
on the Chief Officer, who by this time was reduced to
a state of coma. Even the Captain, who while
mending the boat had been far more exposed to the
sun than any of the others, had not altogether escaped

ODENWALD

Neckargemünd

Neckarsteinach

Hirschhorn

Rauabach

Dilsberg

Station

Neckar

Neckarhausen

Station

Station

Kapelle

Jagelsbach

Station

Pleutersbach

Neckarwimmersbach

Eberbach

Rokenau

Katzenbuckel

Stolzeneck

1934

Lindach

Schloss

Zwingenberg

Minneburg

Neckargerbach

Station

Woods

Guttenbach

Binau

Obrigheim

Dudesheim

Neckarelz

Station

Neckar

Neckarzimmern

M.D.

Hornberg

Böttingen

Hassmersheim

Heinsheim

Gundelsheim

0 1 2 3 4 5 6 7 8 9 10 Kilometres

N

from its effects. It was therefore decided to land
and rest for some hours in the shade of the luxuriant
woods opposite the village of Binau, till the rays
of the sun had become less fierce. In the course
of the afternoon the Chaplain and the Interpreter
crossed over to the village and procured a large can
of fresh milk, with which they assuaged their thirst
for the rest of the day.

Putting off again about six o'clock, when it had
grown somewhat cooler, they paddled on through
similar but still finer scenery, past the ruin of
Minneburg on the left and the restored castle of
Zwingenberg on the right, till they sighted the
wonderfully picturesque old town of Eberbach.
Here they might very well have put up for the night;
for not only are there two very good inns, but the
Katzenbuckel, a mountain nearly 2000 feet high and
the loftiest point in the Odenwald, is near at hand
and well deserves to be ascended for the panoramic
view it commands. Reluctantly drifting past this
attractive place, they rowed on in the vain hope of
reaching Heidelberg, still twenty miles away, that
night. But they had not done more than half
this distance before it had grown so dark that it was
impossible to see the channel, and the boat struck
several times, though fortunately without serious
results, against boulders which appeared to be
strewn about the bed of the river in this part of its
course. It was now nearly ten o'clock, and Heidel-

berg could still not be much less than ten miles
distant.   Having to row slowly and cautiously in the
dark, they could not expect to arrive till after midnight.   Landing would be difficult, not to say hazardous, while the hotels would probably all be closed.
Besides, the Chief Officer, who lay on the stern seat,
was in so lethargic a condition as to be altogether
incapable of steering.   To row on would thus be
doubly risky.   All these considerations decided the
crew to abandon the attempt and to put in at the
first place they could.   Guided by some lights that
presently became visible, they cautiously edged
into the stony bank.   A bargee who happened to be
about came down in response to their shouts, in-
forming them, to their great satisfaction, that the
place was Neckarsteinach.   Leaving the boat in his
charge till next morning, they made their way up to
the *Harfe*, an excellent inn, much frequented by
students from Heidelberg, and filled with pictures
illustrative of German student life.   It has a pleasant
terrace on the Neckar, commanding a good view of
the river.

Next day the crew were afloat soon after ten o'clock;
and allowing themselves to drift had leisure to
admire from the best point of view the beautiful
scenery of Neckarsteinach, with its many castles
perched on the surrounding heights.   As they rowed
on the hills grew grander and higher than ever.   At
one point, where the stream takes a sharp bend to the

north, they seem to close in altogether, leaving
apparently no exit for the river. Rising dark and
precipitous from the water's edge, they seemed to the
voyager at their base to tower up to the sky. It was
here that the Captain, by way of antithesis to the
German word *himmelhoch* (high as heaven), with
great promptitude invented the epithet "hell-deep"
to describe the appearance of the dark waters at the
foot of those beetling heights.

Grand scenery such as this probably showed to
the greatest advantage under a lowering sky. The
present one was, indeed, the first dull day the crew
had experienced since the start. All the others had
in fact been cloudless.

A row of an hour and a half from Neckarsteinach
brought the voyagers to Heidelberg, which, as they
approached, looked surpassingly beautiful. The cox
of a rowing-boat has a great advantage over the rest of
the crew when nearing a lovely scene like this. They
landed at the swimming-baths, giving the boat and
camping baggage into the charge of the proprietor.

The Chief Officer being still very unwell, a council
of war decided that he should drive up to the *Schloss*
Hotel, accompanied by the Chaplain, in the hope that
a day's rest might restore him to his usual health.
A Heidelberg doctor who was called in pronounced
his patient to be suffering from Neckar fever, a
malady which he said prevailed during hot weather
in the river valley. He prescribed a complete rest in

bed for three days, besides various other remedies, the latter no doubt being futile.

The other three, after having a swim at the baths, joined the Chaplain at the hotel. Here they dined and spent the afternoon in the grounds, where a military concert thronged with visitors was going on. Having decided to camp out that night, the same three set off again when it was already growing dusk, and paddling down a couple of miles encamped in the dark after effecting a rather difficult landing on the right bank. They were unaware at the time that a towing-path ran along the top of the bank just above the tent. But for the vigilance of the Captain, whom the other two were startled to see suddenly dashing out in the early twilight, they would all at once have found their abode collapsing over their prostrate forms. For the rope of a barge that was being towed upstream by horses was about to catch the guys of the tent, when the Captain by his timely spring fended it off with an oar. The bargee seemed indifferent to the havoc he might have created, or even to the three fists that were shaken at him from the tent-door by the white-robed figures of their owners. The bargee nature, even in Germany, where it is decidedly superior to what it is in England, cannot be described as very elevated at the best of times. There is a lack of human sympathy about them, perhaps because they are a class living and moving apart from the rest of their kind.

Schwabenheim

Station

Wieblingen

Neckar

Camp

Station

Neuenheim

Station

HEIDELBERG

Station

2

Schlierbach

Station

Ziegelhausen

Neckar

Sandstone
Quarry

Ziegelhütte

Elsenz

Station

Kleingemünd

NECKAR-
GEMÜND

Rainbach

Stanfords Geog.l Estab.t

0   1   2   3   4   5 Kilometres

The excitement caused by this alarm had hardly
subsided when another vessel in tow appeared on the
scene. The present bargee on sight of the camp
suddenly slackened his rope just in front. He
then urged on his horses, expecting apparently to
clear the tent by the rebound. The rope would,
however, on the contrary, have struck with all the
greater force. The Captain luckily managed to catch
it with the blade of his oar and so to avert the stroke.
This was decidedly not the place to choose for
an undisturbed and secure encampment. Even
nocturnal rafts and chain-steamers were preferable to
this sort of thing. Such incidents show how important it is to select your ground while it is yet
light.

After breakfast the three friends struck the tent
in a more legitimate sense, and repacking the boat
returned to Heidelberg. Owing to the great force of
the stream in this part they were obliged to tow
most of the way. When they arrived at the hotel
they were delighted to find that the invalid had
sufficiently recovered to be able to resume the
voyage that day. A thunderstorm breaking out
early in the afternoon, they delayed in the hope that
the wet would clear away. But as the hours wore on
and there was no sign of the rain abating, they at
length started off in a tolerably steady downpour.
Rowing till a short distance beyond Ladenburg, they
selected a camping ground on the left bank below a

plantation of hops. The rain now ceased, and
though the grass was saturated with moisture the
inside of the tent remained perfectly dry owing to
the waterproof ground-sheet. Nor was the gloomi-
ness of the evening by any means reflected in the
minds or the conversation of the campers. The
usual game of Nap concluded the night's entertain-
ment before the crew lay down to rest.

The next morning, which was again fine, was the
last on the Neckar; for they were now only nine
miles from its mouth. The total distance of about
120 miles had occupied eight full days, and of
these, two had practically been wasted. Nevertheless,
in order to derive the greatest possible amount of
enjoyment from the trip, it would probably have
been best to devote ten days to navigating this
beautiful river.

As some hours had to be spent in drying their
clothes, which had been drenched on the preceding
evening, the voyagers were not afloat till noon. The
flatness and uninteresting character of the scenery
here was relieved only by a view of the distant
Heidelberg hills in the background. For immediately below that beautiful town the Neckar enters a
plain, which it traverses for the remaining seventeen
miles of its course.

At Mannheim the crew landed to lunch and buy
provisions for the evening's camp. They then re-
embarked and rowing about a mile and a half farther

R. RHEIN

Station

MANNHEIM

Neckar

N

Ferr.

Feudenheim

Seckenheim

Station

Ilvesheim

Station

Neckarhausen

Station

LADENBURG

Edingen

Neckar

Schwabenheim

Stanfords 'o.gl Estab[t]

0   1   2   3   4   5 Kilometres

reached the extreme point of the tongue of land formed by the confluence of the Rhine and the Neckar; and with a few strokes shot into the broad expanse of the main river, now about three times the breadth of its tributary. The contrast between its milky waters—so characteristic of glacial rivers—and the dark and clear stream of the Neckar, was at first very marked, as they flowed for some distance side by side; but soon they combined to produce a uniform greenish hue, which the Rhine seems to retain during the remainder of its course.

CHAPTER V

THE RHINE

" Und zu Schiffe, wie grüssen die Burgen so schön
  Und die Stadt mit dem ew'gen Dom !
Zu den Bergen, wie klimmst du zu schwindelnden Höhn
  Und blickst hinab in den Strom !"—SIMROCK.

Uninteresting scenery below Mannheim—Break an oar—Worms—
Historical and legendary associations—Rowing-club—Camp
below Worms—Visit of gendarme—The Interpreter's irrita-
tion—Flings one of his garments into the Rhine—Nierstein—
Futile attempt to camp on an island—Nieder-Walluf—Fine
scenery—Statue of Germania at Niederwald—Romantic ruins—
Rhine inferior to some other German rivers in natural beauty
—Bacharach—Dangerous race with a steamer—Bathe opposite
Lurlei rocks—St. Goar—Boppard—Coblenz.

THE stream being fairly strong the voyagers rowed
steadily on, for there was absolutely no inducement
to linger here. The scenery is intensely dreary, consisting of nothing but long sandy reaches. The
high abrupt banks, mostly bare, show here and there
a sparse growth of willow bushes, the unspeakable
dulness of which is only occasionally diversified
by the monotonous poplar. The utterly depressing
effect of these desolate wastes is enhanced by the

fact that not a single human habitation comes into
view all the way from Mannheim to Worms, a
distance of twelve miles. There are several sandy
islands in the channel, covered with scrubby bushes.
One of these must be over one mile in length,
being formed by a more or less stagnant arm of the
river, which forms a great loop on the right, some
three miles above Worms. The whole character of
this tract is similar to the flat parts of the Danube
below Linz. And yet the impression produced on
the mind is very unlike. This may partly be owing
to the different light in which the two rivers are
seen; for on the Danube the voyager is steering
towards the south-east, while on the Rhine he is
making for the north or north-west. The difference
may also in part be due to the totally dissimilar
associations these streams arouse in the mind, the
Rhine being always suggestive of Teutonic, and the
Danube of Roman civilisation.

The only object in all this region that attracted the
attention of the crew was a sandy beach of dazzling
whiteness; so greatly, indeed, were they taken with
it, that they ran ashore in order to enjoy from it their
first bathe in the waters of the Rhine. As they
were approaching the region of Worms a steamer
going upstream passed close to the boat. Considering
it incumbent on them to display their prowess, they
made a spurt. It was then that the Captain, taking a
mighty stroke, snapped his oar short off at the row-

lock. Retaining his balance as well as his presence
of mind, he at once gaily waved the stump before
the astonished gaze of the passengers, as if to inti-
mate that this little feat was one of quite ordinary
occurrence, and immediately substituting another oar,
rowed on as if nothing had happened. This was the
only spare oar in the boat, and by great good luck
belonged to the same side as the broken one.

Passing under the bridge of boats at Worms, they
landed on the other side. Their main object in
stopping here was to pay a flying visit to that ancient
city, so famous in history and romance. The ground
on which the visitor here stands teems with the
memory of mighty events as well as the deeds of
great legendary heroes. The Roman name of Worms,
Barbetomagus, seems to point to a Celtic origin. In
early times the place became a settlement of the
Teutonic tribe of the Vangiones under Roman protection. Having been sacked by the Huns under
Attila, it was occupied in the fifth century by the
Burgundians, who made it their capital, and three or
four centuries later was frequently the residence of
Charlemagne and his successors. Many Imperial
Diets were held here, the most celebrated having
been that at which Luther appeared and defended
his doctrines in 1521.

Its venerable Romanesque cathedral, which was
begun in the eighth century, but not completed till
the beginning of the twelfth, ranks among the finest

specimens of that style of architecture in Germany. It has four round towers, two large domes, and a choir at each end. Like the cathedral of Strassburg, it is built of red sandstone.

Worms has declined greatly from its ancient glory, for in the days of the Hohenstaufen emperor, Frederick Barbarossa, it could boast a population of 70,000 souls, while the present number of its inhabitants is only 22,000. It was, however, still worse off at the beginning of this century when, in consequence of the continual ravages of war during nearly two centuries, its population had sunk as low as 5000.

The town is situated in a very fertile vine-growing region, celebrated as the Wonnegau (mead of joy) in the lays of the Minnesingers.' Its most famous vintage is known as Liebfrauenmilch, produced on vineyards near the Liebfrauenkirche.

Worms is the very centre of the legendary cycle of the *Nibelungenlied*. That epic describes it as the home of the Burgundian king Gunther, whose sister Kriemhilde wedded the brave Siegfried. The very name of the place points to the prowess of that mighty hero; for it was so called from the worm or dragon which he slew in mortal combat. Formerly many relics of the mythical hero were preserved here, among others his lance, nearly eighty feet long, being shown in the cathedral! Here, too, in the space before the cathedral, that deadly quarrel

arose between Brunhilde and Kriemhilde, which in
its final issue brought about the annihilation of the
Nibelungen at the court of Attila.

Carlyle, in his essay on the *Nibelungenlied*, is
wrong in saying that the author of that epic represents Worms as lying "not in its true position, but
at some distance from the river; a proof at least that
he was never there and probably sang and lived
in some very distant region." The town is actually
three-quarters of a mile from the river. The frequent
reference, moreover, which the poet makes to the
sandy shore[1] is at all events far more appropriate
here than the same term applied to the shingly
beach of the Danube, near Ingolstadt, where the
Nibelungen crossed on their way to the land of the
Huns.

The plan of the voyagers as to visiting the
town was, for all but one of them, put an end to
by an unforeseen occurrence. Hardly had they set
foot on the strand when they were pounced upon by
several members of the Worms rowing-club, whose
boathouse was close to the landing-place. They
were thus constrained to adjourn to a neighbouring
Wirthshaus, of which the *Sportsmänner* were no
doubt the chief frequenters, and were here entertained
with beer by their new friends. The Chaplain alone
had energy and strength of mind enough to tear
himself away and utilise the remaining hour or so of

[1] *e.g. für Worms: bj den sant*, outside Worms, upon the sand.

daylight to make off and view the cathedral, which
lies at a distance of about a mile from the bridge
of boats. On the Interpreter therefore fell all the
onus of the rather wearing duty of listening to
and answering, as best he could, the innumerable
questions on rowing matters, such as the merits of
sliding seats, with which he was incessantly plied.
His interrogators stuck to the subject throughout the
lengthy conversation with all the unbounded enthusiasm which is so conspicuous on the Continent
wherever rowing has recently established a footing.
The other three members of the crew taking refuge
in their ignorance of the language—though the Captain might easily have contributed many German
nouns and some verbs to the discussion—had as
good a time as was consistent with the almost intolerable stuffiness of the smoke-laden atmosphere. Without allowing the conversation to flag, their brethren of
the oar conducted the strangers to view their boats,
which they displayed with great pride. One of these
was a smart-looking and well-finished light four, but
there was just a touch of clumsiness about her lines.
They did not possess an eight. Though he saw one
or two six-oars, the writer believes that none of the
boat-clubs he came across on the rivers described
in these pages own eights, with the exception no
doubt of those at Mainz and at Frankfort-on-the-
Main.

At length the Chaplain, the much-longed for, re-

II

turned. The united crew thereupon arose and took
a cordial leave of their new and well-meaning friends,
gently but firmly declining their pressing invitation
to stay at Worms for the night and attend a full
meeting of the rowing-club to be convoked in their
honour. For they well knew that this meant con-
suming vast quantities of beer in an atmosphere
charged with tobacco smoke, a process certain to
produce an aggravated condition of *Katzenjammer*
next morning. The game was decidedly not worth
the candle.

As it was already growing dusk when they got
afloat, they rowed on only a short way and encamped on the open left bank some distance below
a factory. The tent was hardly up when a country
policeman (*Landgendarme*), armed with a sword,
appeared on the scene to ascertain that none of the
Imperial laws were being infringed. After minutely
inspecting, on the plea of official duty, the tent with
its multifarious paraphernalia and discovering nothing
contraband, he gradually relaxed his austerity under
the influence of tobacco and beer, and finally departed
conferring his protection on the encampment.

In order that the floor of the tent should not be
littered the Captain always rigged up a clothes-line between the three poles. Among the articles of apparel
thereon suspended was a pair of drawers belonging
to the Interpreter. For some unaccountable reason
the satire of the remaining members of the crew

had fixed itself upon this unoffending garment. It had become the mark at which all the shafts of their evening and morning wit were directed, and had already acquired the permanent epithet of "Damoclean." The Interpreter was getting rather sore on the subject, and beginning to regard these witticisms almost in the light of personal affronts; but when on this particular evening some one having made a renewed reference to the insecurity of sleepers under "those Damoclean drawers," Bow cut in with the remark, "Don't call them Damoclean, they're d——d dirty," it was more than human nature could bear. The incensed owner immediately started up, and tearing them down from the rope rushed out into the darkness. Wrapping the offending garment round a brick, which lay close by, he flung it with a loud splash into the depths of the stream. There, along with the hoard of the Nibelungen and many other treasures, it lies at the bottom of the Rhine, awaiting the day when it shall be brought to light by the operations of the steam-dredger. Returning to the tent panting with emotion, he shouted, with a general wave of the hand taking in the four satirists, "Well, I hope you are satisfied now, for you will never set eyes on those drawers again." The silence of some minutes' duration which followed this outburst probably expressed assent.

It was nearly eleven o'clock next morning by the time the voyagers were afloat. The day was again a

brilliant one, calm and intensely hot. The river,
though now much more winding in its course, preserved the same utterly dreary character, and the
rowers were beginning to long for the sight of even a
few hillocks to vary the monotony of the banks. At
length in the neighbourhood of Oppenheim actual
hills were seen to approach the river, the left bank
of which they follow for the remaining twelve miles
of its course till Mainz. The town of Oppenheim
lies picturesquely on a height rising from the Rhine
and is commanded by an old ruined castle. Then
the first vineyards hitherto visible from the river
came into view on the terraced slopes of the low
hills at Nierstein. Here the crew stopped for lunch
in the intense heat of the early afternoon, and drank
some of the well-known local wine. Niersteiner
seems to be a good deal thought of in Germany,
but owing to its acidity it is certainly inferior in
flavour to the best kinds of Rhenish wine.

One of the advantages of a boating excursion on
the Rhine and its three tributaries, the Main, the
Neckar, and the Moselle, is the opportunity it affords
of acquiring a vast experience on the spot of the best
German wines, and often at a price hardly above that
of beer. The latter beverage is in fact rather at a
discount in those regions, and can rarely be obtained
good.

Starting off again at four o'clock they rowed past
Mainz soon after six, and taking the channel on the

extreme right put in for provisions below one of the
terraced hotels at Biebrich, some two and a half miles
farther down, intending to camp on an island about
a mile and a half in length just beyond. The
dilatoriness of the waiter unfortunately spoilt their
plans, for it was already beginning to grow dark
by the time they were able to put off again. Near
Biebrich there are, besides a small one, three long
islands in the Rhine, all about a mile and a half in
length. It was on the last of these they proposed
to camp for the night. Had they not foolishly put
off buying victuals till the evening it would have
been preferable, while there was still daylight, to land
and select a camping ground on one of the two first
islands, the Ingelheimerau and the Petersau, between
which the steamboat channel lies. The latter is a
historical spot, for here Charlemagne's son, the
Emperor Louis the Pious, died in 840. As it was,
they found a reef of rocks running along close to
the shore of the island and for a considerable distance
beyond its point, which rendered landing on the
right bank impossible. The project of rowing up on
the other side was at last reluctantly abandoned as
being too risky, owing to the strength of the current
and the increasing darkness. They were all the more
disappointed, as they had set their hearts on camping
on one of the islands of the Rhine at the very outset
of the expedition, while speeding along the left
bank in the train on the way to Heidelberg. By

this time, the task of landing even at a town they
found to be no easy matter in the darkness, with a
strong stream running and numerous buoys and
boats moored in the way. At length, however,
they managed to run in safely to Nieder-Walluf,
an ancient little town with three good inns, on
the right bank a mile and a half beyond the end
of the island. Nieder-Walluf is the eastern extremity
of the Rheingau, the region twelve miles long and five
broad which extends along the northern bank of the
Rhine, and is famous for producing some of the
choicest wines in the world.

The next day, which was Sunday, the crew were
up early, getting afloat before half-past seven. It
was a glorious morning, the sun being very hot even
at that early hour. The surface of the river was
like a mirror, as, breakfasting in the boat, they
drifted down that magnificent reach, which flows
almost due west as far as the mouth of the Nahe
near Bingen.

There are two long islands opposite Eltville and
Hattenheim. On the latter of these they landed for
a short time after breakfast, at a delightful spot, and
so enjoyed the experience if not of camping at least
of having been ashore on one of those charming
islands of the Rhine.

As they drifted past, looking up at the colossal
statue of Germania, only recently completed, which
rises on the slope of the Niederwald just below

Rüdesheim and exactly opposite Bingen, they were
puzzled to make out what it was the figure held aloft
in her outstretched hand; nor was it possible to
ascertain this with a field-glass, owing to the unsteadi-
ness of the boat. It is of course the Imperial Crown
of Germany.

After this point, where the river turns due north,
the finest scenery on the Rhine begins, one romantic
old castle following the other in rapid succession.
There are at least twenty of these in the distance of
forty miles to Coblenz. This part of the Rhine's
course is so well known as a steamboat route and is
so fully described in the guide-books, that it would
be superfluous to give an account of it in these pages.
Fine though this scenery certainly is, there can be no
doubt that it owes its reputation for beauty of a very
high order in no small degree to the many charming
ruins which rise from its rocky heights, as well as to
its general accessibility to the traveller. The Neckar,
the Main, the Moselle, and the Danube have their
picturesque ruins too, but these, except in certain
regions, occur only at long intervals. Otherwise the
Rhine with its steep and barren banks, generally
destitute of wood, and with its continual terraced
vineyards, cannot be said to equal in natural
romantic beauty the finest parts of any of those
four rivers.

With a view to enjoying the charm of the Rhine
to its full extent there can be no doubt that a rowing-

boat is a far better vessel to go down it in than
a steamer can be. For on the one hand the oarsman can linger or land wherever and whenever he
pleases, and on the other, as his pace is far slower,
he is not hurried past the scenery at such speed
that only a blurred impression of it is left on the
memory.

In broad daylight only three points in the
distance between Mainz and Coblenz are at all
dangerous for small boats, and even they are safe
enough if the right channel be taken and no steamers
are in the way. The latter enemies of the oarsman
or the canoeist certainly add to the risk of navigation. The first of the bad places is the Binger Loch,
a narrow rocky channel with a swift rapid. This
the voyagers passed without any incident, soon after
coming to Assmannshausen, a village famous for its
red wine. The Captain here expressed some curiosity
as to whether the place had received its name from
the unusual dulness of the inhabitants, possibly induced by excessive addiction to their local wine, or
whether its appellation was rather due to the facilities
it affords, in the matter of donkeys and guides, to
tourists wishing to visit the Niederwald.

The second bad place was the comparatively
narrow channel on the right near Bacharach. When
approaching this the rowers suddenly saw coming
round the corner behind a large steamer crowded
with Sunday passengers. Cox at the same time

caught sight of a tug with barges in tow toiling up
in the opposite direction. Now, then, was the time
to strain every nerve, before the large steamer caught
them up and the tug entered the narrow channel. The
steamboat behind of course gained at every stroke of
her paddles, and her bows were already beginning to
overlap the stern of the four, the passengers meanwhile crowding to her sides, eager to see the result of
the chase. Then with a final spurt the oarsmen shot
past the end of the reef into the broad expanse beyond, only just before the steamer drew level with
her paddles and the tug entered the channel above.
Had they been caught between the two they would
most probably either have been swamped or wrecked
on the reef.

At noon the voyagers had for some time been
looking out for a suitable bathing-place, but the
stream was everywhere far too swift. At length, just
before reaching the point round which St. Goarshausen
comes into view, they discovered a fine deep backwater,
nearly opposite the mouth of a tunnel on the left
bank, where a large ferry-punt was moored. Disembarking into this, they all stripped and dived off
her edge into the cool depths below. Here they
disported themselves for some time opposite the
Lurlei rocks, which rise precipitously from the water's
edge to a height of over 400 feet on the other side.
But as they gazed upwards, the barren promontory
seen in the glaring midday sunlight seemed to have

none of the romance with which it has been invested by Heine's beautiful ballad.

The third place dangerous to small boats is a reef, called *die Bank*, in midstream, a short way from the Lurlei rocks. The best channel is on the extreme right, but the crew, not knowing this at the time, just escaped coming to grief by keeping too close to the shallows in the centre of the river.

Having landed at St. Goar and enjoyed a one o'clock *table d'hôte* at an inn almost opposite the steamboat pier, they rowed on again till they went ashore at Boppard to assuage with beer the thirst brought on by the intense heat of the afternoon.

It was already growing dusk as they approached Coblenz. Having passed safely through the bridge of boats, a feat which requires some delicate steering, for the space between the boats is narrow and the stream runs very strong, they landed near the steamboat pier not much before eight o'clock. Thus ended one of the most delightful days the writer ever experienced on any of the rivers described in these pages. The total distance rowed that day from Nieder-Walluf to Coblenz was fifty-two miles.

Having without delay made arrangements for the conveyance of the boat by cart to the goods station of the Moselle railway, the voyagers took up their quarters for the night in one of the huge hotels which are built along the bank of the Rhine.

CHAPTER VI

THE MOSELLE

" Et praeceps Anio ac Tiburni lucus et uda
*Mobilibus pomaria rivis."—*HORACE.

EARLY on the morning of 19th August two or three
members of the crew made arrangements at the
Mosel-Bahnhof for the despatch of the boat as
express luggage (*Eilgut*) to Trèves, so as to enable
them to launch her there some time on the following
day. After lingering a few hours at Coblenz, the
five friends themselves started off for Trèves by a

convenient train, reaching their destination at about
four o'clock. They thus had the advantage of seeing
the valley of the Moselle, at all events for the last
quarter of the distance between Trèves and Coblenz,
from a point of view somewhat different to that of
the downward voyage upon which they were about
to embark. For the railway closely follows the left
bank of the Moselle for thirty miles. After Cochem,
however, it quits the river owing to its tortuousness
above that point, the distance by water between
Cochem and Trèves being nearly ninety, whereas
that by rail is scarcely forty miles.

On their arrival the travellers took up their
quarters in the *Rothe Haus* (Red House), a hotel
situated in the market-place, and so called because
of its present colour. It was formerly the Town
Hall, and is upwards of 400 years old.

Trèves (or Trier), which has a population of
about 25,000, lies charmingly in the valley of the
Moselle on the right bank of the river, and is
surrounded by magnificent wooded heights. It is
probably the most ancient town in Germany, having
originally been the seat of the Gallic tribe of the
Treveri, from whom it obviously derives its name. It
then became a Roman settlement and was in the fourth
century often the residence of the Roman emperors.

Containing as it does so many and interesting
remains of this period, it is a place that ought not to
be visited in a hurry. The best scenery of the

Moselle also begins here. It is therefore excellently adapted to be the starting-point of a boating excursion. The scenery of the river is fine all the way down to its mouth—a distance of about 120 miles —in some stretches being extremely beautiful, while the good part of the Rhine is not more than forty miles long.

The chief characteristics of the Moselle are lofty and richly wooded hills along its banks, the many great curves and loops formed by the course of the stream in the ninety miles below Trèves, and the lovely side-valleys (of which there are six or eight) opening on it at various points. Of all the rivers described in these pages the Main resembles it most. In the region of the Spessart that river has hilly and magnificently wooded banks, and at least two beautiful side-valleys. It also winds greatly in a certain sense ; but its course is rather a zigzag from east to west, the reaches between the angles being comparatively straight.

One great advantage of the Moselle from the boating man's point of view, an advantage which very forcibly strikes the voyager fresh from the busy steamboat traffic of the Rhine, is the wonderful quiet and peacefulness of its valley.

Unlike the Neckar, the Werra, the Main, and the Upper Danube, the Moselle has between Trèves and Coblenz absolutely no obstruction in the way of weirs or locks to retard the progress of the navigator.

A boating trip in Germany might very well be limited to this river alone, for a series of delightful little walking tours up the side-valleys might be combined with the voyage. The rowing part of the excursion might be prolonged either by starting from Metz, though the scenery all the way to Trèves is said to be uninteresting, or by the more arduous undertaking of rowing up from the mouth to Trèves, and then down again.

The voyagers made the best use of their time in visiting the lions of the place,—the Porta Nigra, a magnificent Roman gate, so called because it has become blackened with age; the Basilica, built entirely of thin Roman bricks; the ruins of the Roman Palace; and the amphitheatre, which is very well preserved, and was capable of holding 30,000 spectators, being thus rather more than one-third of the size of the Colosseum at Rome.

Unfortunately they found no time before starting to visit the famous Igel Monument, as it is situated at a distance of seven miles from the town. It is a Roman funeral column, seventy-five feet high, erected in the third century, and covered with Latin inscriptions, which have, however, for the most part become illegible through the ravages of time.

In the evening, as it was growing dusk, the friends took a stroll on the Moselle bridge. This must be the oldest structure of the kind in Germany, for the

masonry of some of its buttresses is Roman. Enjoying the calm of the evening and the beauty of the
surrounding scenery, they stood leaning on the stone
parapet of a recess in the middle of the bridge. The
inhabitants of Trèves here for the first time struck
them as being extraordinarily polite towards strangers,
for every man invariably took off his hat as he passed.
The Britons, not to be outdone in courtesy, regularly returned the salute, a process which from
constant repetition began after a while to grow
irksome. The First Officer now remarked that he
really thought the English custom of bowing to ladies
only was greatly to be preferred to the continental
usage. He at the same time expressed a conviction
that the hat which, in consequence of his old one
having been hopelessly ruined in the boat, he
had been reluctantly compelled to buy that very
morning at Coblenz—he did not like German hats
—would not last out till the end of the voyage, if
he were obliged to appear during the hours of daylight in any of the other towns of the Moselle valley.
One of the friends after a time accidentally looked
up, and for the first time noticed that they had
been standing immediately below a figure of the
Virgin Mary. They now remembered they were
in a Roman Catholic town, and moved on feeling
some inches shorter than before. The First Officer's
hat was still quite presentable—for a German one, as
he would have said—when he reached Coblenz.

Next morning the Captain having provided him-self with a good-sized basket, proceeded into the market-place for the purpose of buying vegetables, fruit, eggs, and other provisions. He created a good deal of amusement as well as admiration while he wandered about among the market-women, airing his German and filling his basket with his various bargains. He was not quite the type of person they were in the habit of dealing with in the capacity of a careful *Hausfrau*.

The boat having arrived at noon, was ordered down to the quay below the bridge. Here her crew found her already in the water when they came at about four o'clock to launch her and pack. Curiously enough the start in nearly all the voyages described in these pages was made late in the afternoon, to be followed soon after by an encampment. Among the crowd assembled to see them off were two Englishmen who had rowed down from Metz in a light pair and a German sculler. Both of these parties they came across again later on in the course of the voyage.

It was half-past five when they at length pushed off from the bank. Hardly had they commenced to row when a loud grating sound, calculated to set the teeth on edge and upset the nervous system gener-ally, began to be heard. As it evidently proceeded from below, the crew at first surmised it to be due to the bottom of the boat scraping on the shingle in the river-bed ; but it was soon shown not to be this, for the water was everywhere proved by sounding to be at least three feet deep. The harder they tried by strenuous rowing to escape from the hateful noise the worse and more intolerable it grew. It would then in the most inexplicable way stop for a few minutes, but only to be renewed with redoubled vigour. As no hypothesis could be framed to account satisfactorily for the mystery, the crew were fain to assume in the meantime that there was some unknown but diabolical contrivance in the river-bed, possibly akin to the steamer chains of the Neckar.

Rowing on for some five miles with this odious accompaniment, they came upon an excellent camping ground on the right bank, some way beyond the village of Pfalzel. The spot was in a fine large open meadow, close to an iron erection about twenty feet high, resembling the Eiffel tower in miniature, and apparently connected in some way with waterworks. The ground had evidently been well selected with a view to privacy, for not a soul was visible anywhere. But hardly had the tent risen, when an unlooked-for visitor in the shape of the official guardian of the field appeared on the scene. His side, however, was, strange to say, not adorned with the customary sword. Striding up to the tent, he proclaimed in a stern voice that the strangers must at once quit the spot, for the ground on which they stood was an

I

imperial meadow (*kaiserliche Wiese*).   The Interpreter, at once adopting a conciliatory attitude,
explained that the trespassers only wished to camp
till next morning, and suggested that they would be
willing to pay compensation for any damage they
might cause on the small corner of the imperial
property which they wore occupying.   He ended
his apology by asking the myrmidon of the imperial
laws to name any sum which he considered equitable
under the circumstances.   After much show of deliberation he at length gave his authoritative sanction
to their remaining for the night on the ground
of which they had taken possession, assessing the
amount of the indemnity with some hesitation at
one mark.   With difficulty repressing a smile, and
simulating internal wrestlings, the Interpreter gravely
handed over the coin specified.   The official then
proceeded solemnly to take down the name, calling, and description of each member of the crew,
stating that he would have to report the case next
day to the court at Trèves.   Thereupon he disappeared, only to return again after a short time with
a view of making sure that the law was not being
infringed in any unforeseen particular.   In proof of
his vigilance he produced a bundle of faggots which
he had just caught a trespasser stealing from the
imperial estate.   Next morning he came back to
watch the proceedings of the crew till they embarked.
The latter were convinced that there was a solid

substratum of curiosity at the bottom of his official
zeal; nor could they help wondering whether the
mark was ever paid into the imperial treasury.

After breakfast the boat was drawn up on the
bank, when the mystery of the harsh music on the
previous evening was at once solved. A piece of
the iron keel about four feet in length had become
detached at the stern in consequence of the screws
by which it was fixed having been broken, and was
now seen to be bent downwards almost at right
angles to the bottom of the boat. Wherever, therefore, the water was less than four feet in depth the
iron had grated on the gravel of the river-bed in the
manner described above. The injury had not been
observed before the start, because the boat had
already been launched when the crew came down
to embark.

The difficult task of repairing this new damage
with inadequate tools having occupied some hours, the
voyagers were not afloat again till half-past twelve.
The light rain which had then already begun to fall
soon turned into a heavy downpour, which continued
steadily without a break for the rest of the day. The
rowers were of course soon drenched to the skin, but
to them this was not of much consequence. The
cox for the time being was much worse off, as he sat
shivering in the chilling rain. By a kind of reaction
not uncommon on such occasions, the dripping
oarsmen seemed to be more cheerful than on days

of brilliant sunshine, as one merry jest followed the
other and peal after peal of laughter re-echoed
among the solitary hills.

Thus beguiling the time, they rowed on for
several hours. The scenery was fine all along, the
dark wooded hills alternating from one bank to the
other. These hills were specially beautiful on the
right bank, above the village of Detzem (the name of
which is derived from the Latin *ad decimum*, because
it is at the tenth mile-stone from Trèves); but a
mist which had begun to gather unfortunately hid
the tops of the higher ridges from view. The river
in this region makes three great curves, the third
forming a narrow loop about five miles round, with a
uniform breadth of not much over half a mile across.
As the voyagers rowed past they were particularly
struck with the prettiness of the village of Leiwen,
which lies nestling among walnut plantations in the
meadow-land on the southern right bank of this
bend.

As they now saw no prospect of the rain ceasing
that day, and could not think of camping in their
present soaking condition unless the evening cleared
up, they finally decided, though they had not yet
done twenty miles, to land and spend the night at
Neumagen, the largest village in this part of the
Moselle. While still debating the question, the
Captain remarked that the very name of the place
seemed to recommend it as a good one for restoring

the inner man. Those of the crew who understood German said nothing, but made a mental note of the Captain's observation as showing the steady progress he was making in the acquisition of the German language.

At Neumagen therefore they landed at about four o'clock, and in a perfect torrent of rain made their way up to the inn, which, though facing the river, is some distance from the bank. The village lies back from the river in a rather cramped position close to the foot of the hills. It was a Roman settlement, its Latin name having been Noviomagus, and many Roman antiquities have been and still are found there. Otherwise the only object of interest about the place is its Gothic church, which is 700 years old.

The little inn, though very plain and barely large enough to accommodate the five oarsmen, they found comfortable enough, perhaps appreciating its shelter after changing their soaking garments more than they would have done in other circumstances.

On coming down to the coffee-room (*Gaststube*) they restored themselves with a cordial, the name of which, if not in itself famous, at least bore testimony to the popularity which aquatics must already have attained on the Moselle. The wall displayed a large advertisement setting forth the merits of this *Rudersport-liqueur* (rowing-sport-liqueur).

As the rain still continued coming down heavily

during the evening the friends were obliged to stay
in after dinner, consoling themselves with a rubber
of whist till bed-time.

The landlady, a very good-natured woman of
about fifty, was evidently much impressed with the
Captain and, greatly to the amusement of the rest of
the crew, singled him out for her marked attentions,
which he, alas! did not seem to value as fully as
they deserved.

Rising next morning refreshed by a long sleep,
the voyagers were rejoiced to find that the rain had
cleared off during the night, leaving a cloudless sky.
The brilliant sunshine lent a very different aspect to
the fine scenery from that which it wore under the
dark lowering rain-clouds of the previous day. Afloat
before nine, they rowed on past Piesport, long famous
for its wine, and round another loop some five miles
in length, but not more than half a mile across the
neck, till they came in sight of the *Braune Berg*,
celebrated for the wine grown on its terraced slopes.

Here they fell in with their German friend
sculling along in his light boat, which resembled a
cross between a dinghey and a whiff, as they are
called on the Isis. He was proceeding along in a
very business-like fashion, with an ostentatious
action and high feather, looking as if he felt that the
eye of the world was on his boat-club's representative
on the Moselle. He was a brawny fellow of six or
seven and twenty, got up in a jersey and white-

flannel knee-breeches with stockings. It would
never have done, according to German notions of
propriety, to display the bare knee. The *tout ensemble*
was that of the English boating-man slightly cari-
catured ; but the effect produced on the natives, who
knew not the original, must have been imposing.
Allowing for a certain excusable air of importance,
due no doubt to the rather recent introduction of
aquatics into Germany, he was really a very good
fellow. At the village of Kesten, where the *Braune
Berg* begins, he parted company with his English
acquaintances and landed, no doubt in order to refresh himself with the local wine.

This incident reminds the writer of a chart of the
Main between Würzburg and Aschaffenburg given
him at the former place, and drawn for the use of a
German four that rowed down the river some three
years ago. On this chart were marked in red ink,
at intervals of every few miles, all the way down,
the times, varying from half an hour to an hour and
a half, spent by the crew at different places in refreshing. This was a thoroughly German mode of
combining the *Wirthshausleben* (restaurant-life) with
the new element of athleticism.

Continuing their voyage the Britons rowed on
through a fine gorge till they reached Berncastel,
with its ruined castle of Landshut rising picturesquely above the town. Here they landed in the
heat of the day to lay in a stock of provisions. This

little town, originally a Roman settlement, situated
at the mouth of the beautiful Tiefenbach valley,
is well known in Germany for two kinds of excellent
wine cultivated on the neighbouring slopes.   From
this point the river flows due west for five miles past
the fine vineyards of Zeltingen, which have a good
reputation for the wine they produce.

Having lunched at the corner of this reach, where
the river turns north, the voyagers, near the village
of Uerzig. rowed past a curious tower with a sun-
dial, said to have been a hermitage at one time
and built into the rocks, which are here of a fine red
colour.

After a short landing for a bathe at an angle of
the river, they continued past some pretty meadows,
followed by a magnificent hill on the right bank, till
they reached Trarbach, a little town lying in a lovely
situation below the ruined castle of the Gräfinburg,
near the end of another long loop formed by the
stream as it doubles round on itself.   In the vineyards along the slopes of the river-valley between
this point and Piesport are grown all the best wines
of the Moselle.   On the bank opposite Trarbach lies
the village of Traben, the latter having been partially
and the former wholly destroyed by fire in the
year 1857.

Allowing themselves to drift down this beautiful
reach, the rowers came in sight, a short way farther
down, of a high ridge, on the top of which a village

and an old fort are picturesquely perched. As the
evening was growing late they stopped at the little
village of Burg to buy milk and some other
necessaries. Then rowing round the next bend of
the river, they ran in to the right bank with a view
to camping for the night. The landing-place was
excellent, for the bank was not more than two feet
high at the water's edge, while the flat ground higher
up was admirably adapted for an encampment. The
grass was very long, but as there were luckily a few
small patches where it had been mown, the tent was
pitched in one of these clearances. One or two of the
mowers being still about, the Interpreter thought it
advisable to anticipate possible objections by asking
for permission to camp for the night. The natives
replied that the strangers might stay wherever and
as long as they liked, apparently not quite under-
standing the point of the question, probably because
the ground was common-land.

Nearly opposite the encampment on the other side
of the river lay a railway station, the line now for
the first time since Trèves coming within sight of
the bank.

Having lighted their lamp when it had grown
dark, the campers found it impossible to go on with
their supper owing to a plague of white-winged
moths which came swarming round them in a dense
cloud, and after scorching their wings dropped by
hundreds into the cups and plates on the table.

Violence and strong language being of no avail, stratagem at last proved successful in abating the nuisance. The large lamp was removed and placed in the bows of the boat, which was a good way off, while a solitary candle was alone retained on the table. The vast majority of the insects were thus diverted by the attraction of the greater light. The appearance of the lamp below was now indeed curious to behold, for it looked not unlike a distant light in winter seen through a storm of snow. Next morning it was found half-buried in a mass of the corpses of these insects, which was five or six inches deep and covered a considerable part of the bottom of the boat. As there must have been millions in the heap it was quite a business clearing them out.

During breakfast next morning the German sculler appeared on the scene, and in response to an invitation joined the party for a short time before continuing on his solitary way. Hardly had he left when the two Englishmen were seen to be rowing down towards the camp. Being hailed they landed, and stayed half an hour or so for a friendly chat and a cup of tea. One of them was a barrister, and seemed to have had considerable experience of canoeing on foreign, especially French rivers. This was the last time the crew from the Isis saw either them or their German acquaintance.

Owing to the delay caused by these visits they

did not get off this morning till quite eleven o'clock. About two miles below the camp, at the pretty village of Pünderich, begins the fourth and probably most beautiful loop formed by the stream of the Moselle below Trèves. It is a circuit of seven and a half miles round a ridge, 360 feet high, on which is situated an old ruin, the Marienburg, while the neck of land is narrower than in any other curve on the Moselle, being less than 600 yards across. There is a good restaurant at the top, as is usual in Germany near ruins commanding fine scenery. The view from there is said to be the best in the valley of the Moselle, the two reaches of the river on each side looking like beautiful lakes. The voyagers having started so late did not land, but contented themselves with enjoying the view of the ruin from below on both sides. This was certainly charming enough. They felt no doubt that the German sculler had ascended the height to refresh at the restaurant ; he must, however, have been off again by this time, for his boat was nowhere to be seen.

Rowing past Zell, which is near the head of the loop, they soon reached Alf, situated at its neck and seventy-two miles by water from Trèves. Bow here remarked that if this place had received its name as an indication that it is equidistant by river from Coblenz and Trèves, its godfathers ought rather to have bestowed the appellation on Burg, that place being exactly sixty-one miles from each of those

towns. He seemed disappointed at no one appearing
to understand his remark.

At this point the railway crosses the Moselle by a
large double bridge, and following the right bank for
some miles recrosses at Elier. It there enters a
tunnel which, being two and three-quarter miles in
length, is the longest in Germany, thus cutting off a
winding curve of twelve miles in the river's course.
Issuing from the tunnel at Cochem, the line closely
follows the left bank till within two miles of Coblenz,
when it again crosses to the right.

In the middle of a narrow bend which the river
makes to the west some three miles below Alf the
voyagers came upon the lonely ruined monastery of
Stuben on the right bank. Having landed to visit it,
they had a good bathe a short way below before
starting off again. They then rowed past the picturesque little village of Ediger, with its many mediaeval
buildings situated on the left bank of this straight
reach, which flows east for four miles. After this the
river makes four considerable winds before reaching
Cochem. Near the corner of the second curve lies
the town of Beilstein, at the base of a rocky hill and
commanded by a large ruined castle. On the right
bank before the last bend is situated Bruttig, a
picturesque little town with mediæval buildings.
Then after the last corner comes a fine reach
three miles long, flowing straight towards Cochem.
This winding curve, which the railway avoids by

the Kaiser - Wilhelms - tunnel already mentioned, contains some of the loveliest bits of scenery on the Moselle.

The small town of Cochem, nestling in an angle at the foot of a side-valley through which the Ender flows into the main river, is perhaps as beautifully situated as any place on the Moselle. Above it rises a very picturesque old castle which was restored about twenty years ago and contains some show-rooms worth visiting.

Here the crew landed to dine at about four o'clock in the afternoon. While dinner was preparing the Interpreter and two other members of the crew strolled about to look at the town. In the course of their peregrinations they came across a photographer's shop, which they entered in order to buy some views of the Moselle. One member of the crew had since the very beginning of the voyage been insisting on the appropriateness of getting the boat and her crew photographed, but his proposals had only met with a negative. He had for some time past resigned himself to his fate, expressing a conviction that the projected group would never come off. It suddenly occurred to the Interpreter that a surprise might be prepared for him. Knowing that the railway followed the left bank of the Moselle from Cochem onwards, he asked the artist whether he could manage to bring his camera with him next morning to a station some five miles farther down the river. The photographer

replied that he could certainly come by the nine
o'clock train, stopping at Pommern, four and a half
miles below Cochem. It was thereupon at once
arranged that he should do so, and be fetched across
in the boat to take the encampment on the opposite
bank.

Having dined, the crew re-embarked as it was
growing dusk. The four who were in the secret
now derived much pleasure from adopting an allusive
style of conversation, the real meaning of which
remained concealed from the object of the plot.
They began to talk of the proposed picture, and
to deplore their negligence in having missed their
last opportunity at Cochem. For as the next day
would terminate the voyage, it would be impossible
to have an encampment photographed. The un-
witting victim, being worked up to a great pitch
of disgust by such remarks, testily observed that
he had said all along the project would turn out
thus in the end. The others then, by way of sooth-
ing him, said that after all it was not a matter of
any great importance, thereby of course only increasing his irritation.

Below Cochem the character of the Moselle
changes; for the windings peculiar to its stream so far
now cease, the remaining thirty miles being more or
less straight. This is of course the reason why the
railway follows it so closely all the way to Coblenz.
The scenery is no longer quite so fine as before, but

its picturesqueness is considerably increased by the comparatively numerous old castles to be seen on its banks; for out of the twenty ruins occurring between Trèves and Coblenz nine are to be found in this tract, though it is only a quarter of the whole distance.

Rowing past Clotten with its castle, the voyagers encamped in the dark on the right bank about four miles below Cochem. The ground chosen turned out to be very fair, and the view was good, especially when looking back on the old ruin rising on the ridge behind.

The morning of the next day, 23d August, was cloudless, and when the campers breakfasted at eight o'clock the heat was already intense.

After breakfast the Interpreter in the course of conversation pointed out a railway station visible on the opposite bank some half mile farther down, and naïvely suggested that a photographer might possibly be found there by rowing across in the boat. The victim of the plot testily remarked that the bare notion of such a thing was raving nonsense, and he, for one, would have nothing to do with encouraging such ridiculous waste of time. After much pressure he was nevertheless induced to accompany two of the others in the boat. They had hardly reached the railway station when the train arrived. A man with a bundle under his arm having got out, one of the two in the secret went up to him and innocently asked if he happened to be a photographer. On his answering in the affirmative, the victim stood rooted to the spot for a considerable period. He afterwards observed that if this plot was meant for a practical joke, it certainly was a very poor one. The victim always considers the practical joke inflicted on him to be poor.

The photographer being ferried across, took the group, including the boat and the tent, successfully enough from a generally picturesque point of view ; but owing to the strong glare the faces all came out so badly that they were hardly ever recognised by friends.

On the eve of this the last day of the voyage the old leak had begun to show signs of renewed activity. The invaluable aid of the versatile Captain had therefore again to be brought into requisition on behalf of the crew. The delay caused by this, together with the photographic episode, deferred the start till noon. Having at last embarked, they rowed straight down to Pommern, landed, and took leave of their friend the photographer. As they had put in just below a picturesque little inn with a pretty arbour overlooking the river, they took the opportunity of trying the local wine, which they found to be cheap and good.

They then leisurely paddled on in the heat of the day past Treis, with its tower on the right at the entrance to a side valley, Moselkern on the left, six and a half miles below Pommern, at the mouth of

the valley of the Eltz, and then the old castle of
Bischofstein rising on the bank opposite the village
of Burgen and the end of the Beyachthal.

Soon after this they allowed themselves to drift
along with a view to lunching in the boat. The
meal, however, was neither long nor enjoyable. For
a motive to speed which they never hitherto experienced now began to assert itself. The intense
heat was evidently causing the rapid decomposition
in the boat of some substance, the exact whereabouts
of which it was impossible to discover. The stench
thus produced became so intolerable, as long as the
boat remained more or less stationary, that the
crew were compelled in self-defence to keep rowing steadily without a break; for as long as she
moved fast the evil odour remained almost, if not
quite, imperceptible. The conclusion which the
friends drew from this experience was that a bad
smell interferes very much not only with the enjoyment of a meal, but even with the appreciation
of fine scenery. They were also inclined to admit
that, if the decaying substance was a piece of cheese,
which they strongly suspected it to be, that luxury
decidedly has its disadvantages as a travelling companion.

Rowing, therefore, at an accelerated pace past the
pretty village of Brodenbach and through the narrow
rocky gorge below, they came in sight of Cobern,
with its two old castles, a small town well situated

K

on the left bank at a bend of the river, nine miles
and a half from Coblenz. A short way below this
place they ran ashore, and disembarking more
speedily than they had ever done before, enjoyed their last bathe at a distance of twenty or
thirty yards to windward of the boat. Having
dressed, they hurriedly took their seats and resumed their oars without the loss of a moment.
Such hot haste is probably never seen except at a
canoe race in a college regatta. Had a foreigner
happened to see the crew getting in and out of the
boat on that occasion he would certainly have said :
" These Englishmen *are* a restless race, and can never
take even their pleasures without hurrying."

As evening came on they found themselves rowing past the Moselle side of Coblenz. Filling up,
as it does, the whole corner of land formed by the
junction of the Rhine and its tributary, the town fully
deserves its name, which, as is well known, is derived
from the Latin *confluentes*. Emerging into the Rhine
and strenuously rowing with a spurt up the mighty
stream, the crew landed some distance up the right
bank soon after seven o'clock.

Thus ended this most delightful expedition,
which while extending over only eighteen days,
appeared owing to its variety to have lasted quite
six weeks. During all this time the weather had
been splendid, with only one day and a half of rain.

The boat was that very evening made over to an

agent for despatch to England, while the crew next
morning went down to Cologne on one of the Rhine
steamers.   Here they regretfully dispersed, the
Captain and First Officer returning direct to England,
Bow going off to visit relations at Bruges, while the
Interpreter and the Chaplain took a steamer to
Düsseldorf, the former on his way to visit for a few
days at Göttingen the scenes of his boyhood.

CHAPTER VII

THE MAIN

"Quod adest memento
Componere aequus : cetera fluminis
Ritu feruntur."—HORACE.

THE morning of 9th September 1888 saw the two would-be navigators of the Main at Bayreuth, but the canoe, though it had been despatched from Dresden four days before, and was to have taken but forty-eight hours on the way, had not yet come. Finding she could not possibly arrive till midnight, they were fain to spend the day as best they could. Their first move was to proceed to the *Anker* Hotel, from the head-waiter of which they had received the only information it had been possible to obtain as to the navigability of the Main from a point so near the source. In starting from here they were, in fact, making an experiment; for they had been fully aware before leaving England that Bayreuth lies only about ten miles below the source of the Red Main, and that the fall in the first fifty miles is upwards of 300 feet. The latter fact in itself was sufficient to prove that the navigation in this part of its course must be difficult if not hazardous. It could not, however, be as dangerous for a canoe as the Danube, the average fall of which is above eight feet per mile between Donaueschingen and Ulm. On the other hand, the Main being but a tributary, was found to contain far less water at a point 320 miles from its mouth than the Danube at Donaueschingen. The information above referred to was conveyed on a post-card to some English friends who, having attended the Wagner festival a month before, had written to the waiter in question asking whether he could ascertain anything about the river near Bayreuth. The reply received was as follows :—

"BAYREUTH, *22th af. August* '88.

"SIR,—Received your kindly letter, and send you now your wished Information. The Frachtzug [goods train] from Dresden to Bayreuth wants 40 until 48 ours because he stops at every little station. To carry at boot in the told size its very easy because the trains are always arranged as the people desires. The Main is usefull from Bamberg to Wuerzburg and farther following line, but not from hier, only lickwise [in places] for little tree's for the countrymann [rafts]. Their are two river hwo been called Main, the withe

and the red. The source from the last one begins 3 ours
outside Bayreuth, and the source from the withe Main beginning near Pegnitz perhaps 100 miles from here near
Nuremberg, and is neither usefull near Bayreuth. This the
best information I could find out for you. Many respect
and remembring to you and your wife.—I remain your
faithful truly,   C—— S——,
                    " Head waiter of Hotel Anker, Bayreuth."

This "information," such as it was, could hardly
be called encouraging. Knowing, however, by long
experience the ignorance of German riparians as to
the nature of their own rivers, the two friends decided
on trying the experiment. Had they been aware
beforehand of the hardships and disasters awaiting
them in the course of the first two days they might
have been deterred from launching their frail bark
at Bayreuth. Meanwhile, pending the arrival of
the canoe, they spent the forenoon in wandering
about the *Eremitage*, a château situated about three
miles from the town, and once the residence of
Frederick the Great's only sister, Markgravine of
Bayreuth. The main building presents a fantastic
appearance owing to the walls being completely
inlaid with stones of various colours. The grounds,
which are laid out in imitation of Versailles, would
be very pleasant if well kept, but as it is have a
desolate and neglected look. At the entrance there
is a notice containing a long list of rules for the
guidance of the public. The most interesting to
strangers were two clauses strictly prohibiting the

hanging up of dirty linen on the statues, and the bathing of dogs in the ornamental waters.

It was a relief to find early next morning that the boat had arrived during the night. Having packed in a basket provisions for two days and a night, and purchased a lamp, besides other requisites for camping out, the crew despatched their Gladstone bags to Bingen on the Rhine, and then proceeded to convey their boat on a truck to a spot just below the town, where two branches of the river unite. Even after the junction the stream looked alarmingly small and shallow. The baggage being arranged in the middle compartment of the canoe, the two ends remained entirely free for the crew. The articles brought from England for camping purposes were a waterproof ground-sheet, two rugs apiece, an inflatable air-bed, a spirit-lamp, saucepan and tea-kettle, tin plates and cups, besides knives, forks, and spoons. A locker fitted in the stern under the poop-seat proved a great convenience for storing away all the utensils as well as odds and ends. It is advisable for those intending to camp out much to take a small tent with them, for unless you are sure of your weather the results of sleeping in the open air are apt to be unpleasant. A Canadian canoe would, however, only hold a tent of the most limited and portable dimensions in addition to the other necessary luggage. A tub-pair or a four-oar, on the other hand, will easily carry in the stern a good-sized tent, such as is described in the chapters on the Werra and the Neckar.

All being now ready, a start was made at about eleven o'clock amid great public enthusiasm. For as this was the first time a boat of any description had been seen at Bayreuth, the excitement caused by so great a novelty was probably second only to that produced by the musical festival. On the day of the embarkation a paragraph to the following effect appeared in the *Bayreuther Tagblatt* :—

Sept. 10.

"To-day there arrived at the Hotel Anker two Englishmen, who intend to navigate the whole course of the Main from here, and then to enter the Rhine. It is doubtful whether the sportsmen (*Sportsmänner*) will succeed in getting down the Main from here ; it is, however, just possible that the fulness of the river at the present time will enable them to accomplish their project."

It subsequently appeared that the distance between Bayreuth and Lichtenfels, about fifty miles, had never been done by boat before. The raft navigation begins at Mainleuss, three miles below the junction of the White and the Red Main, and about twenty from Bayreuth. These first twenty miles were therefore altogether virgin waters. The whole length of the Main is 330 miles from the source to its junction with the Rhine. In the first fifty miles there are twenty weirs with their corresponding mills (about the same number as for more than double

Maineck

Mill
Weir

Mainroth

Rothwinder Mill
Weir

Main

Weir

Mainleuss

Station 280

Polz

3 Waterwheels

To Kulmbach

Mill

Steinenhausen
Weir

White Main

Melkendorf

To
Kulmbach

N

Waterwheel

Red Main

Waterwheel

Mill

Unter
Zeblitz
Ober

Lanzenreuth

Mill

Gessmannsreuth

Dreschen

Large number
of waterwheels

Langenstadt

Langenstadt

Mill

Water
wheel

Mill

Neuenreuth

Waterwheel

Camp

Alt drossenfeld

Weir

Neu-
drossenfeld

Red Main

Dreschenau

Mill

Neuen Ples

Alten Ples

Mill

Unterkonnersreuth

Mill

Honersreuth
Mill

Mill

Station

BAYREUTH
333

Stanford's Geog. Estab.

0   1   2   3   4   5 Kilometres

the distance on the Werra and the Danube), besides
other obstructions which will be described later. In
the upper waters, before the junction of the two
branches, there are continual rapids and many
shallows which it would be absolutely impossible to
navigate in anything but a canoe. A dry season
might render them impracticable even for so light a
boat as that. Below Lichtenfels, on the other hand,
for a distance of 270 miles, the Main is probably
one of the best rivers (not regulated by locks)
in Europe for rowing on. With the exception
of one weir, about five miles below Lichtenfels,
and of two locks, the one at Schweinfurt and
the other at Würzburg, there are no obstacles what-
ever. The scenery for nearly a hundred miles
above Aschaffenburg will compare for continuous
beauty with that of any other German river. The
Main has the additional advantage of having a
clear and placid stream, in which a fine bathe may
be enjoyed almost anywhere, and of possessing ideal
banks for landing and camping. This does not apply
to the Elbe, the Weser, the Danube, the Rhine, or
the Moselle in anything like the same degree. Between Kitzingen and Würzburg there lie several
picturesque mediaeval walled towns and villages,
probably unknown to the tourist and unlike any
to be seen on other German rivers. The Main is the
only German stream the current of which is not too
rapid to row against with comparative ease. It would

make a very pleasant trip to go up the 240 miles
from Mainz to Bamberg, a distance which could without trouble be accomplished in a fortnight, thence
through the *Ludwigs-Canal* into the Danube, and
finish with a row down to Vienna, Buda-Pesth, or
the Black Sea, according as time and circumstances
permitted.

But to return to Bayreuth. Waving their farewells to the assembled crowd, the two friends swiftly
paddled down the rapid current, while the tiny Union
Jack fixed in the bows fluttered gaily in the breeze.
The large contingent of the juvenile population which
accompanied them on the bank till the first mill was
reached could not have kept up with them but for
the extraordinary meanderings of the stream at this
point. So short, indeed, were the windings that no
other kind of boat could have got round them.
After lifting the canoe across at three mills and stopping all agricultural proceedings on the banks till
they were out of sight, they landed for lunch at a
lonely and beautiful spot where the Main receives a
tiny tributary at the base of a pine-clad hill.

Wherever there is a mill on the upper Main
the river divides into two arms, the weir always
coming first. It invariably proved better to cross
at the latter, as the weir branch has more water
and its bank is generally lower and more convenient
for the purpose. This is probably due to the fact
that the weirs are built across the natural bed of the

river, while the mill branch is an artificial cutting. Having at the second crossing chosen the mill-stream, the canoeists, after a few yards' paddling, entered a sort of tunnel through reeds growing to the height of about ten feet. This channel, which, owing to the dense growth was not more than three feet broad, and seemed nearly a mile long, had probably never before been penetrated by man since its construction.

As each mill was passed the volume of water in the stream was found to have visibly increased.

Immediately after a deep weir at a place called Neu-Drossenfeld, there comes a magnificent broad reach with absolutely no current. This branch, leaving the town some way off on the right, widens out into a sheet of water resembling a lake, fringed with a luxuriant growth of trees. The cause of this phenomenon is a second weir with a very deep fall at the next place, Alt-Drossenfeld. The absence of a boat of any kind on so fine a piece of water could not fail to strike one as a singular thing.

Below this second weir there followed a succession of rapids, which were passed without mishap; but a cascade with a fall of about three feet over rocks seemed too hazardous to attempt off-hand. After a close examination from the bank, however, it was determined to run the risk. So, keeping as close to the right bank as possible, the canoeists shot merrily down without even touching, much to the delight of a number of peasants, who had assembled on the

hillside, no doubt fully expecting to witness the
ruin of the adventurers. Raising a cheer, the latter
disappeared from their sight, as a rapid swiftly
carried them round the next bend of the stream.
Soon afterwards so beautiful a spot came into view
that it was without further delay chosen as a
camping ground, though the hour was as yet only
five o'clock. It was a strip of bright green meadow
dotted with haycocks and flanked by a steep ridge
thickly wooded with pine. There was also a good
landing-place here, and deep water for a bathe before
breakfast. Of the latter advantage the two campers
were, however, by no means inclined to avail themselves next morning.

This had, indeed, been a delightful day ; and no
forebodings of impending evil arose to mar the enjoyment of that beautiful evening. There was, it
is true, a few hundred yards farther down stream,
an object looking in the distance like a disused mill,
but its diabolical nature was not revealed till the
next day. It turned out to be a water-wheel, the
worst enemy the navigator of the Upper Main has
to contend with.

On landing the campers first proceeded to collect
all the hay in the field—it is to be hoped not very
much against the wishes of the owners—into two
large heaps close to the bank. By turning the canoe
over and supporting her ends on these, they formed a
sort of roof, and by hanging the waterproof cover of

the boat over one side, transformed the whole into
quite a comfortable cabin. Thus their vehicle by day
became their shelter by night. Having turned in
early, after an excellent supper, they must have slept
for nearly three hours. Suddenly, about one o'clock,
an explosive sound, something like the bursting of
a balloon, terminated their slumbers for that night.
Peering into the darkness they caught a glimpse of
the dim forms of their umbrellas careering away
towards the river. The Interpreter dashed out barefoot in pursuit, but for his pains only got well
drenched in the rain, which was now coming down
heavily. The umbrellas had been set up to protect,
in case of wet, a number of articles left outside the
cabin. They had broken away from their moorings
in a sudden gust of wind. The necessity of bringing
the now exposed property under shelter increased the
discomfort caused by the rising wind, which was now
driving the rain in on the unprotected side of the
boat. The ambition of the two friends was now not
so much to sleep as to keep tolerably dry. They had
cause to be thankful that their insecure roof did not
collapse over their devoted heads, or turn over and
leave their prostrate forms exposed to the full fury
of the elements. Dawn at last slowly broke, but
brought only the prospect of a drenching day. To
cook breakfast amid the general dampness and with
hardly any shelter from the blast required no small
amount of patience; for even the preliminary of

striking a match was successful only when the whole
stock was almost entirely exhausted. There was a
certain amount of consolation in discovering that the
umbrellas had not vanished for ever. One of them
was found caught in a bush some way down the bank,
while the other lay dimly discernible, like a huge
tortoise, at the bottom of the river. The latter was
at length fished up with some trouble and a boat-
hook. Keeping their things dry by the ingenious
use of the recovered umbrellas, and packing their
bark on what could now only ironically be termed
dry land, the soaking friends launched her at about
8.30. In a few minutes they reached the first of the
dozen or more water-wheels they were destined to
come across on that eventful day. The country
through which the Main passes between the camping-
ground and the confluence, a distance of perhaps
eleven miles, is flat meadow-land. For the purpose
of irrigating the fields huge wheels, with a bucket
attached to each paddle, have been constructed so as
to revolve close to the bank and discharge the water
they raise into a wooden channel, from which it is
dispersed over the land.

However beneficial these erections may be to
agriculture, they are to the navigator undoubtedly
the most hateful obstacles that can well be imagined. In order that the stream may be sufficiently
strong to turn the wheel, it is dammed up with
large stones right across, excepting the space of a few

feet immediately opposite the wheel. The banks
are always highest at the parts chosen for the
erection of these obstructions. They are at the same
time almost invariably so steep as nearly to pre-
clude the possibility of pulling the boat over. The
unfortunate crew were therefore reduced to the
deplorable necessity of wading up to their middle
and making a channel by rolling the boulders down
the stream. This process generally entails a delay
of twenty minutes, besides being extremely exhausting. If the wheel happens to be turning at the
time, the unwary worker is liable to be severely
doused by an intermittent but heavy shower-bath.
The progress of any future canoeist on these waters
will be much easier, unless the local irrigators have
discovered and repaired the mysterious breaches
in their dams. This they have most likely done,
for they must have found out during the summer
of 1889 that their wheels for some unaccountable
reason refused to turn, thus reducing their fields to a
condition of drought.

Four mills and several plank bridges, built so
close to the surface of the water as to prevent a
boat passing under them, entailed a large addition
to the porterage on that day. It will therefore be
readily believed that when about noon, in a very
winding part of the river, there could be descried
across the fields a series of five or six of these
hateful black objects at short intervals, the two

friends could not find it in their hearts to bless the inventor of water-wheels. They also agreed that never had navvy worked so hard for his living as they were labouring that day.

At about four in the afternoon they came at length to a stationary wheel, at the side of which the stream rushed smooth and swift through an opening three or four feet wide. An uninterrupted immunity from disaster on the Danube and the Elbe had made the crew so over-confident that they had altogether omitted the precaution of tying in their luggage as superfluous on this voyage. Nemesis was now at hand. Glad to be saved another porterage, they gaily made for the gap, but found when too late that the strong slant of the stream towards the wheel would prevent the canoe from taking the fall straight. She consequently struck the wheel broadside, and, tilting over, filled before her crew could realise the situation. By a great stroke of good fortune the lurch had thrown both of them into the water. The canoe would otherwise have turned completely over, and sent the bags, one of which contained the Interpreter's watch and money, to the bottom. The depth and swiftness of the river would have precluded all chance of recovering anything that had sunk by diving. As it was, only the loose things, such as coats, cushions, and paddles, were washed out, and went rapidly floating down stream.

The banks were here so steep and bushy that

the shipwrecked friends had to swim a considerable
distance, snatching up their floating property as they
went, before they could land and pull their water-
logged craft ashore. To their relief they found she
had sustained no injury. Cox had to mourn the loss,
among other things, of the same foot of a pair of
boots and boating-shoes. He was thus compelled to
wear along with a black boot a yellow boating-shoe
on the wrong foot, a by no means prepossessing
combination. The only two hats he possessed had
been washed away by the stream. So he sat for
some time on a sandbank in a woebegone condition,
unable to arouse himself to action. The hats, as
well as a waterproof coat, were, however, luckily
found sometime afterwards, stopped by the dam of
the next water-wheel. This was the only occasion
on which a water-wheel did not exercise a baleful
influence.

The unlucky voyagers had been thoroughly
drenched before starting that morning, and, though
the rain had ceased in the forenoon, had remained
wet all day owing to their repeated wadings. Their
blankets and cushions, too, had been soaked by the
rain during the night. They had therefore decided
in the morning to put up at some village for the
night in order to get their things dried. Their
present plight rendered this step imperative. The
accident caused a long delay, so that though there
was but one more water-wheel to pass, and the

distance did not exceed a couple of miles, the mill
of Steinhausen, just above the junction of the Red
and the White Main, was not reached till close upon
sunset. The miller, a handsome and pleasant man,
with whom the strangers subsequently struck up a
great friendship, took charge of the boat and much
of their soaking property, sending the remainder in
a wheelbarrow to the neighbouring village of Melkendorf.

Here there was quite a respectable inn, in which
a vast room with six windows was assigned to the
unexpected arrivals. The iron stove was lighted,
but proved to be a very bad substitute for an
open fire, as far as drying capacity was concerned;
for in spite of all efforts most of the clothes were
still damp next day. To some of these the brilliant
red of Baedeker had, they were grieved to find, been
transferred, and remained adhering for all time. The
bank-notes, which had been reduced almost to a pulp,
required very delicate manipulation in drying, but
were ultimately restored to a presentable form and
recognised as legal tenders. The friends retired to
bed as early as possible, for what they had gone
through that day was more calculated to exhaust
than almost any other river experience they had ever
known.

Next morning, after taking leave of the miller and
his family, whose faces they never expected to see
again, they started from the mill at Steinhausen at

about nine o'clock. This time they carefully secured
the heavier articles of luggage with a rope, though
in so doing they could not help a sneaking con-
sciousness of resembling the man who locks the
stable-door after his horse has been stolen. The
Interpreter nevertheless had a presentiment that
something was going to happen, and kept on his
coat which contained his watch and money.

After the junction with the White Main a few
hundred yards below the mill, the volume of water
is greatly increased, the river now flowing with a
deep and steady stream. There still being three
water-wheels to pass, the spirits of the canoeists
were naturally not quite so high as they otherwise
would have been. They had paddled down rapidly
for about two miles when the first of these hated foes
came into sight. This one seemed blacker than the
rest, having a particularly deadly look as it went
on revolving rapidly. Here too there was a clear
channel several feet wide, though a large stake just
under water close to the wheel was calculated to
arouse misgivings. A pig-headed rashness impelled
the adventurers to imperil their safety a second time.
To avoid the danger of the Scylla of the dam on the
left, they made the fatal mistake of keeping too close
to the Charybdis of the wheel on the right. This was
a much worse place than the scene of the previous
day's disaster, owing to the greater depth and rush of
water. Impending ruin was seen when it was too

late to avert the stroke. The stern struck the stake
with an ominous crash. The canoe instantly heeled
over, filled, and began to sink beneath her occupants.
When the water was nearly up to their necks they
plunged into the stream, but in so doing unfortunately
overturned the boat completely. The luggage which
was tied in consequently hung downwards, while all
the loose articles either sank or were rapidly carried
away by the current. The Interpreter managed with
great difficulty to bring the canoe, which in her present
condition was extremely heavy, to land and drag her
up the steep bank. Cox had meanwhile scrambled up,
and running along plunged in again to rescue such of
their belongings as had gone careering down stream.

The Interpreter escaped lightly with the final
loss of his umbrella. Cox, on the other hand, had
seen the last of his stylograph pen, his stick, umbrella,
and mackintosh, some of which had been gallantly
rescued only the day before. His watch, too, registered
the exact moment of his immersion. He was for
some time under the impression that he had lost his
valuable field-glass here; but by a process of strenuous
retrospective thought, he ascertained that he had left
it buried in one of the heaps of hay which had
supported the canoe during the previous night.
From this discovery he derived, strange to say, a
kind of mixed consolation. Such was the price paid
for the privilege of camping on that beautiful meadow
in storm and rain.

A loss deplored by both in common was that
of a pound of tea, which was completely ruined by
the submersion. It had been bought at the last moment before starting from Victoria Station for three
and sixpence. Its value had gone up, in consequence
of disagreeable interviews with custom-house officials
on the German and the Bohemian frontier, to about
six shillings. Its owners had only had two brews
of it—at the encampment on the first night—so that
each cup had cost about one and sixpence. The two
friends partially comforted themselves with the reflec-
tion that after all this is not so much more than is paid
for a cup of tea at some London restaurants. Could,
however, the mental worry connected with endeavours
not to leave it behind, and with the insolence of
Bohemian custom-house officers, have been assessed
on the same scale as wounded affections in breach of
promise cases, the value of each cup, on a moderate
computation, must have been about ten shillings.

The most distressing part of the shipwreck was the
discovery that the boat had been so severely damaged
as to be incapable of floating for five minutes. The
only consoling thought in the whole business was
that the fact of striking the stake had probably saved
the adventurers from the more serious disaster of
being completely broken on the wheel as it revolved.
Even the present condition of the boat might, it
was feared, cut short the voyage at this point. In
any case, all further prospect of camping was at an

end, owing to the loss of nearly all the necessary
appliances.

The obvious thing to do in the meantime was to
have the boat transported to Kulmbach, a town of
some size about five miles distant, where there was
some chance of the damage being repaired. Cox, who
from his long swim in the cold water while rescu-
ing the paddles, cushions, and other property, felt the
risk of taking a severe chill, restored his circulation
by running back to the mill at full speed. He
returned with three of the miller's men, who conveyed the boat and the saturated luggage to Steinhausen and later in the day brought them on to
Kulmbach in one of the miller's waggons. The crew
themselves, soaking as they were, walked direct to
the town, and finding out the best joiner in the place
directed him how to patch up the canoe.

By applying continual pressure they succeeded in
having her ready by eight o'clock next morning.
Putting her on a cart and getting on themselves,
they then drove back to Steinhausen and actually
managed to start off again by nine o'clock from the
same spot as on the day before. For the loss of a
day and much property they were to some extent compensated by making the acquaintance of a picturesque
town, famous, moreover, for the excellence of its beer.
Though a place of only a few thousand inhabitants,
it is said to contain upwards of forty breweries.

Before departing the strangers presented their

friend the miller with a beer-glass adorned with a
likeness of the late Emperor Frederick.   He will
probably long remember their visit to Steinhausen
as one of the events of his life.

As a set off against his previous immunity from
loss, the Interpreter was grieved to find on examining
his handbag at Kulmbach the day before, that a valuable pearl breast-pin which he had carefully deposited
in it before the fatal start had disappeared.   He had
heard of pearls being soluble in wine, but never of
their melting away even in the strongest river water.
especially along with their setting.   Millers' assist-
ants have long had the reputation in German literature
of being persons singularly unreliable in the presence
of portable property.   This was the only case, in all
the voyages described in these pages, of anything
having been thievishly appropriated.

The *Kulmbacher Tagblatt* on the following day
contained a paragraph which was copied by most of
the South German papers.   The translation is as
follows :—

KULMBACH, *13th September.*

"The two Englishmen who a few days ago arrived at
Bayreuth, in order to navigate the Main in a boat from there
to its mouth, have it is true arrived here, but have not had
much luck with their voyage.   Once they had to pass the
night in their boat, which, built of cedar wood, is very elegant,
and measures 4½ metres in length and 85 centimetres in
breadth.   Then yesterday they fell into the water with all
their possessions, so that they became as wet as poodles

(*pudelnass*). On continuing their voyage the gentlemen met
with their worst piece of ill-luck near Polz for there they
damaged their boat so severely that it had to be brought here.
It was all Herr Schreinermeister Huhnlein could do to repair
the damage by 12 o'clock last night. The two Englishmen,
very fine gentlemen (*sehr feine Herren*), the one an Oxford
Professor, the other a Captain, who are said to have already
navigated the whole of the Danube this year, spent the night at
the Hotel Hirsch and continued their voyage at 9 o'clock this
morning, but are said again to have come to grief at Polz.
What a fine thing a Main voyage of this kind must be!"

The goal of that day's voyage was Lichtenfels. As
the distance is nearly thirty miles, with three water-
wheels and eight weirs to bar one's progress, the
adventurers had their work cut out for them. This
time they did not trifle with the water-wheels, but
with dogged determination dragged the canoe up the
steep banks, regardless of toil.

At Mainleuss, the first mill below Steinhausen,
where the raft navigation begins, they found the
river blocked, and were delayed for some time till
the raftsmen cleared a passage for them.

For every two or three miles below each weir the
stream, on this stretch of river, is swift, sweeping
round the bends in long rapids, till a smooth broad
reach with little or no current betrays the nearness
of another dam.

The scenery for the greater part of the distance is
pretty, the banks being well wooded in places. The
largest town on the way is Burgkundstadt, lying

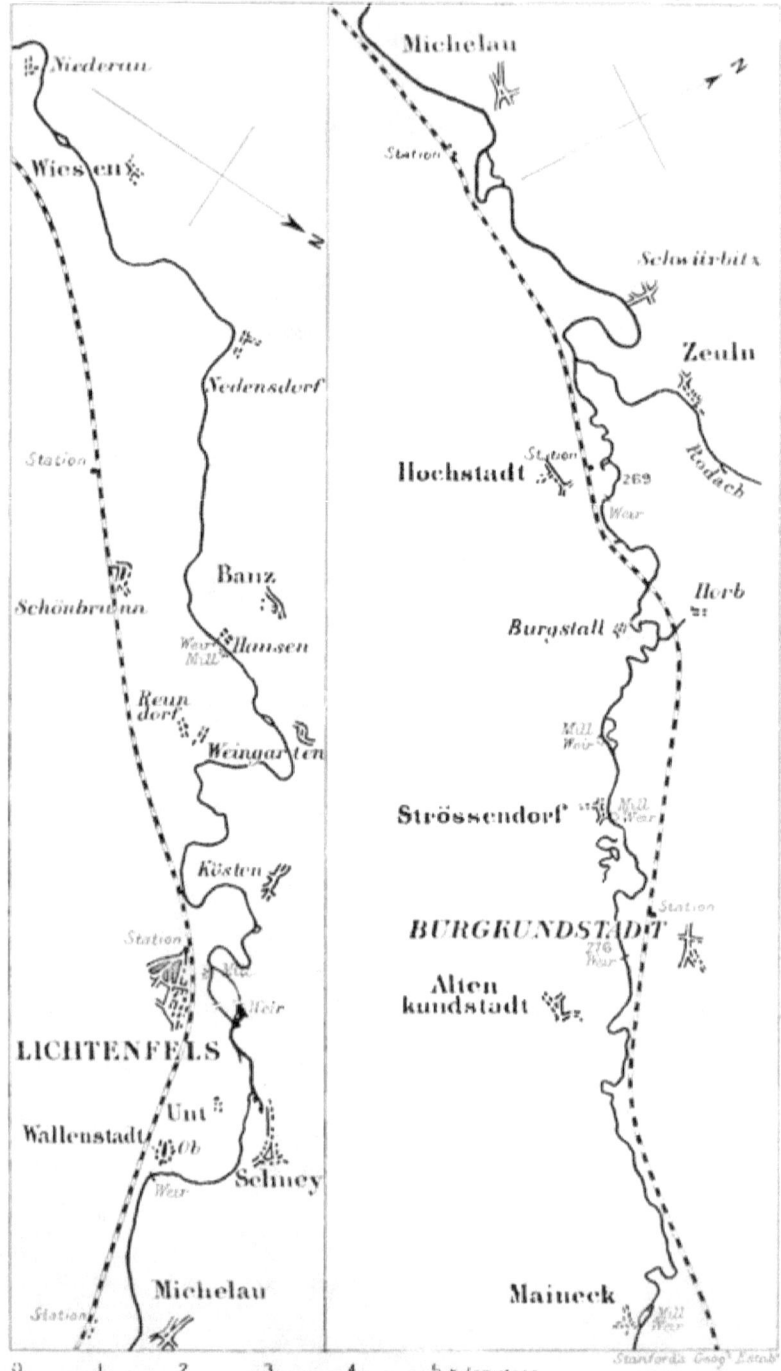

Niederau

Wiesen

Nedensdorf

Station

Schönbrunn

Banz

Weir
Mill   Hausen

Reun
dorf

Weingarten

Kösten

Station

Weir

Weir

LICHTENFELS

Unt

Wallenstadt   Ob

Weir   Schney

Michelau

Michelau

Station

Schwürbitz

Zeuln

Rodach

Hochstadt   Station   269

Weir

Herb

Burgstall

Mill
Weir

Strössendorf   Mill
Weir

BURGKUNDSTADT   Station

Alten
kundstadt   276
Weir

Maineck   Mill
Weir

Stanford's Geog¹ Estab¹

0   1   2   3   4   5   kilometres

picturesquely on the hillside some distance from the
right bank and about ten miles from Steinhausen.
Soon after comes a charming broad calm reach,
fringed with trees and extending to the weir below a
village called Strössendorf. The situation of the latter
place on the slope of the left bank is one of rare beauty.
From Hochstadt to Wallenstadt, the last weir above
Lichtenfels, there is no obstruction for a distance of
about seven miles. After receiving the waters of the
Rodach a mile and a half below Hochstadt the Main
is already a fine river as broad as the Thames below
Nuneham.

With only a short break at noon for a bathe
and lunch in a pretty reach above Maineck, the
canoeists managed by dint of unremitting exertions
to reach Lichtenfels by nightfall. As they paddled
noiselessly and swiftly over the mirrored surface of
the river, the view of the town in the clear calm
twilight, with the crescent moon above a dark background of wooded hill, was wonderfully fine. By
taking the millstream they penetrated close up to
the centre of the town, and leaving their boat in
charge of the miller made their way through a
crowd of spectators up to their hotel in the market-
place.

Starting next morning before eight they reached
the last weir on the Main at Hausen in an hour and
a quarter. This was a morning of rare loveliness,
the sky being cloudless and the air calm and fresh.

Nothing perhaps produces so keen an enjoyment of
mere existence as a row on a fine river in an early
autumn morning, when the air is clear and crisp and
laden with the scent of newly cut hay.

The friends disembarked at Hausen and ascended
through the woods to the handsome château of Banz,
which crowns a hill rising to a height of 1500 feet
above the Main. They enjoyed a hearty breakfast at
the top, where, as is usual in Germany on hills commanding a fine view, there is a good restaurant. The
panorama of the river and the fertile country stretching away to the distant hills is very charming.

Resuming their voyage at eleven, and landing for
a bathe and lunch on an excellent beach near the
railway station of Zapfendorf, the canoeists reached
Bischberg at least an hour before sunset, much sooner
than they had anticipated. The scenery from Banz
to this point is rather uninteresting, with the exception of a fine reach extending due south from the
point where the Bannach, a considerable tributary,
joins the Main. The right bank here is formed by a
richly wooded hill, while the river is extremely broad,
though proportionately shallow. The shade afforded
by this ridge proved very refreshing in the intense
heat of the afternoon.

Bischberg is a small village situated at the junction of the Regnitz with the Main, and about four
miles by road from Bamberg, which lies on the
tributary. Leaving the canoe in charge of a ferry-

man, the voyagers were obliged, owing to the
absence of anything in the shape of a porter or cab,
to trudge along the high-road carrying their bags,
rather a fatiguing process at the fag-end of a day.
While crossing one of the bridges they were
addressed with sympathetic inquiries by a gentleman who had identified the wayfarers by the
accounts in the papers, and took a special interest
in their voyage as a native of Bayreuth, its starting-
point. At their hotel, the *Drei Kronen*, where they
met an Oxford friend, the cool Bavarian beer, in its
stone pots, seemed more than usually delightful after
the toil and heat of the day.

The *Ludwigs-Canal*, which joins the Danube at
Kelheim, enters the Regnitz at Bamberg. The latter
place being the starting-point of the large navigation on the Main, the distance in kilometres is
marked all the way down the bank to the mouth
of the river opposite Mainz.

The following day was to be an easy one, the
distance to Schweinfurt, the next stopping-place,
being a stretch of only thirty-three miles, free from
all obstacles. The largest town on the way, about
twenty miles from Bischberg, is Hassfurt. Entering
through an opening in the embankment here and
disembarking in a kind of backwater behind it, the
crew visited the interesting *Rittercapelle*, a fine
Gothic chapel, dating from the fourteenth century,
and adorned with many curious monuments both

without and within. The only other towns of any
size are Ober- and Unter- Theres, the rather imposing
buildings of which attract the attention of the passing voyager. Some way below the latter there is a
fine wood on the left bank, which would make an
ideal camping ground. Well worthy of notice is the
Mainberg, a château most picturesquely perched on
a height rising from the right bank. Its site is one
of the finest on the Main, commanding as it does a
view of the magnificent reach extending for nearly
two miles down to Schweinfurt.

On arriving at their destination the crew left
their boat in charge of the weir-keeper (*Wehrmann*)
at a convenient place just above the bridge. There
is a weir at Schweinfurt for rafts to pass down, and
a huge lock for barges on the other side. The chief
hotel, the *Deutsche Haus*, was found to be situated
close to the landing-place. The town was full of
soldiers who were quartered there and had just
returned from their manœuvres. The thunder of
the artillery had been audible from the river during
the course of the day.

At a military concert to which they went after
dinner the strangers entered into conversation with
some Germans, who, they found to their surprise,
were acquainted with the *Log of the Waterlily*, an
account of a voyage made by an English four between Mainz and Würzburg nearly forty years ago.

The dwellers on the Main are beginning to avail

themselves of the advantages of their river. For not
only has Würzburg its rowing clubs, but even
Schweinfurt and Hassfurt, besides some other towns,
have one each; to say nothing of Frankfort, which
has for several years been the centre of the German
boating world.

There is some very good Franconian wine to be
had at Schweinfurt. The best appears to be Hol-
berger Riesling, grown near Volkach, a small town
some twenty miles farther down the river.

The crew were up betimes, and having the canoe
carried over the bridge to a stair below the lock,
were afloat before eight. They were prepared for a
long day of fifty-four miles, a distance which turned
out to be even more exhausting than they had anticipated. In the morning there was a dense mist,
which did not clear off till eleven o'clock. The
scenery consequently remained practically invisible
for three hours. The fog at length lifted only to
leave a cloudy and lowering sky for the rest of the
day. As it rained, though not heavily, for the last
three hours and a half of daylight, and a strong
adverse wind blew steadily for the last eight or nine
miles, this proved a depressing as well as an exhausting day.

After the mist had disappeared one bank and
sometimes both turned out to be clothed with vines,
which continued nearly all the way to Würzburg.
At Volkach the river makes a long loop of several

miles, its neck being formed by a narrow vine-clad
ridge.   This bend resembles in length and shape that
formed by the Moselle at Alf.   It is here that some
of the best Franconian wine grows.

The two friends had paddled thirty-three miles
before they landed for lunch, a short distance below
Kitzingen, a very picturesque town on the right
bank of what would make a splendid piece of water
for a rowing course.

In the next ten miles they passed several towns
and villages, the appearance of which is still entirely
mediaeval.   They were especially struck by a village
named Sulzfeld about three miles below Kitzingen.
It is surrounded by a wall forming almost a perfect
square.   Its effect, as seen from the river, is very
peculiar.   The wall on this side is built close to the
water's edge, having quaint gateways and towers,
while the gables of the houses inside show over the
top.   Another of these relics of the Middle Ages is
Ochsenfurt, a place which interested the voyagers
particularly as being a namesake of their own
University.

At this point the river, which has been flowing
due west for six or seven miles after its southerly
course from Schweinfurt, turns up to the north.
Owing to the wind now blowing straight in their
teeth, the friends had to strain every nerve to accomplish the last eight or nine miles before darkness
set in.   They were somewhat delayed by two or

three mills occurring in this part of the river. The stream here being very broad, is divided by a long dam, which thus forms a *cul de sac* on the side where the mill is situated. Owing to the distance one is apt to go down the wrong channel by mistake in the dusk, though the mill branch soon betrays itself by its lack of current.

It had become so dark by the time the canoeists approached Würzburg that they had to strain their eyes very hard as they cautiously paddled along. At last they discovered a landing-stair on the quay, which turned out to be exactly in front of the *Schwan*, the best hotel at Würzburg. To have their boat conveyed into its courtyard and safely locked up for the night was the work of no more than ten minutes. They felt that eleven hours' hard exercise on a very unfavourable day deserved the reward of a good rest. They were, however, not too tired to appreciate, from the windows of the *Schwan*, the beautiful night-view of the river and of the castle, which crowns a lofty hill on the opposite bank.

They did not set off as early as usual, thinking it worth while, before leaving, to have a look at the cathedral and some of the other sights of the town.

There is a weir-dam at Würzburg, which runs some distance up the middle of the river from the bridge. The canoe had to be launched on the other side of this after being taken across in a punt.

From Würzburg the river flows for about thirty

miles to the north with a slight trend to the west,
till it again begins to turn south at Gemünden.
On the slopes of the right bank, some two or three
miles below Würzburg and opposite Zell, are situated
the vineyards in which the famous *Steinwein* grows.

The scenery gradually improves till Karlstadt, a
picturesque mediaeval-looking town, opposite which,
on the left bank, there is a fine cliff crowned by an
imposing ruin.   From this point onwards, especially
as Gemünden is approached, the banks become more
and more beautiful, and for nearly one hundred miles
there is a continuous stretch of some of the finest
river scenery in Europe.   Gemünden, so-called because situated at the mouths of the Sinn and Saale,
lies in an angle of the hills, with a picturesque ruin
on the slope above the town.   It would have been
far pleasanter to stop here than at Lohr, the goal of
this day's voyage, ten miles farther down, but doing
so would have entailed the almost impossible distance of fifty-five miles to Miltenberg for the following day.   Scenery more charming of its kind than
that below Gemünden it would be hard to imagine.
The autumn tints of the luxuriant foliage, with
which the hills are covered, contrasting with the
bright green strips of meadow along the water's
edge, and the occasional red sandstone cliffs reflected
in the clear calm surface of the broad river, produced a harmony of colouring of surpassing loveliness.   A few miles below Gemünden on the left

there rise out of the woods on a lonely ridge the
ruins of a castle once inhabited by robber knights.
Had their only motive been a love of charming
scenery, they could not have chosen a finer site for
their stronghold.

The sun was about to set when the voyagers
arrived at Lohr. The day had been so perfect and
the scenery so lovely that their forty miles' paddle
seemed to be over all too soon. The town lies some
way from the river, and there is no place where a
boat can be safely left. However, there happened
to be a barge moored to the bank for the night,
and the owner gladly undertook to take charge
of the canoe till morning. The landlady of the
inn, the *Post*, told her guests that in the old coach-
ing days many of their countrymen used to stay
at Lohr, making the place their headquarters for
excursions to the neighbouring valleys of the
Spessart Forest; but the railway had changed all
that, and strangers were nowadays few and far
between.

The morning of the 18th was gloriously fine. The
friends paddled along briskly, enjoying to the full
the charm of the scenery, as the light wreaths of mist
were exhaled by the woods under the influence of the
early sunbeams. Some sixteen miles below Lohr on the
right bank they passed the large château of Triefen-
stein, the architecture of which, like that of many a
German *Schloss*, is somewhat suggestive of barracks.

M

This defect is, however, greatly compensated for by its position in the midst of a beautiful park.

Ten miles farther down lies Wertheim, a small town of about 4000 inhabitants, situated at the mouth of the Tauber, and commanded by the red sandstone ruin of a stronghold destroyed in the Thirty Years' War. This old castle is supposed to resemble that of Heidelberg, but the likeness is certainly remote. As they regretfully drifted past this pretty town with its charming riverside inn, the voyagers thought of the many delightful days that might have been spent there had they been able to spare the time to stay. Wertheim would certainly be an ideal place for a reading party provided with a boat to pass a month or two in. About five miles farther down on the left bank there is as magnificent camping ground—extending for several miles—as the heart of the adventurer could desire. The two friends had the bad luck to land for their midday bathe and lunch just before reaching this beautiful tract.

Ten miles below Wertheim they passed the picturesque town of Stadtprozelten, with its fine old castle; and, some distance farther, a lonely ruin rising from the trees in a reach without a trace of human habitation. There is something peculiarly melancholy about a solitary ruin surrounded by waving woods, especially perhaps when seen on a bright sunny afternoon. Few sights are so suggestive of the thought *sic transit gloria mundi*.

The direction of the river here being mostly due west, the glitter of the sunlight on the water in front is so dazzling in the afternoon as to render it almost impossible to see where one is going. About nine miles above Miltenberg, however, the stream turns south, and the shade of the hills on the right bank affords a welcome relief from the glare. At the end of one of these southerly reaches there comes into view while yet a long way off one of the most beautiful places on the Main. This is Freudenberg, a small town nestling at the foot of a hill which juts out from a richly wooded valley. The front of this hill, looking towards the river, is shaped like the side of a pyramid, the apex being crowned by a ruin. From this point two old walls run down the edges of the face, thus enclosing the town at the base. The space between the walls above the town is now covered with trees.

The sun was going down as the voyagers landed at Miltenberg, the distance being forty-five miles by river from Lohr. The situation is as fine as that of any other place on the Main. The town lies in the southern angle of the river, where it turns north towards Aschaffenburg, high and richly wooded hills forming its background. Though the population is hardly 4000, the town extends for about a mile along the bank. It is a very old place, having been known to the Romans, who worked the sandstone quarries in the neighbourhood. As there seemed to be no inn near the bank, the friends left the boat

with a ferryman and made their way inland to the
Engel hotel. As they paddled down next day they
passed at the extreme end of the town a good-sized
and pleasant-looking inn, the *Rose*, very conveniently
situated on the bank for the voyager.

One of the crew having unfortunately to be back
in England on the 21st of September, it was resolved
to conclude the voyage on this the 19th at Aschaffenburg, which lies about twenty-four miles below
Miltenberg. The original plan was to finish the
trip at Bingen on the Rhine ; but to do this would
have required an extra day, the distance from Aschaffenburg being more than sixty miles. The scenery
after Miltenberg begins to fall off, though Aschaffenburg itself, where the good part of the Main ends, is
finely situated. This place they reached in about
four hours, landing at the swimming-baths. The
proprietor being a carpenter by trade and evidently
a practical man, undertook to make a case for the
canoe himself, and finished his task in three hours.
She was accordingly despatched to England that
same afternoon through an agent, and arrived safely
after the unusually long period of five weeks.

That night the two friends spent at Bingen. The
broad stream of the Rhine bathed in the bright
moonlight was indeed a glorious sight. Next morning Cox returned by rail *viâ* Cologne to England,
while the Interpreter, not being in such a hurry,
took one of the Rhine steamers to Königswinter,

and passed the evening on the Drachenfels. From here he saw the sun set at six o'clock in gorgeous splendour over the plain stretching far away beyond the Rhine, while the full moon rose in unclouded beauty over the dark woods of the Seven Mountains in the east.

CHAPTER VIII

THE MOLDAU AND THE ELBE

THE boat, as well as the crew, was the same on this
voyage as that which had gone down the Danube
two years before, and which navigated the Main as
described in the previous chapter.   Packed in a light
case, the canoe was despatched in the first week of
August 1888, so as to ensure her arrival at Prague by
1st September.   It would probably have been well
worth while starting from Budweis, more than a
hundred miles farther up the Moldau ; for, according
to the account given by the Bohemians, the river is
broad and the scenery fine all the way from there to
Prague.   There was, however, no time to do this, as
the friends intended after reaching Dresden to send

their craft by rail to Bayreuth, and to navigate the Main from thence to its mouth—a distance of more than 300 miles. The chief difficulty in the way of rowing down the upper Moldau would be linguistic. For German would hardly be of any use in those regions, and an Englishman who speaks Bohemian fluently is rather a *rara aris*. In order to avoid being checkmated in one sense it would thus be almost necessary to be so in another [1] on such an expedition.

The freight charges for the transit of boats by the slow route seem to be very arbitrary. The charge for sending the canoe to Prague was £3 : 18s.; while the return journey from Aschaffenburg, a considerably shorter distance, cost upwards of £5, and that from Vienna, though several hundred miles longer, only £2 : 11s. The expense of sending a four to Cannstatt had been about £5; but that of transporting a pair-oar (a smaller boat) to Meiningen, a shorter distance, was more than £6. Let not these remarks be construed as a covert recommendation of the express route. Such a suspicion ought to be dispelled by the perusal of the chapter on the Danube. That route suffers from two disadvantages. It encourages the intending voyager to believe that it is more rapid than the other; while the expense is more than twice as great; that is, if an estimate has previously been obtained. But if the latter precaution be not taken, it had better be

[1] See Index.

left to men of the Jubilee Plunger type to ascertain what the charge may be.

The travellers reached Prague at about six o'clock on the morning of the 31st of August, after a railway journey from Mainz of sixteen hours, in what is probably the slowest train in Europe. Arriving in a thick drizzle after a sleepless night is not a cheerful thing. Nor was the prospect of having to hunt for the boat in ten different places calculated to raise the spirits. For Prague possesses five railway stations lying far asunder and having a goods department in a separate building belonging to each. A vast amount of trouble might have been saved by addressing the boat to any one of these stations in particular. The friends were especially unlucky in their search, not discovering the canoe till they had trudged about in the rain for over three hours. There was some consolation, however, in the fact that the station of the *Nordwestbahn*, where she was ultimately found, was by far the most conveniently situated for their purposes, being close to the bank of the river below the town.

The next thing was to settle the custom-house officials—a task calculated to try severely the temper of even a patient man. Apparently no business is transacted by them in the forenoon after 11.30. If any matter seems likely to occupy more than half an hour they refuse to take it in hand after eleven, deferring it either till the afternoon, or more likely,

till the next day. The most speedy method to
attain one's ends here is to keep one's temper, but
to part with two or three guldens, a coin which is
said to exercise more than ordinary fascination on
the mind of the official Bohemian. The latter fact
was not understood by the two friends till it was
too late to apply the knowledge. They would never
have ventured at the time to make any offer to such
distinguished-looking individuals attired in imposing
uniforms. Their eyes were opened when, at the
close of the business, one of these officers, who had
dogged their footsteps, asked for a small gratuity in
the most abject manner.

The proceedings, then, were phenomenally slow.
At first there seemed to be no prospect of starting
that day. However, long and persistent, though
amiable expostulations, aided no doubt by curiosity,
at length resulted in the opening of the case just
before eleven o'clock. There was evidently a lurk-
ing suspicion that the boat was made of tin (*Blech*),
but after much tapping it was officially ascertained
(*constatiert*) to be of wood. It was accordingly
taxed about 16s. as manufactured wood (*Holzwaare*).
The next step was to adduce plausible arguments
to show that the journey had not been undertaken
for the special purpose of selling the canoe in
Bohemia. The scepticism of the officials having at
last been overcome, they affixed to one of the thwarts
a small leaden disc, which, together with a docu-

ment about two feet square and covered with cabal-
istic signs, entitled the owners to have the amount of
the duty refunded at the Saxon frontier.   A necessary
condition of repayment, however, seemed to be that
the voyagers should land nowhere till Schandau was
reached—a distance of 110 miles.   This condition the
friends of course undertook with alacrity to fulfil.   By
dint of unrelaxing perseverance the custom-house was
cleared within the regulation time.   The next delay
was caused by the necessity of finding and paying the
agent to whom the canoe was consigned.   He was at last
run to earth by the employment of numerous cabs.

Having donned their flannels at a small inn close
at hand, the crew launched their bark at a stone
stair almost opposite the station, and hoisting a small
Union Jack in the bows, were actually afloat soon
after half-past one.   The promptitude of all their
proceedings evidently surprised the custom-house
officers not a little.

The rain had fortunately ceased by this time, but
the sky remained overcast for the rest of the day.
Owing to the boat leaking a good deal on starting
she was run ashore after a mile or two and carefully
rubbed all over with a cake of soap.   This filled up
all the cracks and kept the water out most effectually.

The Moldau is a fine broad river flowing with a
steady stream of about two miles and a half an hour.
The scenery is decidedly good, consisting in great part
of bold rocky hills, mostly destitute of vegetation.

The distance from Prague to the junction with the Elbe below Melnik is about thirty-five miles. It can be paddled by a Canadian canoe in less than six hours, while a four-oar could easily accomplish it in five.

The only place between Prague and Melnik where it is possible to put up is Kralup, a small Czech town on the left bank, about twenty miles from Prague and just below a fine railway bridge which here spans the river. It is, however, not a convenient place for landing, as, though a boat may be left with the proprietor of the river baths, the town lies some way inland. Nor has it anything interesting or picturesque to recommend it. Between Prague and this place there are two very swift and turbulent rapids, the first about five and the second ten miles below Prague. The former looked as if it would swamp the boat, yet she managed to get through almost dry; for a Canadian canoe seems capable of riding waves of any size to be encountered on rivers, as long as she is pointed straight.

The inn at Kralup turned out to be very respectable, the cooking and the wine being surprisingly good. The landlady was the only person in the establishment who could speak German with any fluency, the head waiter having but a slight smattering of that language. The strangers were rather taken aback next morning at seeing and hearing a barrel-organist performing on his instrument outside one of the bedroom doors on the first floor. This

may, for all they know, be a common method of
stimulating or satisfying the national craving for
music in Bohemia.

The scenery after Kralup falls off somewhat, but
improves again as Melnik is approached. As you
row down a long and broad reach, which is almost
straight and bordered with beautiful woods on the
right bank, the view of Melnik nestling on the
hillside, with its castle rising from a prominent
and lofty rock, is very picturesque. The town is
situated on the right bank at an angle, where the
river after an easterly course of some ten miles turns
due north. Any party rowing down the Moldau
ought certainly to make a point of staying a night at
Melnik. It is a very convenient place for landing,
as a boat might be moored almost immediately below
the inn. The wine of this region, too, is not to be
despised. To be obliged to drift past this pretty
place was indeed a disappointment. But the delays
of the custom-house, combined with the shortness of
the days, had necessitated a stay at Kralup on the
previous night.

About two miles and a half below Melnik the
Moldau divides into two arms, thus forming a good-
sized island, at the other end of which its waters join
those of the Elbe. The proper channel must be the
extreme right of the eastern branch; but as this
looked shallow at a distance, it was decided to follow
the western arm. It became apparent when too late

to turn that the stream was barred by a low weir in connection with a disused mill. The boat was accordingly steered straight for it, but when half over stuck on a beam. Here she remained balancing, but at length slid over on the other side without being upset or in any way damaged. Incidents of this kind justify some anxiety, owing to the frail build of a Canadian canoe.

About a mile below the junction quite an ideal bower for a midday rest was discovered among the trees on the left bank. Here the voyagers landed, bathed, and enjoyed a hearty lunch, washed down with excellent Bohemian wine. A lounge like this on a beautiful bank is perhaps the most enjoyable part of the day on a rowing expedition.

For the distance from Melnik to Dresden, which is about a hundred miles, a crew should allow themselves at least a week. This would enable them to see all the finest parts of the Saxon Switzerland at their leisure. The best places to stay at are Leitmeritz, Tetschen or Bodenbach, Herrnskretschen and Schandau. The scenery between Melnik and Leitmeritz would be uninteresting were it not for the numerous peaks coming into view in the far distance towards the north, and reminding the voyager that he is approaching the region of the Saxon Switzerland.

At Leitmeritz the main branch of the river on the left should be followed till the swimming baths on the right bank are reached. Here a boat can be left in charge of the *Bademeister*, who will also take good care of any other property that may be entrusted to him. For these services he will consider a florin a princely reward. None of the hotels are near the river. The *Krebs*, which is close to the market-place and was chosen by the two friends, is probably the best. It would be a pity to leave Leitmeritz without climbing one of the hills near Kundratitz, as a fine view of the surrounding country and of the winding course of the Elbe can be obtained from them. The ascent does not occupy more than an hour, the greater part of the distance leading through the pleasant orchards which surround Leitmeritz, and which have caused the district to be called the Paradise of Bohemia.

Leitmeritz lies just within the border of the German-speaking part of Bohemia, which occupies the north-western regions of that country, and may be marked off from the Czech-speaking portion by a line drawn from Reichenberg through Leitmeritz, Saatz, and Pilsen, to Furth on the Bavarian frontier.

A start was made soon after noon, the day being both threatening and chilly. A few miles farther down, at Lobositz, the river turned due north, in the very teeth of the wind, which being unusually strong rendered the broad expanse of the river lumpy and greatly retarded the progress of the canoe. The banks nearly all the way to Aussig, about twelve miles, especially the last half of the distance, are very beautiful. The clouds were lowering all day as the voyagers paddled hard against the wind. But scenery such as you here pass through looks perhaps more impressive under the frown of heaven than in the bright sunshine of a cloudless sky.

On the right bank, about a mile above Aussig, there comes into view a fine old ruined castle, most appropriately named the Schreckenstein, which is perched on a beetling crag overhanging the river. It should not be passed without a visit, which need not occupy more than half an hour. There is, as is usual in Germany at least, a restaurant affiliated to the ruin. Those who, like the two canoeists, are in too great a hurry to eat or drink anything there are charged a fee for visiting the place. They are not allowed to practise what the Germans call *Localschinderei* [1] with impunity. Landing at the foot of the rock is not quite easy, owing to the swiftness of the stream at this point and the shallowness of the water on a stone dam which runs parallel with the right bank for some distance. The railway must then be crossed, and the vigilance of an official who is posted there eluded.

---

[1] This is a technical term of restaurant life which implies sitting in the premises for a prolonged period without ordering any refreshment. A very near approach to this breach of good form was made by the man who on entering a *Wirthshaus* with a large family, and being asked by the waiter what he wished to order, replied, "One glass of beer and eight chairs."

Hardly had the two strangers stepped across the rails when this lynx-eyed guardian hurried up with as much speed as was compatible with his dignity, and informed them in a tone of great severity that it was strictly forbidden (*streng verboten*) to cross the line. The Interpreter endeavoured to turn away the wrath of the irate official by asking some rather irrelevant questions; but the latter knew nothing about the distance to Aussig nor anything at all connected with the river; in fact his knowledge was solely limited to the rule that it was strictly forbidden (*streng verboten*) to cross the rails.

Aussig extends for a considerable distance along the left bank of the Elbe. It is the great coal harbour of Bohemia. Huge barges are moored a long way down the bank, and lines of railway trucks are drawn up in front of them continually disgorging their swarthy contents. Bohemian coal seems to be of a peculiarly soft and grimy nature. All travellers by rail in those regions must have noticed the dense volumes of brown smoke which issue from the funnels of the locomotives, and the vast size of the blacks coming through any window that may have been left open in an unguarded moment. It will, therefore, be readily believed that Aussig is far and away the ugliest port of Seaboard Bohemia. Baedeker makes a sly hit at the place when he advises travellers " who happen to be detained here " to visit a certain point in the neighbourhood.

The two voyagers were obliged to land at Aussig
owing to the approach of darkness. They put up
at the Steamboat Hotel, choosing this because its
nearness to the landing-slip enabled them to convey the canoe with ease to the shelter of the yard.
They had good reason to repent their choice. Half
an hour in bed convinced them that this inn, as
regards the night at least, is situated in the noisiest
spot in Europe. Goods trains were being shunted
about and kept sounding dismal bells at short
intervals all night long; and at a very early hour
trucks began ceaselessly discharging torrents of coal
immediately below the hotel windows. The fact
that it blew great guns all night, and that the
windows in consequence rattled incessantly, made
little or no difference under the circumstances. Nor
did the Interpreter derive any advantage from
passing the night, by way of experiment, on an air-
bed, laid out on the floor, which he had brought with
him for camping purposes on the Main. Future
navigators of the Elbe, who happen to have read
these lines, will know how to treat Aussig and
especially the Steamboat Hotel.

The would-be sleepers rose unrefreshed. The wind
had abated, but the rain was coming down in torrents.
A start was made at half-past eight, when it looked
something like clearing. The friends would gladly
have shaken the coal-dust from off their feet before
departing, but there was only grimy mud. This

they wiped off. Their hopes as to the rain were not
to be fulfilled. In about half an hour it recommenced
coming down, and poured steadily for the rest of
the day without a break.

In two hours Tetschen was reached. On the
opposite bank lies Bodenbach, beautifully situated
on the slope of a high and thickly wooded hill.
Even the heavy rain could not mar the beauty of
the scenery, which from here onwards is far finer
than anything between this point and Prague. The
large amount of moisture in the air had in fact brought
out the varied shades of green in the landscape with
unusual vividness. The friends here allowed themselves to drift down with the stream, looking regretfully at the many inns on both sides, so charmingly
situated close to the river's brink—ideal spots for
voyagers to land and spend the night.

Reluctantly resuming their paddles, they continued on their way through an almost uninhabited
region. The river here grows narrower, flowing
between high defiles clothed with a dense growth of
pine-wood. These forests furnish trees for enormous
rafts, several of which were passed moored along
the banks. The bright yellow of the Elbe, the dark
green of the woods, and the sombre grey of the sky
formed a striking combination of colour.

At half-past twelve Herrnskretschen came in
sight, a small place on the right bank with a large
hotel situated close to the water's edge. There

is an excellent landing-place here in a small side-stream at the very foot of the hotel. Being anxious to visit the Prebischthor, which is only an hour's walk from here, the canoeists decided on making this their halting stage for the night. A four hours' drenching, too, appeared to be sufficient for one day. The luggage, which was covered with a waterproof sheet in the middle of the boat, had, it was a comfort to know, remained perfectly dry.

After changing and lunching at the *Herrenhaus*, as the hotel is called, the friends started for the Prebischthor in a perfect downpour of rain, which, however, did not cause much inconvenience. The road, winding through the forest all the way, is very beautiful. The green of the mosses and ferns, which grow here in extreme luxuriance, had assumed that almost dazzling brilliance which is only to be seen on gloomy days after long-continued rain. There was hardly any view at the top owing to the thick mist, which only partially cleared away before the strangers left. This height is, however, well worth ascending, if only to see the huge natural arch of stone, which the visitor can pass over as well as under. The formation of the rocks rising around in isolated pinnacles of great altitude is very remarkable, and represents best what is most typical of the scenery of the Saxon Switzerland.

The voyagers were up early to look out on one of the most lovely mornings they had ever seen. The sky

was cloudless, and there was that keen crispness in
the air which is only felt after heavy rain has cleared
away. Having breakfasted in the open air, they embarked soon after eight. The river, on the surface
of which there was not a ripple, looked perfect in the
slanting rays of the early sun, which left the dark
pine-woods on the right in misty shadow. There is
perhaps nothing like a bright fresh autumn morning
to make one feel the " fierce joy of living" in its full
extent.

Schandau being reached in an hour—alas! too soon
—the boat was left at the swimming-baths some way
above the steamboat pier. There are at Schandau
several large hotels with pleasant gardens in front,
and close to the river bank. Crossing in a ferry-boat
to the opposite bank, the friends set off for the
Pabststein, to which a walk through open sandy
country brought them in an hour and a half. There
is a fine view of the surrounding region from this
height, but, strange to say, the Elbe is almost, if not
quite, invisible. They got back to Schandau only
just in time to catch the Austrian officials before
the custom-house closed at half-past twelve. The
amount refunded seemed to be somewhat in excess
of the sum paid at Prague; but the two friends
held their peace, and said in their hearts the thing
could not be.

Leaving Schandau at 2.30 they paddled hard,
passing by the twin heights of the Lilienstein and

Königstein, between which the river flows, till they reached Wehlen about four o'clock. They were occasionally delayed by passing steamboats, which are among the worst enemies of Canadian canoes. The latter will, it is true, ride out the largest steamer waves with impunity if lying to stem on. But it would be fatal to take such waves broadside. It is even hazardous to continue paddling when pointing straight, as the canoe in that case comes down on the next wave with a splash, ships a quantity of water over the bows, and runs the risk of being swamped outright.

At Wehlen the voyagers again left their bark in charge at the river baths, and hurried off to visit the beautiful Uttewaldengrund with its Devil's kitchen, thence ascending to the Bastei. The view from this height of the river below is magnificent. There was, however, not much time to enjoy the charm of the scenery, it being necessary to hasten back to Wehlen, so as to reach Pirna before darkness set in. For an old German schoolfellow of the Interpreter—one of the two who had shared his boating adventures on the Werra in boyhood—now a flourishing young physician at Pirna—was expecting the cruisers at half-past six. With five and a half miles still left to do they started off at 6.20, when the sun was about to set, and, straining every nerve, managed the distance in exactly forty minutes. They had never paddled as fast as this in their lives, for this

was at the rate of eight and a quarter miles an hour.
They found their friend waiting for them in the
gathering shadows at the river baths. This meeting
after many years was celebrated that night in what
to some Philistines might have appeared immoderate
potations of Rhine wine.

Their host, with his young wife and two little
boys, next morning escorted his friends down to the
landing-place. It was rather startling to find that
the river had risen about ten feet during the night,
so that the baths, which were close to the bank on
the previous evening, were now far out in the stream,
and could only be reached by means of a punt.
Having carefully packed the canoe, and waving their
farewells to their friends on the shore, the voyagers
soon committed their bark to the now turbulent
stream. The boys, who were greatly pleased with the
two little English flags fixed in the bows and stern,
which fluttered merrily in the breeze, kept looking
after them till they vanished from sight.

The cause of the sudden rise in the river, which
flooded the banks all the way to Dresden, was an
unusually heavy fall of rain in Bohemia. Dresden
was reached in considerably under two hours' easy
paddling, though the distance is about twelve miles.
The terrace of Helbig's well-known restaurant was
under water, and, as it turned out afterwards, a large
number of tables and chairs had been carried away by
the surging waves. The stream had become so swift

that all bathing had been put a stop to in the
swimming-baths. This sort of thing is said to occur
frequently at Dresden. The canoe was with some
difficulty brought to a standstill at one of the river
baths, and thence without loss of time packed off to
the goods station and despatched to Bayreuth. The
crew thus hoped to be able to start down the Main
on their homeward voyage in four days' time.

CHAPTER IX

THE DANUBE

" Wenn ich dann zu Nacht alleine
Dichtend in die Wellen schau',
Steigt beim blanken Mondenscheine
Auf die schmucke Wasserfrau
Aus der Donau,
Aus der schönen, blauen Donau."—BECK.

Raison d'être of this voyage—A Canadian canoe despatched—The
crew reach Donaueschingen—Non-arrival of the boat—False
alarm and strange coincidence—The "Source of the Danube"
—A week's delay—The start—Obstructions on the Danube
before Ulm — Camp near Geisingen — Immendingen — Mysterious disappearance of most of the water of the Danube—
Tuttlingen — Magnificent scenery between Mühlheim and
Sigmaringen—Bath Rock—Beuron—Belated—Stop at Thiergarten — Sigmaringen — Its beautiful situation — Dangerous
rapids at Scheer—Camp near Mengen—Sleepless night—Toilsome day—Surprised by darkness—Narrow escape at the
mouth of the Iller — Dangerous bridge and landing — Ulm
reached at last in safety—The Danube navigable below Ulm—
Characteristics of the river—Monotonous scenery—Dillingen—
Blenheim — Donauwörth — Neuburg — Ingolstadt — Excursion
to Munich—Pföring, where the Nibelungen crossed the
Danube — Roman camp of Abusina — Beautiful scenery near
Weltenburg and Kelheim—The Befreiungshalle—Regensburg
—Narrow escape from being swamped below bridge—The Walhalla—Straubing—Tortuousness and sluggishness of the river

here—Bogen—Deggendorf—The Bavarian Forest—Vilshofen
—Rocks in the river—Passau—Its beautiful situation—Grand
scenery between Passau and Linz—Austrian custom-house at
Engelhartszell—Linz—Grein—The Strudel—The Wirbel—
Dangerous navigation—Mahrbach—Peculiar ferry-boats—
Monastery of Melk—Dürrenstein, the prison of Richard I.—
Stein—The Interpreter finishes the voyage alone—Risky
navigation—Arrives in safety below his hotel at Vienna.

AT the end of September 1886 Vienna was to be the
meeting-place of a congress which the Interpreter was
anxious to attend. It occured to him that for a man
of his tastes the pleasantest way of reaching that
capital would be to paddle down the Danube from a
place as near the source as possible. He soon found
a companion for the projected expedition in the
person of the oarsman who, two years before, had
held the post of Honorary Chaplain on the Neckar,
the Rhine, and the Moselle. After a good deal of
deliberation Donaueschingen in the Grand Duchy of
Baden was fixed upon as the starting-point. A
Canadian canoe purchased by the Interpreter the year
before was selected as the most suitable craft for a
voyage beginning so close to the source of the great
river. That frail bark was therefore packed in a
light wooden case and despatched by the express
route on the 19th of August. This, according to the
statement of the agents, would ensure her arrival at
her destination within eight days at an estimated
cost of £6 : 10s. The friends had at first intended to
take the canoe with them as luggage, but having
discovered when rather late that this would be im-

possible, had resolved to send her the quick and expensive way, so as to be certain of finding her on reaching Donaueschingen. This arrangement, as will be seen, they found to be a complete failure.

It was with light hearts that they steamed out of Victoria Station on the evening of 1st September, hoping to launch the *Flora* on the 3rd. What was, then, their chagrin, on their arrival to find no sign of their boat. By a complication of telegrams to London, Mannheim, and Cologne they at last succeeded in ascertaining the bare fact that she had already passed through the latter city. But as to when she was likely to reach Donaueschingen they had in the meantime to content themselves with conjectures. They at first found some excitement in going to meet every goods train that came in, but repeated failure soon caused this amusement to pall. At length late on the second night their hopes rose to a high pitch when the station-master hastening up to them, said, " Your boats have arrived." " Our boat, you mean," said the Interpreter, correcting him. " No," replied the official, " your boats have arrived." His positiveness naturally suggested that though the canoe had come she had turned up in two pieces. The anguish caused by such reflections gave place to amazement at the sight of two ordinary canoes lying on the platform. The friends could hardly believe their eyes, and at first inclined to the suspicion that for their own smart craft these two vessels of a baser sort had been substituted by some unknown but malignant machinator. The mystery was, however, soon cleared up. The canoes turned out to belong to two Hamburgers, who by a strange coincidence—for no boat had arrived at Donaueschingen for several years past—had fixed on this place as the starting-point of a similar expedition at exactly the same time as the two Englishmen. The latter after this incident became callous, and making the best of the delay, undertook various excursions from day to day into the neighbouring regions. Of one evening walk from Triberg to Hornberg in the Black Forest and of another from the Falls of the Rhine to Neuhausen along the left bank of the river in the bright moonlight, they will long retain pleasant memories.

Donaueschingen is a nice little town situated on the banks of the Brigach, a small stream rising in the Black Forest, and flowing down the valley traversed by the railway from Triberg. Below the windows of the *Schützenhof*, the hotel at which the two friends stayed, this little river is not more than six or eight inches deep; but about a mile and a half farther, where it is joined by the Brege, a slightly larger stream, the volume of water is already considerable. The Danube really begins at the junction, but the Princes of Fürstenberg have endeavoured to anticipate the name by 2000 yards. For they have christened as the "Source of the Danube" a spring of beautifully clear water which rises in the grounds of their palace at Donaueschingen. This spring, enclosed in a stone basin, is connected with the Brigach by means of an underground conduit about a hundred yards in length. The palace contains some interesting art and other collections, besides a good library. The chief treasure of the latter is one of the three best extant manuscripts of the *Nibelungenlied*. The librarian pointed out among other curiosities an oriental manuscript, written in a character to which he had hitherto been unable to obtain any clue.

There is a good swimming-bath in the park. This the two friends had all to themselves, as the water had been too cold for the natives during the past fortnight or three weeks.

Innumerable pilgrimages to the station were at last rewarded on the eighth day by the glad tidings that the canoe had actually arrived. She was unpacked without further loss of time and launched at some stone steps immediately below the bridge and close to the hotel. A preliminary paddle having shown her to be practically uninjured by the long journey, her crew embarked on their adventurous voyage within three hours of her arrival. A thunder-shower, which happened to come on at the time, did not deter a large proportion of the population from remaining to witness their departure. The rain soon passed off, giving place to a glorious evening. The great clearness of the stream, as it swiftly flowed over

Heuberg

Tuttlingen

Weir

Weir   Rapids

Tunnel
Station

Möhringen

Weir
Weir

Rapids
Mill
Weir

Immendingen

Station

Station   Camp
Mill
Weir

Geisingen

Mill
Weir

Gutmadingen

Weir

Neidingen

Pfohren

Bath

Donaueschingen

Station

Station

from Triberg

R. Brigach

R. Brege

0   1   2   3   4   5   6   7   8   9   10   Kilometres

the shingly bottom, gave it the appearance of being too shallow even for a canoe. There was, however, enough water and to spare. Below the confluence the infant Danube already seemed quite a good-sized river, and at the village of Pforen, only three miles from Donaueschingen, it had spread itself out to such an extent as to resemble a lake rather than an insignificant stream still 2000 miles from its mouth.

Some miles farther down, near Neidingen, occurred the first weir, the crossing at which presented no difficulties, as the bank was low and grassy. At Gutmadingen, where a striking Romanesque building attracts the attention, the river winds considerably with a broad and smooth stream. The scenery here is fine, the entire horizon being an unbroken line of hills partly wooded with fir. A glassy reach some distance above Geisingen indicated that an obstruction of some kind was near at hand. This turned out to be a mill, where the river divided, the second branch flowing to a weir. It was a bad enough place for transporting even a canoe, to say nothing of a heavier boat. The miller, who it soon appeared had been five years in America, and was glad to have an opportunity of airing his "English," informed the canoeists that two Americans had some weeks before gone down the Danube from Donaueschingen on a raft, which they had spent no less than five hours in dragging across at this particular point.

What a time they must have had with the
twenty-five weirs and mills of the Upper Danube
before reaching the unobstructed waters in the region
of Ulm! For there are no sluices here, as on the
Werra, for the passage of rafts, this not being a
forest tract. A pair-oar is probably the largest kind
of rowing boat capable of navigating the Danube
above Sigmaringen; but its crew would have to do a
good deal of wading in the shallows below Immendingen and to be very careful in the rocky region of
rapids below Mühlheim. They would also find the
porterage very irksome. Nor is there much pleasure
in rowing where there are many rapids. For these
being generally near one bank or the other neces-
sitate the continual shipping of the oars, which run
some risk of being broken or injured in the process.
A Canadian canoe is by far the most satisfactory
kind of craft in such upper waters, because all the
crew see where they are going, and can keep close to
the bank without shifting their paddles. That the
Upper Danube must abound in rapids is evident
from the fact that the fall in the first 120 miles, the
distance between Donaueschingen and Ulm, is
upwards of 1000 feet, being an average of eight feet
four inches per mile.

The voyagers had now accomplished a distance
of about ten miles, a steady three hours' paddle
from Donaueschingen. As it was by this time growing dark, they resolved on stopping to buy some

necessary provisions at Geisingen, and afterwards
encamping a short way farther down. The Interpreter accordingly trudged a good distance up into
the village, and, after sundry wanderings in the dusk,
discovered the abode of a cheeseman (*Käser*) named
Schwartz, who sold him as much in the way of
milk, butter, and eggs as he wanted. He was rather
surprised at the small amount of attention he attracted
among the human inhabitants ; but the commotion
he caused among the dogs of the village was proportionately great, some of them being only with
difficulty restrained from taking undue liberties with
his calves.

The two friends then paddled some hundred yards
beyond the village in splendid moonlight, when the
sound of rushing waters ahead warned them to land.
The noise proceeded from a paddle-weir connected
with a mill. A few yards above this they ran ashore,
pulling the canoe up on the bank. A sort of encampment was extemporised by spreading the waterproof canvas cover of the boat on the grass, arranging
the three cushions thereon, and turning the canoe
half over so as to form a kind of shelter on one side.
Having prepared supper, and afterwards played a
game of Nap, the campers, at about eleven o'clock,
turned in—if the term can be applied to sleeping with
nothing but the starry heavens above your head—
by wrapping themselves in their blankets and stretching themselves at full length, feet to feet. The moon,

now almost full, for some hours traversed an almost cloudless sky. The view of the distant hills skirting the plain, on which the rather wakeful sleepers lay, looked quite beautiful as the far-off heights stood out bathed in the hazy and silvery light. A mist gradually crept up, which after a time grew so dense as to shroud everything from view save the star-spangled sky above. Neither of the friends managed to get much sleep, partly owing to the hardness of the ground, but chiefly because it sloped too much in a lateral direction, as they discovered too late.

They arose at half-past five to find their blankets perfectly white with rime. Cox now repaired to the village to procure bread and milk, while the Interpreter sponged out the canoe and varnished her outside, as she had shown signs of leaking slightly the night before. It would have been a better plan to rub her carefully over with a cake of soap, since varnish takes so long to dry.

Soon after eight o'clock the sun came out hot, quickly dispelling the mist and drying the blankets, which were soaked with dew. The morning had now become delightfully warm and bright, while the river was as smooth as glass. Having breakfasted at their leisure, so as to allow the varnish to dry, the voyagers started off again shortly before ten o'clock. After a mile or so they stuck for the first time in a shallow rapid under a small wooden bridge, and were compelled to get out and wade for some distance.

At Immendingen, which they reached in an hour's time, they had a long and tedious porterage, occupying fully half an hour. Their labours were somewhat lightened by a small truck on two wheels which they had brought with them from England for such emergencies. To this the stern of the canoe was attached, while her crew pulled her along by the bows. A student of Indian literature on seeing this contrivance might well have regarded it as specially designed to disprove a Hindoo proverb which, to illustrate the futility of attempting the impossible, asserts that a cart cannot go on water, nor a boat on dry land.

After Immendingen there came into view on the right some fine wooded hills, which looked particularly grand under the dark clouds of an impending thunderstorm. In this beautiful reach occurred the first real rapid with rough waves. Down this the *Flora* gaily sped to the accompaniment of a loud thunder-clap. Had Faust been a man of boating tastes and experienced that exhilarating rush, he would assuredly have sealed his fate by saying to that moment, "Delay awhile, thou art so fair." The storm now burst and drenched the two friends to the skin before they could reach the shelter of some trees on the bank. When the torrent had ceased they emptied the canoe, which was already half full of water, and proceeded on their way.

Now began a series of extremely shallow rapids, which necessitated continual wading. For the Danube

in the neighbourhood of Immendingen suddenly and
mysteriously dwindles into a stream which is shallower
and more insignificant than the Brigach at Donaueschingen. This is due to a great part of its water
escaping through fissures in the soil. Experiments
with dyes are said to have established the fact that
the waters thus disappearing give rise, by a subterranean channel, to the Aach, a tributary of the
Rhine flowing towards the south. There may thus
some day be an opportunity for a modern Sinbad the
Sailor to make an underground voyage of discovery.

In the region between Immendingen and Thiergarten several of those curious roofed wooden bridges
occur, which are also to be seen on the upper course
of the Neckar. There are a good many points of
similarity between the higher parts of these two
rivers, as is indeed natural, considering that their
sources lie very close together on the watershed of
the Black Forest.

Just above a village named Möhringen occurred
what is probably the worst of the twenty-five crossings
on the Upper Danube. The labour of the porterage
was, however, greatly lessened by five men who willingly lent a helping hand. After this followed a succession of shallows, which involved renewed wading,
the monotony of this drudgery being relieved only by
the excitement of a magnificent rapid before the next
mill was reached. The excitement of course depended chiefly on the uncertainty as to whether the

canoe would be ripped up by a stone or a snag during her downward rush.

The river as it approaches Tuttlingen becomes very broad, but at the same time so uniformly shallow as to barely float a canoe in any part of the channel. Though it was only just five o'clock in the afternoon the two friends decided on stopping here in order to ensure a good night's rest, this being the only place for a long distance at which there was any prospect of obtaining even tolerable quarters.

The town of Tuttlingen is built close up to the river, with side streets coming down to the bank. Opposite one of these the canoeists landed at a kind of jetty frequented by washerwomen. Cox now ran up to the *Post* in the market-place and soon brought back the boots (*Hausknecht*) with a hand-truck. On this the boat was transported to the inn with as much expedition as the denseness of the crowd which had assembled in the interval would allow.

As the canoe had still shown signs of leaking slightly in the course of the day, the Interpreter, before turning in, varnished her afresh in the shed where she was housed. The night was beautifully clear, and the quaint old market-place looked wonderfully picturesque in the bright light of the moon.

The ruins of the neighbouring castle of Honburg, destroyed in the Thirty Years' War, would have been well worth visiting next morning for the good view which it commands. The voyagers found no

time for this, having the prospect of a long day of
thirty-seven miles, presumably with many obstructions,
before them, as they were anxious to reach Sigmaringen by nightfall.   They were accordingly afloat by
seven o'clock, and paddled briskly down a fine reach
to the next weir.   The mist still lay on the river,
unfortunately hiding from view what was evidently
a fine wooded ridge on the right bank.

The valley of the Danube between Mühlheim and
Sigmaringen, a distance of about thirty miles, can
boast of scenery which is probably as magnificent
as that of any river in Europe.   The only part of the
Danube itself which can compare with it is that
between Passau and Linz; but most of those who
have seen both will probably agree in giving the
preference to this region of the Upper Danube.   The
river here winds through narrow rocky gorges, in
which grey crags, rising precipitously to a great height,
alternate with woods of the most luxuriant growth.
A road follows the Danube all the way from Sigmaringen to Tuttlingen; but this, besides the drawback
of passing through eight tunnels, labours under the
disadvantage of affording but a one-sided view.   The
full beauty of the scenery can only be enjoyed from
the river itself.   That is perhaps the reason why it
does not enjoy the reputation it deserves.

For some distance below Mühlheim the course of
the river is a perpetual series of rapids over and
between rocks and boulders.   On one occasion the

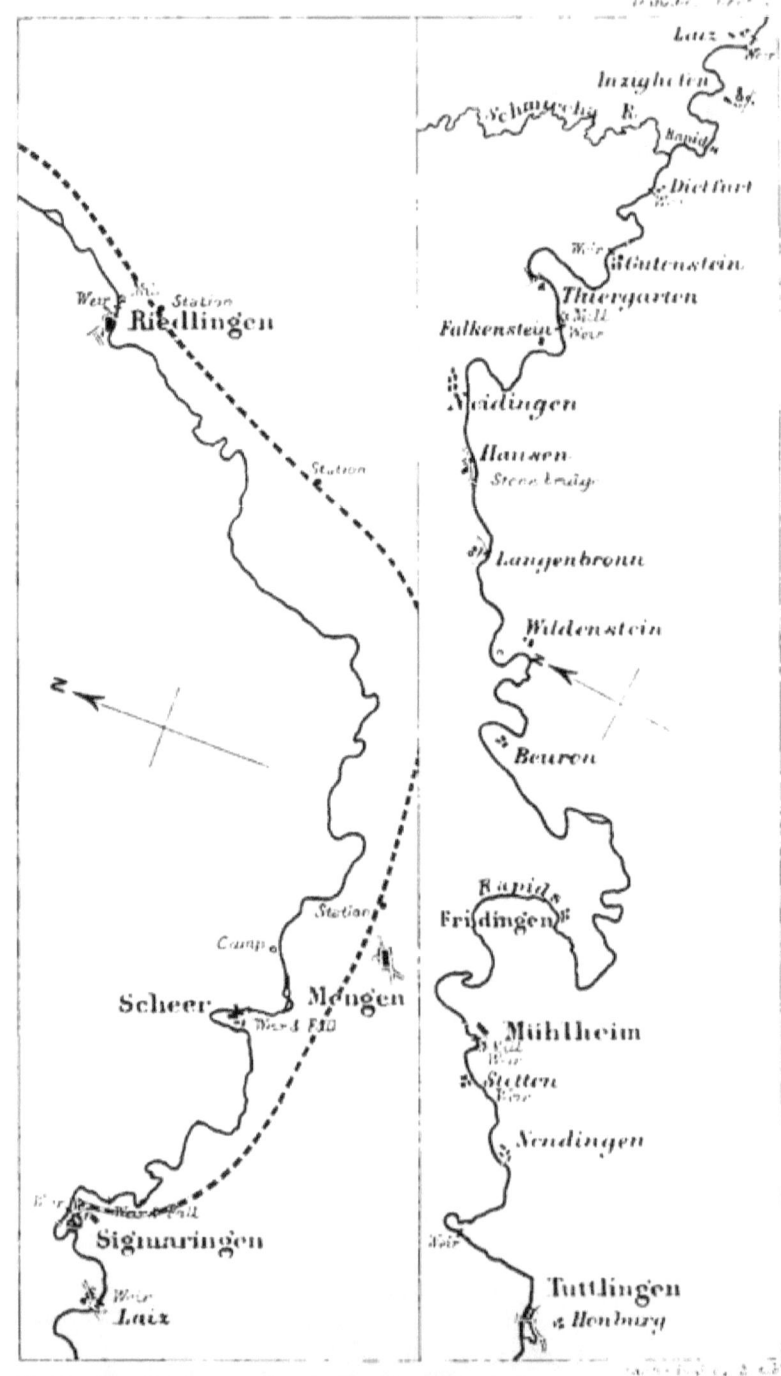

Laiz

Inzigkofen

Schmeechic R.

Rapids

Dietfurt

Weir

Gutenstein

Thiergarten

Mill
Weir

Falkenstein

Weir
Station

Riedlingen

Neidingen

Hausen

Stone bridge

Station

Langenbronn

Wildenstein

N

Beuron

Rapids

Fridingen

Station

Camp

Scheer

Mengen

Weir & Mill

Mühlheim

Mill
Weir

Stetten

Weir

Nendingen

Weir & Mill

Sigmaringen

Weir

Weir

Laiz

Tuttlingen

Honburg

0 1 2 3 4 5 6 7 8 9 10 Kilometres.

canoe was by the merest accident carried down
exactly between two ugly rocks under the surface
and only just far enough apart to admit of her
passing. Had she struck, she would have been
irreparably damaged, the voyage thus coming to a
premature end on its third day.

Two or three miles above Beuron the friends
stopped for their midday rest in a reach of the
most enchanting beauty. Opposite them in the
middle of the river lay a fine large rock overgrown
at the top with grass and a few shrubs and small
trees, and surrounded with deep still water. Round
this they swam many times in the deliciously cool
river, which was doubly refreshing in the fierce rays
of the noontide sun. Hitherto no doubt anonymous,
it now received the name of the Bath Rock. Lovely
though this spot was, the friends could not help
admitting that it was surpassed in magnificence by a
broad lake-like reach of which they came in sight a
few hundred yards lower down. The water here was
like a mirror and of such depth as to assume a beautiful bluish-green tinge—like that of the Danube below
Weltenburg—at the foot of a cliff rising sheer to a
great height, and reminding one rather of a rocky
precipice on a sea-coast than the bank of a river still
so near its source.

About eighteen miles from Tuttlingen lies the
monastery of Beuron on the right bank of the river.
As there is an excellent inn here, it would be a

capital place even for pedestrians to make their
headquarters with a view to exploring the rare
beauties of the Danube. It would be a very paradise
to the British landscape painter in search of lovely
river scenery. Were it but always brilliant summer
weather as it then was, how easily could such men
there begin to forget their native land and say—

> "Our island home
> Is far beyond the wave ; we will no longer roam."

A mile and a half beyond Beuron is the castle of
Wildenstein on the right bank, and about the same
distance farther on the village of Langenbronn,
dominated by the old château of Wernwag, the view
from which is said to be very fine. At the top there
is the inevitable inn, which in this case is described
as being excellent.

Another mile and a half farther down lies Hausen,
where an old ruin rises on a height and the Danube
is spanned by a stone bridge.

Near the ruin of the Falkenstein, three miles and
a half lower down, the voyagers came to a weir
involving a very long porterage, in which they were
glad of the help of two very friendly natives. As it
was now growing dark and Sigmaringen was still ten
miles off, all hope of reaching that town was given
up, and Thiergarten, a small place hardly a mile
farther on, was fixed on for that night's resting-place.
To get even thus far was bad enough, owing to the

rapids on the way and the numerous rocks scattered about the river-bed. However, Thiergarten was at last reached in safety nearly an hour and a half after sunset. On the bridge crossing the river here the forms of two or three men could be dimly made out in the darkness. Being hailed, they hurried down with great alacrity to the shingly beach, where the canoe had been run ashore. One of these men took a long time to get over his surprise at this occurrence. which was, he said, an exact repetition of what had happened three or four nights before. At the identical hour, as he was then leaning over the parapet, voices had addressed him from the dark surface of the water below, asking whether the place was Thiergarten. These were the voices of the two Hamburgers, who had also been belated, and one of whom having upset a short way above had arrived in a woeful plight.

Locking the canoe up in a shed hard by, the two friends made their way up to the inn, which was also close to the bridge. They found it to be very primitive but sufficient for their modest wants.

On the following morning, which was fresh. bright, and free from mist, they were afloat again by half-past seven. After passing many rapids and two weirs, they stopped on the right bank, which was still saturated with dew, at a point nearly opposite a railway station where the Schmiecha runs into the Danube, and enjoyed a most invigorating bathe in

the smooth deep water of this short reach. Some
way farther on the river turns to the right, flowing
past high bare grey cliffs. In one of the rapids here
the canoe stuck and was strained, but fortunately
got off again without any more serious damage.
Below the weir at the village of Laiz the stream
widens out into a broad calm expanse of water
without any perceptible current, and resembling a
beautiful lake. The wooded southern shore of the
Danube, which rises steeply from the water's edge, is
charmingly laid out and forms the park of Inzig-
hofen. This combination of mountain, wood, and
flood produces a very lovely effect.

At Sigmaringen, which lies at the end of this
splendid reach, the voyagers arrived under the
broiling midday sun. Leaving the *Flora* at the
swimming-baths, which they found completely deserted, they walked up through the town, carrying
their paddles in their hands, to the *Deutsche Haus*,
where they had intended to pass the previous night.
The Interpreter had corresponded with the landlady
before leaving England, having at first thought of
beginning the voyage at this point.

There are few towns so beautifully situated on a
river as Sigmaringen, with its castle crowning a rock
which rises abruptly from the Danube on a small
peninsula formed by a curve of the river. Though
its population is less than 4000, its many important-
looking public buildings give it quite the appearance

of a small capital. This it practically is, being the residence of the princes of Hohenzollern.

The palace contains an excellent museum and a good picture gallery, representing chiefly the early German school of painting. Taken all in all, there is probably no town in Germany which would prove so charming as the headquarters of a reading party, especially if they were provided with a boat. The latter, it is almost needless to say, could not be obtained at Sigmaringen itself, but an arrangement might no doubt easily be made with the leading boat-builder at Frankfort-on-the-Main to send one there. The best method of doing this would be to take Frankfort on the way and select a suitable craft on the spot. The distance to Sigmaringen being short, the transit would not occupy more than three or four days. This plan would be far cheaper than sending a boat out from England. Not only would the cost of the journey be saved, but also the amount of hire for the additional six or seven weeks required for transmission to and from Germany.

After an excellent *table d'hôte* at the *Deutsche Haus* the crew of the *Flora* re-embarked soon after two o'clock and almost immediately shot the centre arch of the stone bridge. This was attended with some risk, as the river just above takes a sudden turn to the left and flows through with a great rush. Then curving round the castle rock it forms a peninsula, near the neck of which is a weir. The crossing here was very easy, the bank being low and grassy.

The beautiful scenery ceases at Sigmaringen. With the exception of the magnificent break between Weltenburg and Kelheim, the banks of the Danube from this point onwards are comparatively tame and uninteresting till Vilshofen, some fifteen miles above Passau, is approached.

At Sigmaringen the railway from the north enters the valley of the Danube and more or less follows the course of the river—the length of which owing to its windings is greater—for a distance of about thirty-six miles, as far as Ehingen.

About a mile beyond Sigmaringen there is right across the river a low weir over which it flows with a fall of about three feet. This the *Flora* shot beautifully, shipping only a small quantity of water over the bows as they plunged into the stream below.

At the small town of Scheer the Danube forms a loop, near the end of which a long, high, and steep weir is built straight across the river. It being impossible to carry the boat over the bank, which is faced with a high wall all along, the crew found it necessary to get out and, wading close to the base of the wall, to lower the canoe gently over the weir by means of the towing-rope into the stream at the bottom. Then clambering cautiously down the slimy surface

and wading some distance in the swift rapid below,
the Interpreter managed to scramble into the bows,
when the water was already up to his waist. Cox
meanwhile having clung on with all his might
behind, and only just able to retain his foothold, then
with great agility leaped on to the stern, like a
horseman into his saddle—no mean feat to accomplish
under the circumstances without upsetting the boat.
The *Flora* now sped down a succession of rough
rapids till she disappeared from the view of the large
crowd which had assembled to witness the performance from the bridge. Having thus escaped unscathed,
they now ran ashore to exchange places, the canoe
having turned round in the rapid below the weir, and
to empty out the water they had shipped while vault-
ing into their seats. As it was a fine evening and no
town of any size was within easy reach, they had
resolved on camping out that night. This would also
enable them to start next morning early enough to
reach Ulm by nightfall—no trifling undertaking considering the distance was upwards of fifty miles with
many obstructions on the way. It was already growing dusk, so they decided to stop on the left bank,
almost opposite the town of Mengen, which is
situated at a considerable distance from the right
bank of the Danube.

A more comfortable encampment than that of the
previous occasion was made by turning the boat over
and fixing the ends in the sides of a trench-like

depression which happened to be in the ground.
This formed a roof resembling that of a cabin and
high enough to admit of the crew sitting upright
underneath. The waterproof sheet was spread below,
the red sail stretched across one side to do duty as a
wall, and the lamp lit and suspended from one of the
thwarts. While the Interpreter was making some of
these arrangements Cox had trudged across the plain
to a village some half-mile distant for the purpose of
buying milk, butter, eggs, and bread. His solitary
figure, clad in uncouth garments, and suddenly emerging from the region of the river naturally attracted a
considerable part of the juvenile population, which
began to follow him on his return. However, by
dint of the hideous grimaces and terrifying antics
which he displayed as he turned to bay in the increasing gloom, he finally scared away even the
boldest spirits, and thus saved the lonely camp from
molestation. The two friends were therefore able to
enjoy their evening meal in peace and quiet on the
solitary plain. In the warm red light produced by
the sail the extemporised cabin looked wonderfully
cozy. The perfect stillness of the night was broken
only by the gentle murmur of the river and the
trumpetings of the indefatigable mosquito. The
moon having risen full-orbed and red, bathed the river
and the surrounding country in her cloudless radiance
for the rest of the night.

    After a game of Nap the campers laid themselves

down to rest; but sleep resolutely refused to steep
their senses in forgetfulness. This was no doubt
chiefly due to the cramped position in which they
were obliged to lie, the space below the canoe not
admitting of both stretching themselves at full length,
while the breadth available was but two feet and a
half, the grass saturated with dew being beyond.
The attentions of the mosquitoes, besides the chilliness
of the night and the brilliance of the moonlight, must
also have contributed their share to this unpleasant
result. The two friends thus enjoyed the doubtful
privilege of observing for once in their lives the
moon traverse the cloudless heavens from her rise in
the east to her setting in the west.

The would-be sleepers arose at five, and after a
good breakfast with an excellent cup of strong tea,
felt perfectly fresh again in spite of their unbroken
wakefulness. It is surprising how little sleep one
seems to need when spending all night and day in
the open air. Even complete sleeplessness, as in the
present case, makes very little difference on the
following day compared with what it would do in
ordinary indoor life.

Embarking at seven the voyagers found the river
flowing with a strong current and sweeping round
the curves in a succession of rough rapids. The more
or less uniform pace of the stream in this part is
due to the regulation of the river-bed and the absence
of any obstruction till Riedlingen, a place more than

twelve miles farther down. This distance was accordingly accomplished at the rate of ten kilometres an hour.

At Riedlingen there is a very broad and high weir, the crossing in consequence being very difficult and roundabout. The canoe had to be carried behind the mill and a considerable distance beyond till she could be launched from a shingly beach below the weir.

The labour of the porterage was considerably lightened here by the miller and several men and boys who willingly lent a helping hand.

The scenery between Riedlingen and Munderkingen is good at two points,—some way from the former place, where the wooded bank makes a fine sweep, and at the most northerly spot in the stretch, where the ruins of the old castle of Rechtenstein rise above the left bank. In this distance, about sixteen miles, there are two weirs. The only possibility of transporting the canoe at the first of these was over a narrow wooden bridge built outside the mill and suddenly turning a corner at right angles. It is doubtful whether any other kind of boat could have been carried round.

After flowing with a southerly curve of about three miles below Unter-Marchthal, the Danube forms a narrow loop at Munderkingen, almost completely surrounding that little town. There are two weirs at this place, but as they are on different

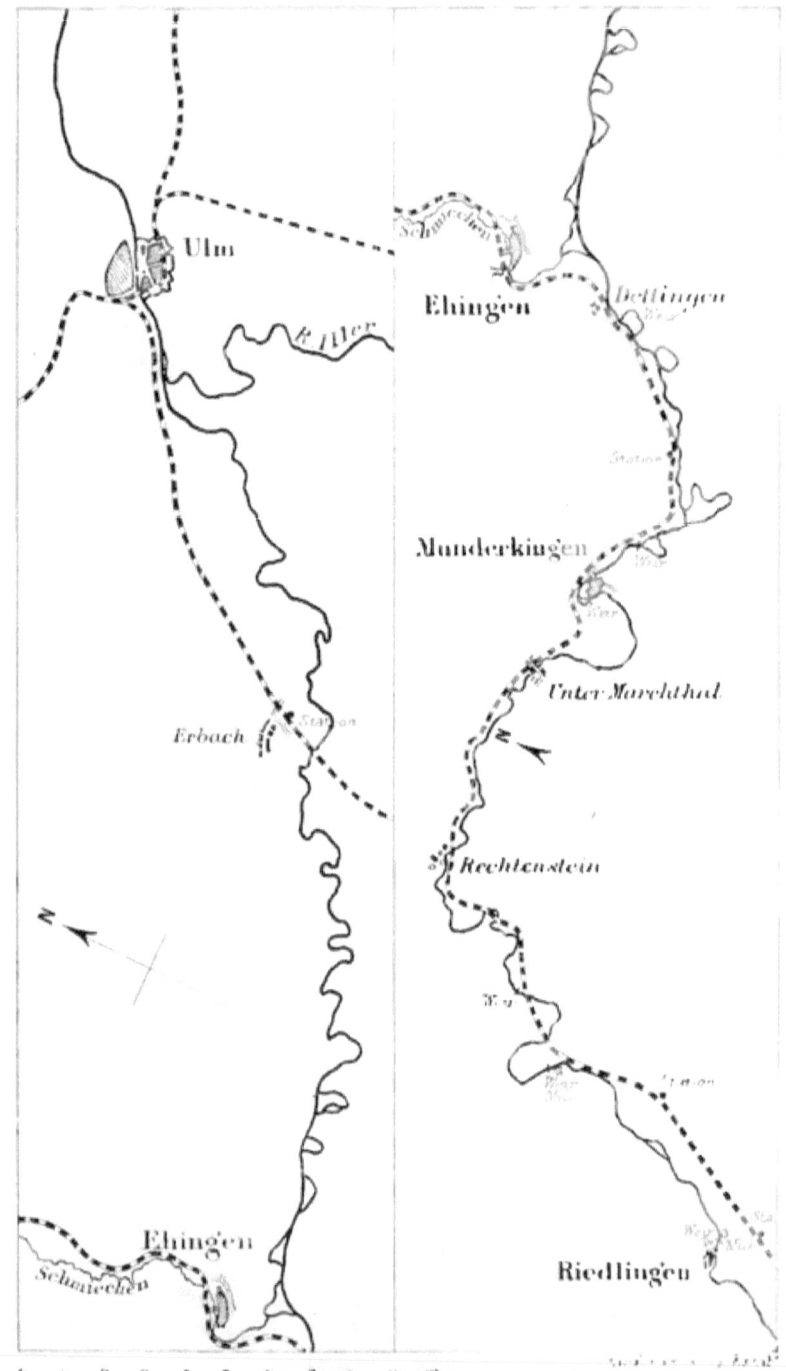

branches of the stream it is only necessary to cross at one or the other. The porterage, however, at the one chosen by the two canoeists proved to be very long, the boat having to be dragged or carried across a large meadow to the left of the town.

After a bathe and lunch on the bank a short way below Munderkingen, the canoeists came about a mile farther down upon their fifth weir, over which there flowed a fine broad sheet of water, the height of the fall being considerable. Another three miles' paddle brought them to what they were told, much to their relief, was the last obstruction on the Danube. This being a weir with a fall of two or three feet, looked as if it might easily be shot by the canoe some ten or twelve feet from the right bank. The crew, however, decided that it would be foolish to run the risk of any accident which might prevent them reaching Ulm that night, and accordingly contented themselves with the rather poor-spirited alternative of pulling their boat over the low, chalky bank. As it was already half-past four, there were only about two hours of daylight left, while the distance still remaining to be accomplished was more than twenty miles. To have to exert oneself to the utmost at the fag-end of a long day following a sleepless night was by no means an inspiriting prospect, especially with a thunderstorm threatening. The latter, however, fortunately passed off, leaving the evening clear and fine.

The unimpeded stream now flowed with a strong

current, the canoe travelling at a rare pace, as her
crew strained every nerve to make the most of the
daylight. Ehingen, a small town about a mile distant from the left bank, and near the confluence of the
Schmiechen with the Danube, was soon passed. The
railway here leaves the river, and making a loop,
runs almost due north for the first seven miles and
does not rejoin the Danube till Ulm. The twelve
miles of river between Ehingen and Erbach are quite
beyond the reach of the railroad. At the latter
place, however, the line from Friedrichshafen to Ulm
crosses the Danube, keeping at a distance of a couple
of miles from the left bank till it again approaches
the river for the last two miles after its confluence
with the Iller.

In the six miles above Erbach the course of the
river winds exceedingly. The voyagers were almost
glad of the necessity to hurry over this stretch, for it
is altogether stale, flat, and unprofitable.

Erbach, a small town situated at a distance of about
a mile from the left bank of the Danube, where the
railway crosses the river, was passed in the distance
at six o'clock. Cox, who had been sitting since the
early morning on the poop of the canoe, was now
growing exhausted, chiefly from want of food, of
which not a morsel remained in the boat. The ad-
visability of trudging up to Erbach was accordingly
discussed, but such weak-kneed counsels being soon
rejected, it was resolved to trust to luck and face the

terrors of the night on an empty stomach till Ulm was reached.

As darkness began to set in it became impossible any longer to take full advantage of the swiftness of the stream. For though the surface of the river was perfectly smooth, and still bright enough to render visible at some distance any obstruction showing above the water, the progress of the canoe now became precarious owing to the shallows occurring every now and then. In one of these she stuck so fast as to compel the crew to get out and wade. By seven o'clock it had grown very dark. About this time the sound of rushing waters suggested the alarming possibility of a waterfall ahead. It turned out, however, to proceed from a tributary which falls into the Danube under a bridge on the left bank. After they had paddled on cautiously for some distance, peering into the gloom, what seemed to be a large island appeared straight in front, the river apparently dividing into two arms to the left and the right. The voyagers, judging by the faint light on the smooth surface of the water, took the latter to be the broader of the two, and accordingly made for this channel. Suddenly they were caught by a swiftly eddying current and driven with great force down the left arm broadside into a large willow, the branches of which hung down into the water. Cox having slid off the poop into the bottom of the boat just in the nick of time, both of them clutched hold of the

branches and thus managed to prevent the canoe
from capsizing.

The cause of the eddies remained a mystery till
later. It then appeared that the supposed right
channel, far from being the main branch of the
river, was a large tributary, the Iller, which joins
the Danube about two miles above Ulm. The spot
where the two voyagers nearly came to grief is said to
be dangerous to boats even in the daytime; how much
more must it be so to a frail bark like a Canadian
canoe in the dark ! The adventurers, thinking they
had had about enough of the supposed main branch,
now resolved to devote themselves to the navigation
of the lesser channel, which alone was in reality
the Danube.

The moon, the long-expected, being one day on
the wane, was now seen to be rising on the right ;
but her light, totally obscured for the first hour by
the thick foliage on the bank, availed the voyagers
nothing that evening. Nevertheless, they felt somewhat reassured by her faint glimmer now and then
showing for a moment between the trunks of the
trees. The lights of Ulm, the long-delayed and
much prayed for, now began to appear in the distance.
Yet the very prospect of arriving was fraught with
almost greater anxiety than that of continuing the
voyage indefinitely in the dark ; for what certainty
was there of finding a landing-place in that dim
light, or even if one were found, of getting ashore

without suffering shipwreck in a stream that ran so
fiercely ?

The sound of rushing water soon betrayed the
nearness of the railway bridge, which was now seen
to be looming darkly close in front. Though Cox
was steering for the middle of one of the arches, it
soon became evident that the force of the current
was carrying the canoe straight towards the right
buttress, against which a large white wave was surging. By frantic efforts aslant the stream, the belated
adventurers just managed to escape being dashed
against it, and to shoot into the arch, almost grazing
its right side as they passed through unscathed.
They were afterwards told at Ulm that this bridge
was considered particularly dangerous to navigation,
and that only a short time before a boat containing
four persons had been driven against one of the
buttresses in broad daylight and upset, some of the
occupants having been drowned. From this point
the Danube seemed to flow with additional swiftness,
now that it was confined between the walled banks
of Ulm. As the adventurers were borne along at a
rapid pace they had no breathing time to reflect on
their hairbreadth escape, having to keep all their
wits about them with a view to landing. Bow after
a few moments descried on the left what looked like
a *Badeanstalt*, and the canoe was at once steered in
that direction. It turned out, when close at hand, to
be one of those floating swimming-baths moored to

the bank which are so common on German rivers
and are the chief refuge of their navigators. As the
current owing to the obstruction of the raft flowed
with redoubled fury past its edge, it would have been
courting disaster to attempt running in alongside.
Had the voyagers possessed a boat-hook it might have
been possible to do this. Though they had specially
ordered one to be packed in the canoe before leaving
England, they had to their chagrin found on her
arrival at Donaueschingen that it had not been sent.
To have a boat-hook is in many cases essential for
landing with a Canadian canoe, it being impossible
to reach far over the side without capsizing, while it
is difficult to lay hold with the bare hand of a smooth
plank or beam as you are being carried past by the
stream. The canoe was accordingly turned and her
crew strained every muscle against the current, as
they gradually edged in towards the raft. Unable to
hold their own, when close up to it, they were carried
astern, grazing along its outer beam. Cox clutched
at the last plank as he drifted past, but was
unable to retain his hold. Bow, however, luckily
managed at the last moment to seize one of the
cross-beams which slightly projected, but in doing so
very nearly upset the canoe, the gunwale of which
was sucked under the planks of the raft by the force
of the current. This swimming-bath was fortunately
the very best kind for landing at; for a platform
about three feet wide ran all along its edge, whereas

the outside partition usually rises straight from the water.

The weary and hungry voyagers soon succeeded in scrambling out upon this platform. They now had time to realise the great risk they had just run. They saw that had they missed this opportunity, the canoe would infallibly have been capsized by running stern foremost into another swimming-bath a few yards lower down, and built farther out into the stream. What would then have happened it is difficult to say. There can, however, be little doubt that, even if the crew had managed to save themselves in that rushing current, the canoe as well as the luggage would have been lost, and the voyage on the Danube thus prematurely cut short. Had they not succeeded in getting ashore at one of these two rafts they would have been swept past the town, to spend the night in the deserted tracts of river below; for with the exception of these swimming-baths there was no other possible landing-place at Ulm for a boat.

Having pulled the canoe out of the water, they turned her over on the open platform in the middle of the raft, laying the cushions and everything but their hand-luggage underneath. They then staggered off with their bags and paddles in quest of their hotel near the centre of the town. The distance seemed interminable to them in their exhausted and encumbered condition as they slowly trudged along the ramparts which form the river-bank.

As a wedding happened to be going on in the hotel,
the nonchalance of the two friends was put to a rather
severe test, when they had to make their way upstairs
in their soiled flannels through the guests in their
gala attire thronging the landing of the first floor.

They had probably never before appreciated a
good supper more thoroughly, though the movements
of the attendant waiter did seem phenomenally slow.
But time, no less than distance, always appears
excessively long to persons in such circumstances.

Next morning the voyagers arose, thoroughly
refreshed by a long and deep sleep, which completely
cancelled the arrears of the previous night. The
greater part of the forenoon they spent in visiting the
magnificent Gothic cathedral and the other sights of
Ulm, besides reading their numerous letters, which
having lain at the Post Office for more than a week,
were now nearly a fortnight old. A thunderstorm
breaking out soon after eleven o'clock delayed their
departure somewhat, so that they were not afloat till
one. When they came down to start, the daughter of
the proprietor of the baths (*Bademeister*) told them that
she, having been the first to arrive in the morning, had
been greatly alarmed when still some way off to see
what she at first supposed to be a whale (*Wallfisch*),
which had lost its way up the Danube, and had some-
how got stranded on the platform of the bathing
establishment !

Ulm is about 120 miles distant by water from

Donaueschingen, and sixty from Sigmaringen. It is 1204 feet above the level of the sea, the fall being upwards of 1000 feet over the whole distance and 656 over the latter half. The average fall for the first sixty miles is therefore six feet, and for the last about eleven feet per mile.

From this point the Danube assumes the character of a large river, being navigable by large vessels from Ulm downwards. The regular service of passenger steamers, which in former days began here, having ceased owing to the competition of the railway, is now limited to the Danube below Passau.

One of the characteristics of the river below Ulm is the continual alternation of the main current from one side to the other. This is due to heaps of shingle deposited by the stream and deflecting it to the other bank, where the process is repeated. It is advisable to avoid the shingly side, not only because there is little or no current there, but because the boat after going a considerable distance is almost certain to get stranded in shallows, from which it is often difficult and tedious to extricate oneself.

Another peculiarity of the Danube below Ulm is a strange seething sound that may in most parts be heard rising from its surface. This is no doubt due to the friction of the gravel as it is rolled along by the swift current at the bottom of the river.

One could not help being struck by the beautiful transparence of the water of the Danube above Ulm,

when one saw the shoals of fish darting off in all
directions as the shadow of the canoe sped across the
river's shingly bed. Even below Ulm it remains
tolerably clear, till the influx of the Inn at Passau
renders it turbid for the rest of its course.

The crew started as usual in view of a considerable
crowd. While paddling down between the high
walls, which, being part of the fortifications, form
the banks on both sides, they had an opportunity of
judging how hopeless would have been the attempt
to land anywhere on the previous night except at
the baths, which they had so fortunately discovered
in the dark. They saw, too, how easily they might
have come to grief against the passenger bridge
lower down, which joins the old city on the left
bank with the new town that has grown up on the
other side.

The rain-clouds having cleared away left a fine
hot afternoon, which rendered that day's voyage
pleasant enough so far. But the scenery was intensely dull and uninteresting, consisting mainly of
long, straight reaches of river fringed with lines of
poplars, not unlike many a continental high road,
with water substituted for land. Of hills and woods
there was not a trace visible anywhere.

Dillingen was fixed upon for that night's resting-
place, as some friends who had gone down the
Danube from Ulm in a rowing-boat the year before
had described the inn at Höchstädt, five miles farther

down, as extremely villainous. Dillingen was, however, not so easy to find; for at the hour and place
at which the town seemed due there was no vestige
of it on the left, where it was marked on the map.
There were, it is true, two deserted swimming-baths
near the bank and a wooden bridge a short way
farther down. As these seemed to be indications of
a town or village of some sort being within measur-
able distance, the crew landed at the second bath to
prospect. As the evening, now approaching the hour
of sunset, had become very gloomy, and not a soul
was visible anywhere in the desolate scene, the effect
produced by this spot on the minds of the voyagers
was depressing enough.

Cox having made his way through a plantation
at the back of the baths, returned after some time
with the news that Dillingen was there, but about
a mile inland. Though a town of some 6000 inhabitants, it appears to consist chiefly of one long
street. It was a place of much greater importance
in former days, having been a university town till
the beginning of this century. There seemed to be
a great dearth of population in the neighbourhood,
but two men were at last found, who helped to carry
the luggage up to the *Bayrische Hof.* This inn
turned out to be a good one. The landlord, who
was a very affable man, informed the strangers that
he had a good trout-stream and shooting to let on
very reasonable terms, which might suit some of

their countrymen, if they only knew about the place.

Setting off soon after eight o'clock next morning they passed Höchstädt in less than an hour's time, and three or four miles farther down the village of Blind-heim (Blenheim), where the Duke of Marlborough and Prince Eugène defeated the Elector of Bavaria and Marshal Tallard in 1704. The inhabitants of this region seem to know nothing of the Duke or of any English troops having taken part in that battle, affirming that it was won by Prince Eugène and his army alone. Such is the value of tradition after the lapse of less than two centuries, and that in a country where the great bulk of the population can read and write.

The scenery in the stretch of eighteen miles between Dillingen and Donauwörth continues to be tame and uninteresting. Stone dams are here and there built parallel with the bank, but at some dis-tance from it, in order to improve the channel. There is an occasional opening in these dams leading into the backwaters which they enclose. Donauwörth, a small town of 4000 inhabitants, is a convenient place for landing, and has an excellent hotel.

The friends did not stop for their midday rest till they had accomplished twenty-five miles at an average speed of over five miles an hour. Soon after resuming their voyage they passed the point where the Lech, one of the largest tributaries of the

Danube during its course in Germany, falls into the river. This stream rises in the north-east corner of Switzerland, close to the source of its sister tributary, the Iller.

After Donauwörth the scenery begins to improve till you approach Neuburg, where a really fine and richly wooded hill comes into view on the right. About four miles above that town lies the château of Steppburg, among the woods on the left. Taking the right of the two branches into which the river divides at Neuburg, and shooting the main arch of a small bridge under which there is a rather dangerous rush of water, the canoeists landed at the foot of a stone stair in the steep, high bank, immediately below their inn, the *Post*. They had expected to reach Ingolstadt before nightfall, but had miscalculated the distance, having been taken in by some dredgers who at their lunching-ground had told them that Neuburg was six kilometres distant instead of twenty, and Ingolstadt fifteen instead of forty. They had accordingly enjoyed a fool's paradise for an hour and a quarter on the bank, believing they would make Ingolstadt in an easy two hours' paddle. The statements of dwellers on rivers regarding distances should invariably be received with distrust, even when there is no reason to doubt the sincerity of such statements.

Neuburg is a pretty town of 8000 inhabitants, situated on the side of a hill rising from the right bank of the Danube. There is here an old castle

of the Dukes of Pfalz-Neuburg, part of it having
been turned into what, like so many other German
châteaus, it most resembles, a barrack.   It has, however, a rather fine vaulted gateway.

At the *Post*, which is a good inn, the two Hamburg canoeists had stopped a few nights before, as
well as the American raftsman some weeks earlier.

Embarking at 8.20, the voyagers by hard work
accomplished the distance of thirteen miles to Ingolstadt in two hours, despite a pretty strong wind
blowing against them most of the way.   They were
anxious to arrive in time to catch a train leaving at
11.25 for Munich.   They had long before planned a
day's excursion to the latter city as a pleasant varia-
tion to the somewhat monotonous character of the
voyage on this part of the Danube.   The proprietor
of the swimming-baths at Ingolstadt luckily happened to be on the spot, but turned out to be a man
of indescribable slowness in his movements.   A boy
was immediately despatched to order a cab—a name,
by the way, suggestive of far greater swiftness than
was proper to the vehicle which it is meant to
designate.   As the voyagers, after changing their
clothes and stowing away the canoe and her contents,
saw no sign of its approach, they hurried up into the
town with their bags, to find the horse still in its
stable.   By dint of the most persevering instigations
they at last managed to get the ancient steed har-
nessed, and by strenuous applications of the whip to

its lean flanks, actually to reach the station on the other side of the river in time for their train, within an hour of their arrival at the baths. This was a performance they might have been proud of, considering the amount of *inertia* they had to overcome, and the fact that the station was no less than two miles off.

After spending a pleasant afternoon in strolling about Munich, and seeing some of its most important art collections, they passed the evening in listening to the opera of *Siegfried*. It was well put on the stage, but to all save Wagnerian specialists must prove rather tedious, owing to the interminableness of the recitative. Its monotony was indeed to some extent relieved by the unintentional humour of the hero's fight with a grotesquely mechanical dragon, and by his attempts to elicit a musical note from the pipe which he had hewn for himself with his sword in the forest. But it seemed a shame to laugh in the midst of Teutons who were looking on and listening with a solemnity surpassing that which is to be seen at most services of the Church. Music has in fact taken the place of religion with a considerable proportion of the population of Germany.

On the afternoon of the following day the two friends returned to spend the night at Ingolstadt. They had time before nightfall to climb the tower of the *Frauenkirche*, and enjoy the extensive bird's-eye view of the surrounding country which it commands.

Starting early next morning, they paddled on for twenty miles till they reached the village of Eining on the right bank, opposite Hienheim. They found it necessary to disembark here on a stone dam which runs parallel with the bank, and past which the stream flows with great swiftness. Leaving the canoe with some misgivings in this unsheltered place, her painter tied to a stone, they walked up to the village with the intention of visiting the recently excavated and well preserved remains of the Roman camp of Abusina, which was close at hand. They were shown all over the site by the schoolmaster of the village, a very intelligent and well-informed man. Cox, being an archaeologist, was much interested, and would have taken full notes of the antiquities had he not been misled by the schoolmaster's description of two Englishmen who had visited Eining a twelve-month ago. The account seemed to tally exactly with the appearance of two friends who had undertaken a walking tour during the previous summer along the *Pfahlgraben*,[1] the Roman frontier moat, and one of whom would undoubtedly have taken down all facts of importance deserving publication. Subsequently it turned out that these friends had not visited the place. This is one of many experiences showing how little dependence can be placed on personal descriptions for purposes of identification.

---

[1] See *A Walk along the Teufelsmauer and Pfahlgraben*, by J. L. G. Mowat, Oxford, 1885.

The woods on the left bank near Hienheim, being the remains of a primæval forest, are said to contain some trees of immense size. A few miles above Eining on the left bank is situated Pföringen. Near this place, called Vergen in the *Nibelungenlied*, the Burgundian king Gunther and his Nibelungen are supposed to have crossed the Danube on their fateful journey to the Court of Attila at Buda. This is one of the most dramatic episodes in the great national epic. The dark-browed Hagen, while wandering solitary and moody along the bank, falls in with some water-witches, who predict that out of all that host the chaplain alone will return safe to Worms. Having ferried across more than 10,000 men with his own hand, Hagen, determined to falsify the prophecy, thrusts the man of God when in midstream into the swiftly flowing Danube, declaring that he at least shall never return. The chaplain, however, miraculously manages to regain the shore they have left. On seeing this, the grim warrior now feels convinced that the Nibelungen are doomed, and steels his heart to meet his fate.

Finding the boat safe on their return, the voyagers paddled on for five miles, till they came in sight of Weltenburg, a Benedictine Abbey founded by a Duke of Bavaria towards the end of the eighth century. It is situated on the right bank at an angle of the river, the shingly beach reaching up to the very building, while the turreted wall of the garden

and orchard extends a considerable distance down
the bank close to the water's edge. The scenery
from a short way above this point down to Kelheim,
a distance of about four miles, is as magnificent as
any on the Danube. The river here flows through
rocky and richly wooded gorges of the most romantic
beauty. The grey crags rise to a height of several
hundred feet from the edge of the deep, smooth
water, which is of a lovely bluish-green tinge. These
defiles looked doubly charming when seen in a kind
of hazy sunlight, which invested the whole scene
with an indescribable splendour. This part of the
Danube bears a striking resemblance to some of
the beautiful reaches below Mühlheim, but has the
advantage of a much broader stream.

There is a ferry at Weltenburg, and boats may be
hired from here down to Kelheim. As this happened
to be a Sunday, and the weather was gorgeously fine,
the river was alive with skiffs, all gay with bunting
and filled with happy holiday-makers enjoying
themselves in that contented way which is so characteristic of Germans in their amusements.

Some way farther down is the monastery of Traun-
thal, beautifully situated on the left bank. There is
here a good open-air restaurant, from which a walk
of less than half an hour through the woods leads to
the *Befreiungshalle*. But as this building lies on
a height immediately above the river at the western
end of Kelheim, it was obviously more convenient

for the voyagers to visit it by paddling down to that point. They had just disembarked when they were startled by hearing something plumping into the water close to the bank. On looking up they saw two youths throwing down stones at the boat from the top of the hill above. Any of these, coming as they did from so great a height, would have gone through the bottom of the canoe had they struck her. Fortunately a policeman was at hand, and a wave of his sword sufficed to put a stop to this dastardly conduct. The two friends then climbed the hillside to inspect the Hall of Liberation, which is a magnificent classical rotunda nearly 200 feet in height. It was founded by the art-loving Lewis I. of Bavaria, and was opened on the fiftieth anniversary of the battle of Leipsic. The interior, which is lined with coloured marble, contains upwards of thirty figures of Victory in Carrara marble, with bronze shields (made of guns taken from the French) between them. The names of victorious German generals and of captured fortresses are inscribed on tablets above the arcades. The floor being of polished marble mosaic, the visitor has to encase his feet in felt slippers before being allowed to walk across. It is advisable to practise some self-restraint while sneezing or blowing one's nose in this building, the echo produced being of so startling a nature as naturally to cause embarrassment to the performer in the presence of strangers.

The top of the hill on which the *Befreiungshalle*

Q

is built commands a distant view of Regensburg lying
far away in the plain to the north-east. There is a
fine passenger bridge across the Danube at Kelheim.
This little town still preserves some of its old walls
and gates. It is situated at the mouth of the Altmühl,
a tributary connecting the Danube with the *Ludwigs-Canal*, the northern end of which joins the Main
near Bamberg. The part of the Altmühl valley lying
nearest Kelheim is said to be very beautiful.

By the time the voyagers had re-embarked it was
already a quarter to three o'clock. To reach Regensburg, their destination, a distance of twenty-two
miles and a half, was therefore all they could expect to do before nightfall. By strenuous paddling
they managed to arrive in three hours and a half,
leaving the canoe for the night at a swimming-bath
on the left. Though this lay at the very beginning
of the town, and on the wrong side of the river, it
was fortunate they stopped here, for there was no
possibility of landing anywhere farther down.

The ancient city of Ratisbon, originally a Celtic
settlement, derives its German name from the
Roman *Castra Regina*. It has a population of
35,000, about 17 per cent being Protestants. It is
finely situated opposite the mouth of the Regen, in
a plain thirty miles in length, and bounded by the
Befreiungshalle above and the Walhalla below
Regensburg. Having been for several centuries
during the Middle Ages the most important city of

South Germany, it was the seat of the Imperial Diet for nearly 150 years, till the dissolution of the German Empire at the beginning of the present century. It contains one of the very earliest ecclesiastical foundations of Germany, the Benedictine Abbey of St. Emmeram, which dates from the middle of the seventh century. What appears to be the most ancient monument preserved in the abbey, that of a Duke of Bavaria, belongs to a period about 300 years later.

The two friends spent a couple of hours next morning in visiting the fine Cathedral, the Town Hall, and the Museum. The latter contains Roman and Merovingian antiquities found in an ancient burying-ground, which was unearthed twenty years ago. They also wandered with much interest through some of the old parts of the city, especially the Street of the Ambassadors (*Gesandtenstrasse*), so called because it contains the houses which were occupied by the envoys to the Imperial Diet. The armorial bearings of their former owners are still to be seen on the front of some of these fine old mediaeval dwellings. Several of them have fortified towers, a peculiarity of domestic architecture not preserved in any other of the mediaeval towns of Germany, not even at Nuremberg. These towers point to the fact that the walled cities of the Middle Ages not only had to defend themselves against external foes, but were also the scene of perpetual internal feuds among their nobles.

A stone bridge, built 700 years ago, and nearly
400 yards in length, unites Regensburg with the
small town of Stadt am Hof, situated on the opposite
bank.   The Danube being divided by two large
islands, called the *Obere* and the *Untere Werth*, into
two channels, the right arm, which is narrow but
has to be taken by the navigator, is spanned by only
four of its arches.   The bridge, though no doubt
very interesting to students of ancient architecture
of this kind, seems to have been specially designed
to confound the canoeist.   It rests on broad and flat
boat-shaped buttresses, the arches themselves being
narrow.   As there is very little water under the
outer arches, the whole force of the stream rushes
through the two in the middle.   While embarking
at the swimming-bath the voyagers had been warned
to be on their guard in shooting the bridge.   As they
rapidly bore down on the formidable structure, Bow
noticed that Cox was steering for the third instead
of the second arch from the right bank.   Across the
former ran an iron bar about two feet above the level
of the water, and probably connected with some repairs
that were being carried on.   Had they passed under
this arch they would infallibly have been wrecked
and probably half decapitated as well.   As it was,
they shot the second arch safely enough ; but on
issuing out on the other side they were instantly
swung round by a kind of whirlpool, produced by
the large volume of water rushing through the

narrow arch and coming in contact with the back-
wash behind the broad buttresses. As the canoe lay
for a moment broadside to the surging current, the
water poured over the gunwale and half filled her
before her crew knew what was happening. As they
managed to retain their balance, she was luckily not
completely swamped. Making rapidly for the bank,
they landed, emptied out the water, and wrung as
best they could the soaking carpet and cushions of
the canoe. Had they known beforehand what the
stream was like below the bridge, they would certainly have tried the arch on the extreme right,
notwithstanding the shallowness of the water.

This little incident caused a blush, derived from
the red cushion upon which he sat, on Bow's flannels,
which ever after produced a deep impression on the
juvenile riverside population till the end of the
voyage.

A short way below the bridge the Regen empties
its turbid waters into the Danube, behind the lower
island, which thus renders the mouth of the affluent
invisible to the navigator of the right channel. On
this tributary a large quantity of timber is floated
down into the Danube from the Bavarian Forest.

Resuming their paddles and passing in an hour's
time the ruins of the castle of Stauf, which crowns
an abrupt rock above the village of Donaustauf, and
was destroyed by the Swedes in the Thirty Years'
War, the voyagers suddenly came in sight of the

Walhalla, an edifice magnificently situated on a hill
upwards of 300 feet in height, and overhanging the
left bank of the river. The spectacle of what seems
a Greek temple, perched on a lonely height, coming
suddenly into view when the mind is still steeped in
the Gothic impressions of a mediæval city, is very
strange. A flight of 250 steps facing the Danube
forms the approach, on the upper part of the hillside,
to the splendid building. This temple of fame, built
of grey marble, and about 250 feet in length, is a
close imitation of the Parthenon. Like the
Befreiungshalle at Kelheim, it was founded by
Lewis I. of Bavaria, having been finished in 1842.
The total cost of the structure is said to have been a
million and a quarter sterling. Besides some beautiful figures of Victory by Rauch, and Battle-maidens
(*Valkyrien*) by Schwanthaler, the hall contains 101
marble busts of celebrated men of Teutonic race.
Carping critics have been heard to object that, for
instance, the insignificant head of a man of theory
like Kant seems singularly out of place in a temple
called the Warriors' Paradise. But after all are not
such great philosophers brave soldiers in the liberation war of humanity? Fault-finders of this type
remind one of the story of the discontented man
who, on meeting a former friend for the first time
in heaven, complained that his halo didn't fit.
They also recall the old *Hofrath* who, with all the
concentrated fire of criticism flashing from his single

eye, and emphasing his remark with his forefinger,
made so profound an impression on the youthful
Goethe by saying, " I can discover flaws even in the
Deity."

The terrace in front of the Walhalla commands a
fine view of the valley of the Danube towards
Regensburg in the west and Straubing far away
towards the south-east, some twenty miles off as
the crow flies. The Walhalla lies close to the
most northerly point reached by the river, the
course of which from Donaueschingen to Vienna, a
distance of 535 miles, represents the upper sides of
a flat triangle. Rising in a north-easterly direction
from below the 48th to slightly above the 49th
parallel of latitude, the Danube turns the angle near
Donaustauf, now flowing about as far to the south-
east till it reaches Vienna. The Walhalla thus
forms a worthy jewel in the diadem of this the
Queen of European rivers.

On re-embarking the friends paddled on for ten
miles before stopping for their midday bathe and
lunch. Unable to allow themselves much time for
a rest, they started off again at 3.20, with a distance
of twenty miles to accomplish in three hours of daylight before arriving at Straubing, their only possible
halting-place. There was now an additional reason
for paddling hard all the way ; for the current had
latterly become extremely sluggish, and the wrigg-
lings of the river as shown on the map for a con-

siderable distance farther down were sufficient to
prove its continued slackness.   The stagnation is
due to the Danube having now entered the plain
of Straubing, which is very extensive and fertile,
being the chief corn-growing district of Bavaria.
The average fall of the river between Regensburg
and Passau is thus only 0·625 feet per mile, but
must be even considerably less in the immediate
neighbourhood of Straubing.   From Ulm to Regensburg the fall is more than twice, while from Passau
to Linz it is four times as great.[1]

When the voyagers were yet a long way from
Straubing what looked like a large town appeared
straight in front, apparently only a short way off in
the middle of the plain.   They concluded it must be
some large place unaccountably omitted on the map.
Suddenly it reappeared, this time apparently not far
from the left bank.   The river then seemed to be
flowing towards its very centre, but after a few minutes
left it behind altogether.   The distance in a straight
line was all the while, as far as could be judged, pretty
much the same.   After this game of hide-and-seek
with the mysterious town had been going on for some
time, the conviction was at last forced on the canoeists
that it could be no other than Straubing itself.   The
cause of the mystification was the extraordinary

---

[1] From Ulm to Regensburg the average fall per mile is 1·5 ; from
Regensburg to Passau, 06·25 ; from Passau to Linz, 2·5 ; from Linz
to Grein, 2·8 ; from Grein to Vienna, 2·876 feet.

convolutions of the stream. These came to an end
at last, Straubing being reached soon after half-past
six, amid the deepening shadows of night.

Though September is, as far as weather is concerned, probably the best month for boating expeditions in Germany, it certainly has its drawbacks.
The voyager, unless camping out regularly, is often
compelled by the shortness of the days to hurry in
order to reach his destination before nightfall. And
the experiences of the two friends before reaching
Ulm had proved the necessity of being rather chary
about navigating unknown waters after dark. A
minor disadvantage of being belated is the certainty
of finding the swimming-baths closed and the difficulty
of discovering the proprietor.

The *Bademeister* at Straubing was, however, easily
found, his cottage being close at hand. Leaving the
canoe and unnecessary luggage in his charge, the two
friends made their way up to the *Post* hotel in the
town, which lies at some little distance from the
river.

Straubing, an ancient city of 13,000 inhabitants,
contains a fine Gothic church 400 years old,
and a tower which dates from the beginning of the
thirteenth century. It was here that Duke Ernest of
Bavaria, infuriated with his son, who had very
imprudently married a barber's daughter, caused that
beautiful lady to be cast into the Danube for the
crime of her birth. In justice to the reigning house

of Wittelsbach it should be stated that this event took place no less than 450 years ago. The members of that house, it will be admitted even by their enemies, would as soon drown themselves as their subjects.

The crew of the *Flora* was afloat soon after eight o'clock on the morning of 21st September. Some young Straubingers having come down to see them off, informed them that an Englishman, a resident in their native town for several years, had a boat of his own, with which he frequently rowed down to Deggendorf, bringing her back by rail. The latter proceeding seemed rather unheroic to his two countrymen, considering the slackness of the stream in this region. Among other accomplishments his admirers mentioned with pride his capacity for drinking large quantities of whisky (*er kann auch kolossal viel Wiski trinken*). The feats of their fellow-townsman in this respect they seemed to be even prouder of than his prowess with the oar.

The current still remained sluggish. The wind, on the other hand, was pretty strong and partly unfavourable, but fortunately fell completely in the course of an hour. The morning, at first gloomy, soon cleared up, turning into one of those days with light fleecy clouds when a landscape generally shows to the greatest advantage.

The scenery began to improve greatly as the voyagers, about six miles from Straubing, began to approach the town of Bogen. The hills of the Bavarian

Forest here come down to the left bank of the Danube, following it more or less closely to Vilshofen, and receding only for some five miles above Deggendorf.

Bogen, lying at the end of a long broad reach with a background of high hills, looked remarkably picturesque as the canoeists paddled straight towards the town. It probably owes its name to the bend which the Danube here makes, as it turns off almost at right angles towards the west. It is situated at the mouth of a tributary of the same name. Curiously enough several of the lesser affluents seem to be called after the towns situated at their confluence with the Danube, instead of the converse, as seems more natural, being the case. This obviously applies to the Regen, from Regensburg (the Roman *Castra Regina*), and to the Vils, from Vilshofen (the Roman *Villa Quintanica*).

A long narrow island at Bogen divides the river into two channels of about equal width. By taking the right branch the navigator obtains a better view of a high hill of conical shape, rising above the town and crowned by a church, the effect of which is very strange and picturesque.

The scenery of the hills on the left bank continues to be good till some way below Deggendorf. This town is situated at the confluence of two tributaries flowing down from the Bavarian Forest. Excellent excursions can be made from here into that mountainous region, some of the peaks of which

command fine views of the Danube valley. This
forest district covers a tract of 1800 square miles,
well wooded in most parts with fir and beech.
One of the chief employments of the natives of the
forest is naturally the timber trade.

The Isar railway from Munich to Pilsen at this
point crosses the river. The Danube line having
followed the course of the river pretty closely from
Ulm to Regensburg, leaves it after the latter place at
a distance of some miles, except at Straubing, till it
touches Vilshofen. From this place to Passau it again
skirts the right bank. But the long stretch of fifty-five
miles between Passau and Linz, which is by far the
most beautiful part of the Danube below Ulm, is, like
the lovely region above Sigmaringen, completely beyond the reach of the railroad.

A mile below Deggendorf the Isar flows into the
Danube, causing a succession of banks of shingle in
the bed of the river. These continue till a short way
above Vilshofen, recommencing at intervals after
Passau. In spite of this and of the many other large
tributaries it has received, the water of the Danube
remains wonderfully clear till it reaches Passau.
Whether it is due to the influx of the Isar or not,
the strength of the current certainly increases after
the confluence.

Having accomplished a distance of fifty kilometres,
the two friends landed on a fine beach flanked with
trees for their bathe in the heat of the day, feeling

they had earned a two-hours' repose by five hours and
a half of steady work. On resuming the voyage at
half-past three, they had thus less than fifteen miles
to paddle before reaching Vilshofen. About two
miles above the latter place there comes into view
among the woods on the left bank a fine old ruin, the
Igersberg, which in bygone days belonged to the
Fugger family, the Rothschilds of Augsburg in the
Middle Ages.

As a number of rocks, some showing and others
being just under the surface, are embedded in the
Danube for two or three miles above Vilshofen, it
would be highly unsafe to navigate that distance
except in broad daylight. This is the first time that
rocks occur in the bed of the river below Ulm.

Finding a convenient swimming-bath above the
bridge which here spans the Danube, the canoeists
landed there at six o'clock, leaving their boat in charge
of the proprietress, the first woman, by the way, whom
they had met with in this capacity. The genial old
soul was highly entertained by the notion of so vast
a river being navigated by a craft so tiny.

Vilshofen is a small town, originally a Roman
settlement, lying at some distance from the right bank.
The voyagers here put up at the *Hotel zum goldenen
Ochsen*, which they found to be comfortable enough.

Rain fell very heavily during the night, but
fortunately cleared away by the morning.

The landlord, in the simplicity of his heart, strongly

advised the crew to take a pilot in the bows of their
boat; for he assured them they would never be able
to find their way alone among the rocks which
bestrew the river bed below Vilshofen. But when
he had come down to the bank and saw the size and
build of their craft, he admitted that his advice could
not be carried out.

They launched their canoe at half-past eight, after
thanking and liberally rewarding the excellent
Badefrau for the care—surpassing that of any
Bademeister they had yet come across—with which
she had washed out the boat and attended to such of
their belongings as required cleaning.

The landlord was quite right in describing the
navigation below Vilshofen as hazardous; for the
rocks, many of them sunken, now become more
plentiful in the river bed than above, being at one
point so numerous that it seemed a mystery how a
steamer could possibly thread its way among them.
There must, of course, be a channel, as tugs ply up
and down the river; but the two friends failed to
find it, getting quite into the thick of the rocks.
This was highly dangerous to a Canadian canoe, for
collision with one of them in that swift stream would
infallibly have ended in shipwreck. The voyagers,
however, with their usual good luck passed through
these perils unscathed. After the worst place the
rocks cease, leaving the course of the river perfectly
clear down to Passau.

The scenery is fine all the way, especially on the left bank, which is bordered by the low wooded hills forming the edge of the Bavarian Forest, and extending to some distance below Passau.

Reaching that town before eleven o'clock, the canoeists luckily decided, as at Regensburg, to disembark at a swimming-bath some way above the town on the left bank. Had they passed this they would have found no other landing-place farther down.

Crossing over by the bridge to the right bank, they walked up to the *Bayrische Hof*, having resolved to spend the rest of the day and the night at this charming spot.

Passau, originally a Roman settlement, named *Castra Batava*, is a town of some 16,000 inhabitants. It is probably more beautifully situated than any other place on the Danube, lying as it does in a hilly and richly wooded region at the confluence of three rivers. The town is built on both sides of the sharp tongue of land which, rising to a ridge of considerable height in the middle, is formed by the influx of the Inn. This tributary is at its mouth upwards of 300 yards in width, considerably broader in fact than the Danube itself. Houses occupy the promontory down to its very extremity. Just beyond the point the Ilz discharges its dark stream into the Danube. The Klosterberg, a height on the left bank, commands a fine view of the meeting of the waters. From there the different colours of the three rivers can be seen most

distinctly. The Inn has the pale milky tint peculiar to
glacial streams, while the inky hue of the Ilz contrasts
strongly with the light green of the Danube.   In no
part of its course does the epithet of " blue," so com-
monly applied to the latter river, seem to be justified,
except possibly in one or two calm deep reaches
below Weltenburg, where its waters, when seen in
the sunlight, have a greenish blue colour.   Of an
almost crystal-like clearness for a considerable distance from its source, it assumes below Ulm a
greenish tinge, gradually becoming more and more
qualified with yellow, till below Passau it acquires
and retains a permanently muddy hue.   It is, however, possible, that from certain bird's-eye points of
view, which the present writer does not know, it
may have a blue appearance.

After receiving the waters of these large tributaries, the Danube, of course, becomes a river of
great size, being by this time 350 miles distant from
its source in the Black Forest.

Splendid views may be obtained from various
heights in the neighbourhood.   One of the best is
from the fortress of Oberhaus, on the opposite side of
the river.   Many pleasant excursions, too, may be
made from Passau into the charming scenery of the
surrounding region.

The two friends unfortunately saw nothing of all
this, being disinclined to walk after sitting for eight
or nine hours a day in the canoe during the last fort-

night. They would in any case have been prevented from doing much in this way by the heavy rain which now came on and continued for the rest of the day. They did not, however, omit to visit some of the sights of the town, notably the cathedral, which, built in the florid Romanesque style of the seventeenth century, occupies the site of an older Gothic edifice.

Neuralgia must be a prevalent malady at Passau, if it is legitimate to draw any conclusion from seeing so many women with their faces tied up as the two friends saw in the course of that day.

After a good night's rest, the voyagers were afloat soon after seven o'clock, having a long day of fifty-six miles before them to Linz. Though the rain with which the morning began ceased in about an hour's time, the sky remained overspread with dark clouds till the end of the day. On passing the tip of the tongue of land on which Passau lies, the crew turned the canoe upstream to enjoy for a few minutes the magnificent view as you look back on the town. The beauty of its situation cannot be fully appreciated till seen from here.

The scenery during nearly the whole of that day's voyage was of surpassing grandeur, the mighty river now flowing between lofty forest-clad hills. Its effect was rather sombre on that dark, lowering day ; and the sense of loneliness, as the tiny bark glided silently along, often for miles without a sign of human habitation on the banks or any sort of traffic on the river

R

itself, became almost oppressive. It was quite a
relief in the most solitary region, that between Obermühl and Untermühl, to fall in with a steamer which
was slowly making its way upstream. The pleasure
of the meeting was, however, not altogether unquali-
fied as far as the canoeists were concerned; for
while riding out the huge waves caused by their
doubtful friend they were carried down broadside by
the swift current and nearly came to grief in the
surf breaking on the shingly beach. On a previous
occasion they had continued paddling while facing
some large steamboat waves. The consequence was,
that the canoe projecting with half her length beyond
one wave came down with a splash on the next,
shipping a quantity of water over the bows, and
having a narrow escape from being swamped.

At Engelhartszell, about fifteen miles below
Passau, the boundary between Austria and Bavaria
comes down through a wooded ravine to the left bank
of the Danube. The right bank is Austrian all the
way from Passau. The crew had been informed
before starting that they would have to land here in
order to clear the custom-house. They had at first
formed the project of running the blockade; but as it
occurred to them that the artillery of the Austrian
Empire might be brought to bear on them, and failing
that, the telegraphic system set working, to their
disadvantage, all down the banks, they resolved on
second thoughts not to attempt an escape. Misled by

a statement in Baedeker, whose work, however, is not meant for the guidance of boating men, they were making for the left bank, when an official in uniform began gesticulating to them to come over to him on the right. So they crossed the broad river slanting upstream and managed to land, not without difficulty, owing to the swiftness of the current. After undergoing a cross-examination and signing various documents, they were requested to pay the toll for passing the frontier, to the amount of thirty kreutzers or about sixpence. This payment conferred on them the privilege of navigating the rest of the Danube without molestation. Whether the charge is in proportion to the tonnage or the number of the crew, or is the same for all vessels alike, did not appear. If the tonnage is the standard, thirty kreutzers must be very nearly the minimum charge.

From Engelhartszell the river flows almost in a straight line for some eight miles, then making four great sweeping bends, all the way through steep, lofty, and wooded defiles of the utmost grandeur. The most magnificent part of the scenery begins near Hayenbach, a ruin lying on a promontory formed by the first sudden curve to the left. The dark precipitous hills forming both banks here rise to the height of 1000 feet. The Danube is now confined in a channel of half its previous width, being proportionately deep and swift. The volume of water passing through these narrow gorges must be enormous. The banks are so steep and the current so rapid that there is no possibility of landing in these solitudes.

The Danube suddenly emerges into a broad plain ten miles long, which begins at Aschach and ends above Ottensheim. This tract is uninteresting, the river losing itself in many channels divided by islands which are thickly overgrown with bushes. Judging by Baedeker's maps one would suppose it to be hard to find the main stream here, and still more so in the stretch between Linz and Grein. It is, however, always perfectly obvious. Having landed for lunch at a solitary spot on the shingly left bank below Aschach, the voyagers quickly passed through this dull region till Ottensheim came into view.

On the hills which here come down to the river lie two ruined castles. One of these was in mediaeval times inhabited by a powerful family, which dominated the whole valley of the Danube between Passau and Linz, but died out in the sixteenth century. A solitary old ruin, which crowns a height rising from the Danube, now alone remains to tell the tale of their forgotten grandeur. The town of Ottensheim, looking as if built on a promontory, while it faces the voyager at the end of a long and broad straight reach, has a very picturesque appearance. The river at this point takes a sudden turn to the right, flowing for the next four miles till it reaches Linz through a thickly wooded defile. The approach to that place, which is rivalled in beauty by Passau alone among all the

towns on the Danube, is very grand. The dark
pine-clad hills looking almost black on that sombre
evening under the lowering clouds, produced a very
impressive effect on the two voyagers.

Arriving at half-past four, they landed at a convenient swimming-bath, where they housed their canoe
for the night. They had thus accomplished a distance
of fifty-six miles in seven hours and a half, exclusive
of stoppages, this being at the average rate of seven
miles and a half. The speed of the current must
therefore be at least three and a half miles an hour.

The hotel *zum rothen Krebs*, a short way farther
down the bank, proved to be a very good one. Its
only drawback, no doubt quite a temporary one, was
the boots (*Hausknecht*), whom Cox brought down to
take up the luggage. He was a man of the most
phenomenal sullenness of temper, on which no amount
of affability could produce the slightest impression.
The two friends came to the charitable conclusion
that he must have been crossed in love recently, but
owing to the uncertainty of this hypothesis they
rewarded him next morning for his grudging services
with only half the gratuity he would otherwise have
received. He cannot have found his manner a paying
one in the long run.

During the night the rain came down in torrents,
but ceased in the early morning. The same thing
occurred several times during the present expedition.
It thus happened that in the course of a voyage of

535 miles, lasting nearly three weeks, the canoeists
passed only two hours in the rain the whole time
they were afloat.   How tourists in Switzerland must
often wish that there could be some permanent
arrangement of the weather like this during the
summer months!

Linz, with a population of 40,000, is the largest
town on the Danube above Vienna, being the capital
of the province of Upper Austria.   On the left bank
opposite lies the town of Urfahr, behind which rises
the Pöstlingberg, a height picturesquely crowned by
a church.

Below Linz the Danube again enters a plain, which
in this case is thirty-two miles long.   The right bank
is flat all along except for a short distance above
Wallsee, though low hills skirt the left bank for
about fifteen miles as far as the town of Mauthhausen,
opposite which the green waters of the Enns enter
the Danube.   The river up to this point is full of
islands, a few being nearly a mile in length.   One of
them can even boast of possessing its château, the
Spielberg.   The main channel, as already indicated, is
easy enough to find.   Many of the branches marked
on Baedeker's map, if not purely imaginary, are at
least perfectly dry.   The stream in this tract is still
swift, and in places rough and surging.   Encounters
with steamers coming upon one suddenly among the
islands are here apt to be unpleasant.

At the end of the plain, near Ardagger, the river

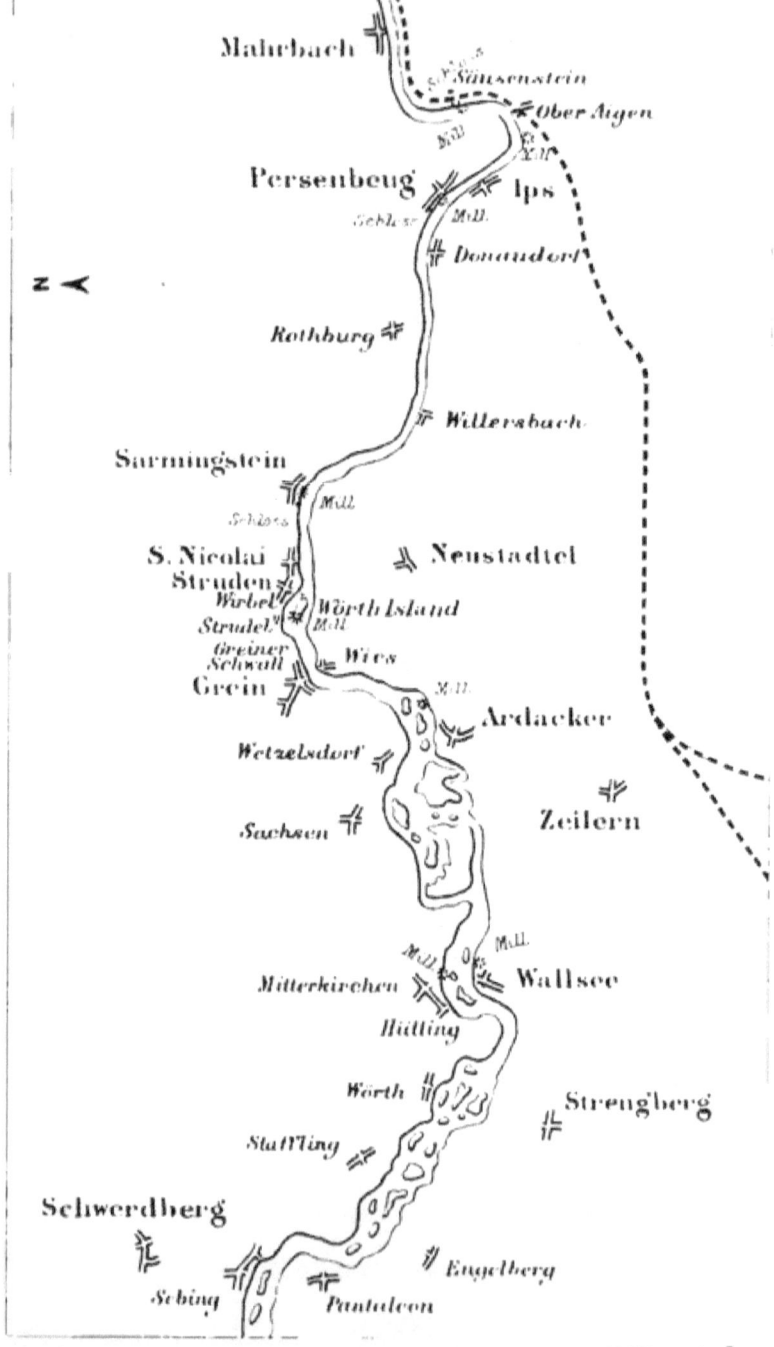

suddenly turns north, entering a narrow gorge formed
by high wooded hills, which contract the channel to
half its previous breadth. The voyagers reached the
picturesque town of Grein at noon. Here they
thought it advisable to land with a view of obtaining
exact information as to the formidable rapids to which
they were now about to entrust their fate. The very
names, *Strudel* (surge) and *Wirbel* (whirlpool), are
sufficient to strike awe into the heart even of an
ancient mariner. On the principle of *omne ignotum
pro magnifico*, the dangers of this gorge had been
grossly exaggerated by the dwellers on the upper
reaches of the Danube. The *Badermeister* at Regensburg, for instance, had described the waves here as
running as high as houses (*häuserhoch*). This notion
of its terrors may, however, in part be based on reminiscences of the old time, now more than forty years
back, when the rocks in the channel, not having yet
been blasted, were really very perilous to navigation.
Similarly, the typical Englishman on the foreign
stage still wears Dundreary whiskers, and can hardly
utter a sentence without saying "goddam." Some raftsmen whom the canoeists had passed that morning had,
besides various warnings, given them directions as to
the right course to steer. But these directions, pre-
supposing, as is so often the case with the uneducated,
a knowledge of the locality, were practically useless.

Landing at Grein was no easy matter. The right
place would have been the steamboat pier; but the

voyagers were swept past it without being able to
stop, owing to the want of a boat-hook. The only
alternative was to run as cautiously as possible into
the bank, consisting of large, rough stones, past which
the stream, already influenced by the suction of the
Greiner Schwall, swiftly flowed. Here they luckily
managed to get ashore without damaging the boat.
They were told at the pier to keep at first as close as
possible to the right bank, which is faced with a low
stone wall, afterwards making for the smoother water
on the left as they passed through the *Wirbel*. A
gentleman who came down to the bank to see them
start seemed much impressed with what he considered their courage in undertaking such dangerous
" sport " in so tiny a craft. To the uninitiated, a
Canadian canoe seen on the bosom of a mighty river
must certainly look very crank, especially when the
steersman, as he always was on this voyage, is
perched on the little poop.

It was very lucky for the two friends that they
had landed to make inquiries, for otherwise they
would have come to grief through the misleading
statements of Baedeker. According to that guide
" the stream is divided by the large island of Wörth,
on the north side of which the main arm descends in
rapids termed the *Strudel*." Now the Danube flows
past this large island on the left side only. There
may have been a regular channel on the right in
bygone times, but nowadays it contains no water

except after heavy rains. A rock some yards in length divides the only remaining branch of the river. The water on the right of this rock is smooth, whereas that on the left is a raging surge in which the canoe would have instantly foundered. The voyagers not seeing the so-called island of Wörth, and naturally mistaking the rock in mid-channel for it, would have steered to the left of the former, and thus run an uncommonly good chance of being drowned. If steamers take this course, every voyage of theirs must amount to a miracle. The height of the water may, however, affect the navigation to some extent.

Immediately below Grein a steep and lofty hill projects at right angles to the northerly course of the Danube, thus deflecting the stream to the east. As the current sweeps round this corner over ridges of rocks, it forms a boiling surf termed the *Greiner Schwall*. The river then suddenly disappears to the left round the end of the spur, pouring the whole volume of its mighty waters into a lofty, steep, and rocky gorge, which, for a distance of some hundred yards, is never more than fifteen yards in breadth. The voyager has hardly passed the *Greiner Schwall*, when he sees before him the rock above mentioned in the middle of the stream. The water all along the right bank is almost perfectly smooth till some way below the rock, though it flows with tremendous velocity. This bit is the so-called *Strudel*, while the surging

rapid a short distance farther on is termed the *Wirbel*.
It is hard to say what would happen were a small
boat suddenly to come upon a steamer in the former
part. Steamers must have their work cut out for
them to toil up these few hundred yards even at a
crawling pace; for the speed of the current can
hardly be less than at the rate of ten miles an hour.

Pushing off from the bank at Grein, not without
some misgivings as to their fate, the adventurers
turned their craft upstream so as to escape the
attraction of the *Schwall*, and paddling with all their
might aslant the current, made for the other side.
Managing to hold their own against the stream till
they were across, they put her head round and keeping within two or three feet of the right bank, shot
past the rock without shipping a drop of water.
Avoiding the rough waves below this point by steering for the smoother water on the left, they were keeping a sharp look-out for the *Wirbel*, when they were
surprised at suddenly finding themselves in perfectly
calm water opposite the lovely little village of St.
Nikolai, which is situated at the end of the narrow
defile. They had thus passed the formidable rapid
without being aware of the fact. Though the canoe
had not taken in any water, a rowing-boat would
probably have shipped a wave or two.

While careering down the rapids, the voyagers
were able only to cast furtive glances on either hand
towards the beetling crags and the picturesque ruins

perched on the rocky heights of this magnificent gorge. The pace at which they travelled was so swift that the whole distance from Grein to St. Nikolai, nearly two miles, seemed to occupy only a few minutes.

When just below the latter spot they fell in with a steamer coming upstream. They were not inspired with as much animosity as usual towards this enemy, being in fact rather grateful to her for not having met them some minutes earlier.

About five miles from Grein they found a quiet backwater and excellent landing-place on the left bank, where they stopped for lunch and a rest.

The river all the way to Ips flows through richly wooded defiles, which, with their mellow autumn tints bathed in the hazy sunlight of the afternoon, formed scenes of surpassing loveliness. The only breaks in their continuity as far as Stein occur in the tract of two or three miles below Ips, where the river makes a loop towards the south, and at Pöchlarn, where the right bank is flat for a few miles.

The town of Ips, the Roman *Pons Isidis*, when it first came in sight, seemed to consist entirely of public buildings, but one or two private houses afterwards made their appearance.

The stream having here grown temporarily slack, again resumes its swiftness as Mahrbach is approached. At the top of a hill 1450 feet high, rising above this place, is situated a church said to be visited by 100,000 pilgrims every year. It is a conspicuous

object from the river for many miles above, and is still
visible from Melk, fifteen miles farther down. The
view it commands is said to be magnificent.

At Mahrbach occurs the first instance on the
Danube of a peculiar kind of ferry, of which there
are several specimens on the Moselle also. A number
of punt-like boats, pointed at both ends, are moored
upstream in a line parallel with the bank, and at a
considerable distance apart. They are connected by
means of a cable running through a kind of mast
fixed in each of them. The combined action of the
heavy ferry-boat, when it has been pushed off, and of
the strong stream, suffices to bring the punts gradually across the river in a curve, thus landing the
passengers automatically at the opposite pier.

A few miles below Mahrbach, on the right bank,
lies Pöchlarn, originally a Roman settlement. Here
the noble Rüdeger, to whom tradition points as the
founder of the ruin on the other side, entertained
not only Kriemhilde on her journey to her future
husband, Etzel, at Ofen (Buda), but also her brothers
and the grim Hagen, when they were, under the
pretext of hospitality, lured to their destruction by
that vengeful queen for the murder of her first husband, the heroic Siegfried. The route from Worms
seems to have been the same on both occasions.
Crossing the Danube near Pforingen below Ingolstadt, it again touched the river at Passau, after that
passing through many places on its banks, such as

Efferdingen, Enns, Pöchlarn, Melk, Mautern, Treis-
mauer, Tulln, and Vienna.

The voyagers were now approaching Melk, the
monastery being visible above the trees on the right.
But though they had been warned, since Melk lies
behind an island, to take the channel at the back of
it, they nevertheless very nearly missed the entrance
to this branch, which surreptitiously sneaks off at
right angles to the main stream. Had they missed
the inner channel they would probably have found it
impossible to paddle up against the current at the
other end of the island. The swimming-bath at
which they landed and left the canoe was kept by
an extremely smart Austrian. The hasty generalisa-
tions, much to the disadvantage of the Bavarians, to
which he gave rise, were afterwards disproved by
many contrary instances.

The length of that day's voyage was ninety-nine
kilometres, or about sixty-two miles. This was the
greatest distance done consecutively on any of the
voyages recorded in these pages, with the exception
of the 105 miles in the last twenty-six hours of the
Weser trip.

After a refreshing bathe the two friends walked
up to their inn, *zum goldenen Ochsen*, which was close
at hand, and proved to be excellent. They received
a large room with a balcony commanding a good view
of the Danube and of the monastery.

After breakfasting on the 25th September the

friends spent an hour or so in visiting this famous
Benedictine Abbey. It is a magnificent edifice, probably the most palatial of its kind in Austria, built on a
rock, nearly 200 feet high, rising sheer from the
river. It contains a fine church and a rich library.
A kind of balcony terrace facing the river affords
a beautiful view of the Danube.

Starting at eleven o'clock the voyagers soon entered
a narrow and charming defile, which continues for
nearly twenty miles till Stein is approached. The
scenery is perhaps best on the right bank. Here,
about five miles from Melk, is an old castle, the
Aggstein, splendidly situated on a rocky height rising
precipitously from the Danube, and once the home
of daring robber knights. Tradition relates that its
owners in the olden time would get rid of trouble-
some prisoners by casting them down from their
stronghold into the waters below. Its situation is
such that they might easily have done so, even
though the tale be not true.

A twelve miles' paddle through this fine scenery
brought the voyagers in sight of the Dürrenstein,
which lies on the left bank in a bend of the river
facing due south. The old ruined castle, perched
on precipitous grey crags of the utmost barren-
ness, which frown down upon the Danube, is well
characterised by its name (Barren Rock). This
arid and desolate spot has a special interest for
Englishmen. It was here that Richard I. was in-

carcerated for more than a year by the Duke of
Austria, till, as tradition has it, he was discovered by
his trusty Blondel. He could not well have been
shut up in a fortress more cut off from the rest of the
world or more impregnable in those days. It must
have been a stronghold of great importance in the
Middle Ages, being the key of Upper Austria and
dominating completely the traffic in the valley of the
Danube. Even had the place itself not attracted
them, the two friends would have felt bound from
patriotic motives to make a pilgrimage up to the
rugged ruin. Landing in a backwater behind a mill
at the foot of the rock, they climbed the height,
spending some time in exploring the old fastness,
the remains of which are considerable, enjoying the
fine view of the Danube which it commands, and
meditating on its historical associations. One could
well imagine, on the spot, with what joy a prisoner
on that solitary rock would have welcomed the
familiar strains of his native land.

Re-embarking at last, the voyagers reached Stein,
which lies on the left bank four miles farther down,
after a paddle of half an hour or so. Though this
town is but twenty miles from Melk, they had decided
on stopping here. For Cox was obliged to cut short
the voyage, finding it necessary to be at Vienna that
night, in order to inspect some collections accessible
to visitors on the following day of the week only.
They accordingly put in at an excellent landing-place

immediately opposite the Hotel *Bittermann*, into the
yard of which they carried up the canoe. There is a
fine view of the Danube from the windows of this inn.

Cox having departed for Vienna by an evening
train, the Interpreter remained behind to finish the
voyage by himself. He was up betimes on the
last day of the voyage to look out on a glorious
morning. He had to shift his seat from the bows
to the now unaccustomed stern, so as to act both as
propeller and steersman. A large stone and all the
luggage were laid in his old place in order to counter-
balance his weight and trim the canoe properly. Not
intending to land till he reached Vienna, a distance
of about forty-eight miles, he supplied himself with a
basket of grapes for lunch in the boat. All being
now ready, he embarked, and pushing off into the
stream, waved his farewells to the inmates of the
hotel assembled on the bank. To them this solitary
voyage in so tiny a vessel on so vast a stream
appeared a most hazardous enterprise.

Below Stein the Danube enters a plain nearly
forty miles in length, and very similar in character
to that between Linz and Grein. The scenery is
equally uninteresting, the river here also dividing into
many channels, which form numerous sandy islands
overgrown with bushes. As the *Wiener Wald* is
approached, where the river takes a turn to the south-
east till it reaches Vienna, the right bank at least
gains considerably in attractiveness.

A number of steamers passing in both directions, and causing large waves, kept up the excitement during the day. The solitary canoeist, however, got on very well till noon, when the wind, which had gradually risen, began to blow very hard straight across the stream, making it very difficult to steer. It was especially bad in the neighbourhood of Tulln, one of the many old Roman settlements on the south side of the Danube. It was, therefore, all the Interpreter could do to prevent the canoe from being blown ashore and damaged on the rough stones of the long dams which are here built along the right bank. Some raftsmen whom he caught up offered to take him in tow, but this offer he politely declined, wishing to complete the voyage unaided. As he turned down the south-eastern reach towards Vienna, the wind, now blowing straight abaft, had risen almost to a gale. The canoe consequently went tearing along through the water. For a single man, or for that matter even a married man, to stop her or even check her speed under these circumstances would have been a sheer impossibility. This state of things threatened to be rather awkward, as the canoe might either come to grief through violent collision with obstacles, or be altogether blown past Vienna when that city seemed to be in the very grasp of her owner. Neither contingency was by any means remote. For while the main branch of the Danube curves away to the left of Vienna, only a narrow straight cutting,

S

with a swift stream running, passes through the city.
The entrance, which is not at all obvious, lies on the
extreme right of the river. Scudding along before
the wind into this narrow channel, the canoeist saw
himself confronted at the very mouth of the cutting
by a steamer coming upstream. He now thought
his fate was sealed, but, as the captain considerately
slackened speed, he managed to ride out the waves
by pointing the canoe at them, though at such close
quarters as almost to touch the side of the steamer.
Soon after another of these enemies appeared in front,
while the canoe was gaining so fast on a barge floating
down-stream that she was bound to run into it, as
the steamboat passed. In this dilemma the Interpreter resolved to keep close to the left bank, which
was very low and bound with beams running along
the edge, and by clutching it, if possible, to arrest the
canoe. This he succeeded in doing. By holding on
he also managed to ride out the waves, though they
came almost broadside. These perils having been
safely avoided, he had now to decide the all-import-
ant question as to how to land. For he could already
see the name of his hotel, the *Métropole*, close at hand
on the *Franz-Josephs-Quai*. Luckily there happened
to be a large swimming-bath on the right, just above
this block of buildings. Quickly turning the corner
into the backwater formed by the obstruction, he
seized one of the beams of the platform, and thus held
Vienna, as it were, in his hand. He arrived at half-

past two, exactly seven hours after leaving Stein. It being Sunday afternoon, a considerable crowd soon assembled, to gaze with much curiosity at the Canadian canoe, which was probably the first that had ever been seen at Vienna. Some of the spectators were astonished to hear that she had come down the Danube all the way from the Black Forest, a distance of nearly 550 miles.

The baths were closed, the water being already too cold for the Viennese; some boys, however, soon fetched the proprietor, who helped to convey the boat inside. After enjoying a refreshing bathe and donning his ordinary clothes, the Interpreter proceeded to his hotel across the road. His arrival at Vienna could hardly have been better timed, for the first meeting of the Congress which he had come to attend was to take place at seven o'clock that very evening. His complexion, too, having now assumed a rich terra cotta hue, would not be inappropriate in an assembly containing a large sprinkling of scholars from the East. It was afterwards stated that he was the only one who had come to this or any other Oriental Congress in a boat of his own.

Thus ended the longest, and in some ways the most delightful, of the voyages described in the foregoing pages.

When the Congress had dispersed a week after, the Interpreter went down by steamer, with two friends, to Buda-Pesth, and after spending some pleasant days there, returned the same way to Vienna. The distance is about 180 miles. The scenery for the first half of the way from Vienna is flat and uninteresting, while in the latter part it is fine, rising in the neighbourhood of Gran to a high degree of beauty.

APPENDIX

I

Meiningen (857 feet), weir just below ; Walldorf (weir
above), 4 m. ; Schwallungen (weir above on the left, mill
farther on to the right), 10 m. ; Wernshausen (weir), 14 m. ;
weir, 16 m. ; Salzungen (two weirs, about ½ m. apart), 24 m.;
Tiefenort (two weirs close together) ; Vacha (mill), 38 m. ;
Philippsthal (mill) ; Lengers (mill), 42½ m. ; Heringen (mill),
45 m.; Widdershausen (mill), 47 m. ; Dankmarshausen (mill),
48½ m. ; Berka (mill), 51 m. ; Gerstungen (mill), 53 m.;
Neustadt (mill), 54 m. ; Sallmannshausen (mill) 54½ m. ;
Herleshausen (station), 58 m. ; Wartha (mill), 59½ m. ;
Spichra (old mill), 62 m. ; Kreuzburg (bridge with rapid),
65 m.; Ebenau, 66 m.; Mihla, 70 m. ; Ebenshausen (mill),
71 m. ; Frankenroda, 73 m.; Falken (mill), 75 m.;
Treffurt, 78 m. ; Burschla, 82 m. ; Wannfried (mill), 86 m. ;
Eschwege (lock), 91 m.; Albungen, 97 m.; Allendorf
(lock), 102 m.; Witzenhausen (bridge with rapid), 113 m. ;
Hedemünden, 120 m.; Münden (380 feet ; lock), 126 m.

II

DISTANCES IN KILOMETRES (= ABOUT ⅝ OF A MILE)
ON THE WESER

Münden	...	Minden	. 203
Bodenfelde	34	Windheim	. 225
Carlshafen	46	Landesbergen	. 252
Höxter	69	Nienburg	. 269
Holzminden	. 81	Hoya	. 302
Bodenwerder	. 112	Intschede	. 333
Hameln	. 138	Uehsen	. 345
Rinteln	. 166	Horstedt	. 353
Vlotho	. 184	Bollen	. 357
Rehme	. 190	Dreye	. 360
Porta	. 198	Bremen	. 372

III

APPROXIMATE DISTANCES (IN MILES) AND OBSTRUCTIONS
ON THE NECKAR

Hofen (weir, easy and straight pull-over), 4 m.; Aldingen (half-weir), $6\frac{3}{4}$ m.: weir (near tributary on the right bank), $9\frac{3}{4}$ m.; Hoheneck, 13 m.; Marbach (mill, with half-lock; great rapid after railway viaduct), 16 m.; Klein-Ingersheim (mill, lock), $22\frac{1}{2}$ m.; third camp (mill, with lock), 27 m.; rapids, 30 m.; Besigheim (lock on branch to the right), 32 m.; Gemmrigheim (half-lock), $34\frac{1}{2}$ m.; Kirchheim, (lock), $36\frac{1}{2}$ m.; Lauffen (half-lock), 41 m.; Heilbronn (weir below bridge), 49 m.; Neckarsulm, 54 m.; Jagstfeld (good hotel, with terrace on bank) 58 m.; Wimpfen, 59 m.; Offenau, $60\frac{1}{2}$ m.; Gundelsheim, 64 m.; Hassmersheim, 67 m.; Neckarzimmern, $68\frac{1}{2}$ m.; Neckarelz, $71\frac{1}{2}$ m.; Binau, 75 m.; Eberbach (two good inns), 80 m.; Hirschhorn (good inn), 87 m.; Neckarhausen, $89\frac{1}{2}$ m.; Neckarsteinach, 93 m.; Heidelberg, 101 m.; Ladenburg, 109 m.; Mannheim, 118 m.

IV

DISTANCES IN MILES ON THE RHINE

Mannheim	...	Lorch	.	$61\frac{3}{4}$
Worms .	12	Rheindiebach	.	$62\frac{1}{2}$
Oppenheim	14	Bacharach	.	64
Nierstein .	16	Caub	.	$65\frac{1}{2}$
Mainz	36	Oberwesel	.	$68\frac{1}{2}$
Biebrich .	40	St. Goar .	.	74
Walluf .	42	Hirzenach	.	$77\frac{3}{4}$
Eltville .	45	Salzig	.	80
Oestrich .	49	Boppard .	.	83
Geisenheim	52	Niederspay	.	$87\frac{1}{2}$
Bingen	55	Rhens	.	89
Rheinstein	58	Capellen .	.	91
		Coblenz		95

V

LIST OF APPROXIMATE DISTANCES (IN MILES) AND OF GOOD INNS ON THE MOSELLE

Trèves (Rothes Haus) ; Pfalzel, 4 m. ; Longwich, 10 m. ; Detzem, 16 m. ; Leiwen, 20 m. ; Neumagen, 25 m. ; Piesport, 29 m. ; Reinsport, 31 m. ; Kesten, 35 m. ; Muhlheim, 38 m. ; Berncastel (Drei Könige ; Post), 41 m. ; Zeltingen, 45 m. ; Uerzig (Post), 48 m. ; Kinheim (Neidhofer) 50 m. ; Croff (Zur Gräfinburg), 53 m. ; Trarbach (Bellevue), 56 m. ; Traben (Clauss), 56 m. ; Enkirch (Anker), 59 m. ; Burg, 61 m. ; Pünderich, $64\frac{1}{2}$ m. ; Marienburg (Restaurant) ; Zell (Fier), $68\frac{1}{2}$ m. ; Alf (Post ; Bad Bertrich ; Burg Arras), 72 m. ; Bremm, 75 m. ; Ediger (Löwen), 78 m. ; Beilstein, 84 m. ; Bruttig, 87 m. ; Cochem (Union), 91 m. ; Pommern, $95\frac{1}{2}$ m. ; Treis (Conzen), 97 m. ; Moselkern (Anker), 99 m. ; Brodenbach (Post), 103 m. ; Cobern (Simonis), 110 m. ; Coblenz, 120 m.

VI

A. APPROXIMATE DISTANCES (IN MILES) AND OBSTRUC-
TIONS ON THE UPPER MAIN

Bayreuth (1180 ft.); Drossenfeld, 9 m.; Steinhausen,
20 m.; Mainleuss (weir), 23 m.; Burgkundstadt (weir),
30 m.; Strössendorf (weir), 31½ m.; Hochstadt, 35 m.;
Wallenstadt (weir), 42 m.; Lichtenfels (weir on right, take
left branch to mill in the town), 45 m.; Hausen (last weir),
50 m.; Zapfendorf (station; good bathing-place), 62; Bischberg (leave boat with ferryman), 74 m.

B. DISTANCES IN KILOMETRES ON THE MAIN FROM
BAMBERG TO MAINZ

```
...  Bamberg.
 53  Schweinfurt (lock, weir).
139  Wurzburg (lock, weir).
166  Karlstadt.
172  Good camping-ground.
180  Gemünden.
193  Lohr (bad landing-place).
234  Werthheim.
247  Stadtprozelten.
266  Miltenberg.
303  Aschaffenburg: stop at Kittel's baths at the
         lower end of the town.
323  Kahl (Bavarian frontier).
329  Hanau.
350  Frankfort.
387  Mainz.
```

VII

APPROXIMATE DISTANCES (IN MILES) ON THE
MOLDAU AND ELBE

```
...  Prague.
 20  Kralup (3 hours 35 minutes by canoe).
```

32½ Melnik (2 hours).

 35 Junction with the Elbe.

 65 Leitmeritz (5 hours).

 77 Aussig (3½ hours).

 95 Bodenbach.

105 Herrnskretschen (3¾ hours).

110 Schandau (1 hour).

118½ Wehlen (1½ hour).

124 Pirna (40 minutes).

135 Dresden (1¾ hour).

VIII

APPROXIMATE DISTANCES (IN MILES) AND OBSTRUCTIONS ON THE UPPER DANUBE

Donaueschingen (2220 ft.) ; Pforen (station ; wooden bridge), 3 m. ; Neidingen (weir, grassy bank), 5 m. ; Gutmadingen, 8 m. : Geisingen (station, short way above mill, river dividing, bad crossing), 10 m. ; short way below Geisingen, paddle weir ; a mile farther small wooden foot-bridge over shallow rapid ; Hintschingen (station) ; Immendingen (long and difficult crossing), 14 m. ; Möhringen (covered wooden bridge ; the worst crossing on the river just above this village ; succession of bad shallows till next crossing : long porterage), 18 m. ; Tuttlingen, 23 m. ; weir, 24½ m. ; Nendingen (shallow rapid), next village (weir, wooden bridge) ; Mühlheim (weir on left, bad crossing over rough stones), 29 m. ; Friedlingen (weir) ; Beuron (wooden covered bridge), 41 m. ; Castle Wildenstein, 43 m. ; Langenbronn (above, the old château of Wernwag, with splendid view and capital inn at the top), 45 m. : Hausen (mill, crossing over grassy slope ; stone bridge across the Danube), 46½ m. ; Neidingen, 48 m. ; ruin of Falkenstein (weir), 50 m. ; Thiergarten, 50¾ m. ; Gutenstein (weir),

53¼ m. ; Dietfurt (weir), 55½ m. ; Laiz (weir, long crossing), 59 m. ; Sigmaringen (boat can be left at bathing-establishment on left bank above bridge ; weir below Schloss), 60½ m. : low weir, 61½ m. ; Scheer (broad and high weir ; nasty bridge) 68½ m. ; camp opposite Mengen, 70 m. ; Riedlingen (weir, long and bad crossing), 83 m. ; weir (difficult crossing) : broad and high weir (easy crossing over grassy bank on the left) ; Munderkingen (two weirs : that on the left had better be taken : long grassy crossing behind mill into millstream), 99 m. ; Dettingen (low weir, fall of about two feet), 103 m. ; Erbach, 115 m. ; Ulm (stop at swimming-bath below railway bridge on left bank), 124 m.

IX

DISTANCES (IN KILOMETRES) ON THE DANUBE FROM ULM TO BUDA-PESTH

... Ulm.

50 Dillingen : stop at second swimming-bath a short way above wooden bridge ; the town is invisible from the river.

78 Donauwörth.

90 Good lunching-ground on left bank.

110 Neuburg : take right branch under stone bridge : landing-stair below Post Hotel.

130 Ingolstadt : stop at swimming-bath on the left bank, opposite 130c kilometre mark.

161 Eining.

172 Kelheim.

208 Regensburg : stop at second swimming-bath on the left bank ; when leaving it is advisable, if in a Canadian canoe, to take the arch on the extreme right of the old bridge.

219 Walhalla.

235 Good lunching-ground ; shallow for bathing.

266 Straubing.

276 Bogen.

302 Deggendorf.

316 Good lunching-ground, but shallow for bathe.

339 Vilshofen : stop at swimming-bath on the right bank just above bridge.

362 Passau (950 ft.) : stop at swimming-bath on left bank above bridge.

410 Obermühl.

452 Linz (813 ft.) : stop at swimming-bath on the right above bridge.

508 Grein (715 ft.).

551 Melk : stop at swimming-bath behind island.

569 Spitz.

625 Tulln.

648 Klosterneuburg.

663 Vienna (436 ft.) : stop at swimming-bath on right bank, just above the Metropole Hotel.

723 Pressburg.

811 Gönyö.

955 Buda-Pesth.

N.B.—The following articles and books on the Danube may be mentioned :—

Article " Danube " in the *Encyclopædia Britannica*, and in the Cyclopædias of Brockhaus and Meyer : Letter by A. F. Peterson on the " Danube from Ulm to Pesth " in *The Field*, September 1885 ; A. Müller, *Die Donau vom Ursprunge bis zu den Mündungen* (1839-1841) ; Peters, *Die Donau und ihr Gebiet* (1876) ; John Macgregor, *A Thousand Miles in the Rob Roy Canoe* (1866) ; *The Water Lily on the Danube* (1853) ; Baedeker's *Southern Germany and Austria*.

LIST OF MAPS

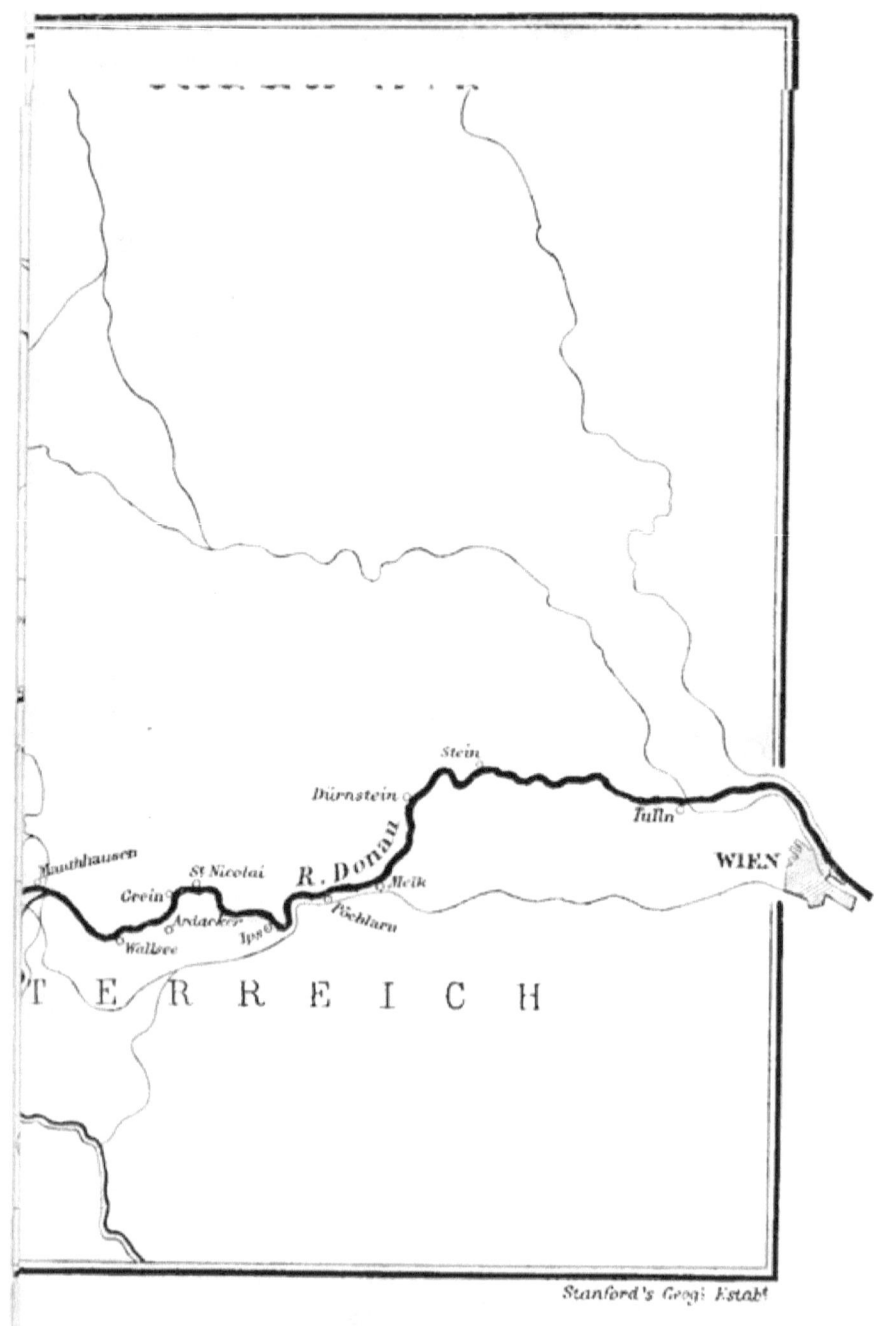

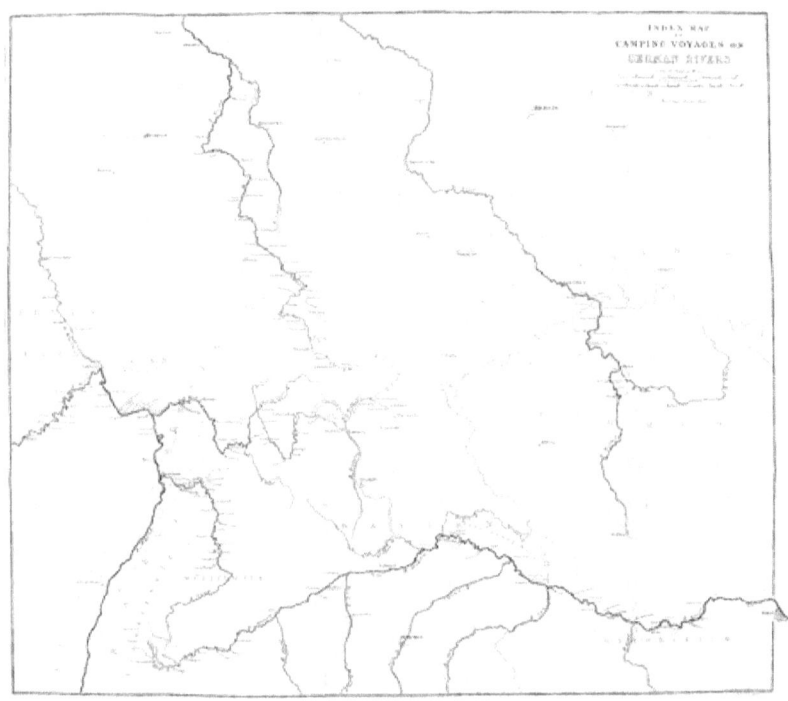

INDEX

T

THE END

Printed by Edward Stanford,
26 and 27 Cockspur Street, Charing Cross, London, S.W.

STANFORD'S TRAVELLING MAPS.

EUROPE.—Stanford's Library and Travelling Map of Europe. Constructed by ALEX. KEITH JOHNSTON, F.R.S.E., F.R.G.S. Scale, 50 miles to an inch; size, 65 inches by 58. The Railways are accurately and distinctly delineated. The Southern Shores of the Mediterranean are included, so that the Overland Route, as far as Suez, may be distinctly traced. Coloured, mounted in 4 sections, in 8vo. morocco case for tourists. £3 : 13 : 6.

EUROPE.—Stanford's Portable Map of Europe, showing the latest Political Boundaries, the Railways, and Submarine Telegraphs. Scale, 105 miles to an inch; size, 33 inches by 30. Coloured and mounted in case, for use of tourists. 10s.

EUROPE.—Stanford's London Atlas Map of Europe. Scale, 110 miles to an inch; size, 26 inches by 22. Mounted in case. 5s.

The following Maps from Stanford's "London Atlas" are sold separately, mounted to fold in case for the pocket, price 5s. each.

Denmark and Schleswig-Holstein.	The Countries around the Mediter-
Iceland.	ranean Sea.
Sweden and Norway.	France in Departments.
German Empire, Western part.	Spain and Portugal.
,, ,, Eastern part.	Italy, North. Sardinia.
Austria—Hungary.	,, South.
Switzerland.	Greece.
The Netherlands and Belgium.	The Balkan Peninsula.

CENTRAL EUROPE.—Stanford's New Map of the Greater Part OF EUROPE, extending from Moscow to the Atlantic, and from the Gulf of Bothnia to the Mediterranean. Scale, 50 miles to an inch; size, 46 inches by 42. Coloured and mounted in case. 25s.

CENTRAL EUROPE.—Davies's Map of Central Europe. Containing all the Railways, with their Stations. The principal Roads, the Rivers, and chief Mountain Ranges are clearly delineated, whilst the scale upon which the map is drawn renders it a distinct and useful guide for tourists. Scale, 24 miles to an inch; size, 47 inches by 38. Mounted in case. 16s.

SWITZERLAND.—The Alpine Club Map of Switzerland. Edited by R. C. NICHOLS, F.S.A. Scale, 4 miles to an inch; size, 60 inches by 43. Four sheets, mounted in case, £2 : 12 : 6; single sheets, 12s.; mounted in case, 15s. The Enlarged Edition of the above, scale 3 miles to an inch, in 8 sheets, sold separately, 1s. 6d. per sheet.

GOVERNMENT SURVEYS.—The Maps issued by the Governments of the various European States so far as published are kept in stock, or can be procured to order.

LONDON: EDWARD STANFORD,
26 and 27 Cockspur Street, Charing Cross, S.W.

BOOKS FOR EUROPEAN TRAVELLERS.

Stanford's Compendium of Geography and Travel.— Europe. Edited by Sir A. C. RAMSAY, LL.D., F.R.S., late Director-General of the Geological Survey of the United Kingdom. With Maps and Illustrations. Large Post 8vo, cloth gilt. 21s.

The Baths and Wells of Europe, with a Sketch of Hydrotherapy, and Hints on Climate, Sea-Bathing, and Popular Cures. By JOHN MACPHERSON, M.D. Third Edition, revised, with a Map. Post 8vo, cloth. 6s. 6d.

Fetridge's Handbook for European Travellers. Three vols. Roan Tuck. Sold separately. Price 16s. each.

Contents :—

> Vol. I. Great Britain, Ireland, France, etc.
> ,, II. Germany, Austria, Italy, etc.
> ,, III. Switzerland, Tyrol, Norway, etc.

The Handy Guide to Norway. By THOMAS B. WILLSON, M.A. With Maps and Appendices on the Flora and History of Norway ; Fishing Notes, and Photography. Second Edition. Revised and enlarged. Small Post 8vo, cloth. 5s.

Through Norway with a Knapsack. By W. MATTIEU WILLIAMS, F.R.A.S., F.C.S., Author of the " Fuel of the Sun," etc. With Map. Crown 8vo, cloth. 6s.

Through Norway with Ladies. By the same Author. With Illustrations and Map. Crown 8vo. 12s.

Nice and its Climate. By Dr. A. BARETY. Translated, with Additions, by CHARLES WEST, M.D., With an Appendix on the Vegetation of the Riviera by Professor ALLMAN, F.R.S., etc. Two Maps. Post 8vo, cloth. 4s. 6d.

Tourist's Guide to the Upper Engadine. Translated from the German of M. CAVIEZEL. By A.M.H. With Coloured Map. Post 8vo, cloth. 5s.

Visitor's Guide to Orvieto. By J. L. BEVIR, M.A. Small Post 8vo, cloth. 3s.

Visitor's Guide to Siena and San Gimignano. By J. L. BEVIR, M.A. With Plan. Small Post 8vo, cloth. 3s.

The Family Guide to Brussels : Comprising General Information for a Family purposing to reside in that city. By R. SCOTT of Brussels. Crown 8vo, cloth gilt. 4s.

LONDON : EDWARD STANFORD,
26 and 27 Cockspur Street, Charing Cross, S.W.